UNDER THE SUN

UNDER THE SUN

a novel by

Susannah Clements

Metokos Press
Narrows, VA 24124

Published by Metokos Press, an affiliate of Metokos Ministries, a parachurch ministry providing *"Encouragement for Small Churches."* Visit us on the web at *www.metokospress.com.*

Cover design by Chip Evans, Walker-Atlanta, Atlanta, GA.

Layout and editing by Diane Hitzfeld, Crestview, FL.

Printed in the United States by Lightning Source, LaVergne, TN.

ISBN 978-0-9742331-2-3

For Matthew Alexander,

thanking God for his life and for his death

and for the sweetness of his spirit.

And for my Grandmother.

Prologue

THE SUNRISE

"The race is not to the swift
or the battle to the strong,
nor does food come to the wise
or wealth to the brilliant
or favor to the learned;
but time and chance happen to them all."

Ecclesiastes 9:11

An island off the coast of Denmark

The shouting woke Mara. Over the steady sound of waves on rocks and the high-pitched hum of night bugs, the shouts were vague but startling. She unwound her legs from her coarse cloak and stumbled sleepily to her feet.

"Father?" she called softly.

She looked around the packed-earth floor of her hut. Elsa was curled up next to the wall, but her father was gone. She wasn't surprised; she had never seen her father sleeping. Mara wondered what had awakened her, and then she heard again the shouting from somewhere outside, somewhere not very far away.

Her father must be where the shouting was.

Mara tugged the wool tunic she had left on the floor that evening over her cord skirt as she slipped into the second room of the hut, but the carved tables and thick stools were empty, arranged neatly in the corners for the night. She pushed her tangled hair—gold even in the moonlight—away from her face as she ventured out into the clearing.

Nights were cold, even in summer, and the stars were achingly bright in the sharp sky.

But there was a strange smell to the night air. Mara took a deeper breath and started to cough. Smoky and thick, like on evenings when the villagers burned the brush.

After three steps on the hard dirt, she tripped over a body. She recognized him immediately; he was the boy without a family who helped her father gather oysters. He had pulled her hair two days ago. The boy was still clutching an ax in his small fist. Mara didn't realize until later that he was dead.

There were two other bodies in the dirt beside the hut, but they were dressed strangely—the men were naked except for their short capes—and their hair, though fair, did not gleam gold, so Mara knew they were not from any of the villages on the island.

She could tell now that the shouting was coming from the village. Their hut, the only one in the village made of stone, was on a hill separated from the others. "A chieftain," her father had said, "must always remind his people that he is separate from them."

Mara could now see smoke sliding up past the roofs of the village and a few stray flames leaping to break the darkness. A hut must be on fire in the village.

Mara could still hear the shouts, and there were more of them. She was sure now that her father was where the shouting was.

Mara ran as fast as she could through the brush that separated their house from the houses of the village. Once, she scraped her bare legs on a low branch; she clapped her left shoulder with her hand to ward off the curse of blood and kept running.

When she could see the village, she stopped and looked down at it, panting. Not just one hut, but many were burning, and as Mara watched, the flames reached another hut. The huts were straw and wood—it wouldn't take long for the fire to destroy them. The heat reached out to Mara like a blow.

Men were fighting in the space between the huts. She could see the golden hair of the villagers clearly through the smoke, and she could see the other men—the strangers. Women were screaming. She wished that they would stop.

She saw her father then, in the red light of the fire. He was just below her at the foot of the hill, and his golden beard was matted with blood. None of the other men in the village wore beards, but her father said it was a sign of honor. Mara watched as a man's head rolled for several paces, severed by a swing of her father's ax.

Mara made a little noise—a soft cry of pride, for her father was the mightiest warrior on the island—but he heard it and swung around.

"Mara! Get away! Go back to the hill and hide!" he bellowed.

Mara turned to run back, instinctively understanding the rough authority in his voice, but before she turned her head she saw another man attack him, and she waited to make sure her father was all right.

"Brant!" her father called to the man fighting a few paces away from him. "Please . . . keep Mara safe." He buried the blade of his ax into the chest of his opponent, and yanked it free as the man fell.

Brant, almost gracefully, cut the throat of the stranger he was fighting with a dagger he drew from his belt, and turned to Mara's father. Brant was gasping for breath, and his broad features were twisted in . . . pain? Mara wasn't sure.

"Don't ask me to flee," he rasped.

Another stranger had lunged for her father, but he said between the swings of his ax, "Please." The stranger died on the word, and her father turned to Brant.

"Please," he repeated.

Brant nodded. He raised his palm to his chieftain. "May the sun always warm you, brother." A strangely calm gesture in the chaos around them.

Mara watched as her father returned the salute—the two men in a space of quiet. "And you, until the sun is devoured by the sea." Mara wondered why they were saying good-bye. She was shaking now, but she knew she wasn't cold. She was dripping from the heat of the fires.

Brant ran toward Mara, his arm stretched out to pick her up. He had almost reached her when he fell before her onto his face.

Mara had not even seen the arrow coming, and it buried itself between his shoulders, pinning his waist-length braid to the bare skin of his back.

"Brant," she gasped, and knelt down beside him.

Brant lifted himself onto his elbows and turned to look at Mara's father, who had seen Brant fall and run toward them. "You will . . ."

"He will be dead." Mara shivered as her father spoke the words of the sacred vow, the vow one made to a dying man. She watched a moment as her father started to look for the man whose arrow had pierced Brant in the back.

"Mara," Brant said. "I must get you away. They will . . . hurt you."
He managed to say this before he collapsed onto his face again.

"But . . ." she began, wishing he would get up to help her.

"Mara," he gasped. "Run! Find Elsa and hide." Mara couldn't
move. Brant's handsome face twisted into something ugly. "Help me
up," he said.

Mara did her best to help as Brant struggled to his feet. He took
four steps before he collapsed again. This time he didn't open his eyes.

"Brant . . ." Mara said softly. She choked back a sob as she felt the
wind pull at her hair, and she knew he wouldn't get up again.

He was her father's brother.

She looked back down at the village. The smoke was even thicker
now. Most of the huts had collapsed. She could see only a few of the
villagers still fighting, dim shadows in the smoke and the fire. The
strangers not fighting were spreading the fire to the remaining huts.
Mara thought she saw a friend's mother lying in her own blood. She
couldn't be sure. The smoke had reached her eyes, stinging them.

Then she saw her father again. He was backed up against a burning
house, but she recognized his silhouette—the tallest man in the
village—and his distinctive stance. He was fighting three men. Two of
them fell as she watched. When he killed the third, he started toward
another man who was bent over a woman. He managed to kill the
stranger before her father died. He was killed, like his brother, from an
arrow in his back.

Mara screamed, but nobody heard her.

She felt the wind again, and sighed with the relief that his spirit, at
least, was safe.

She turned around to run back to her house to find Elsa, like Brant
had said. Then she stopped.

Only last week that her father had taken her down to the sea and
talked to her for more than an hour. She was the chieftain's daughter,
he had said; he had no son. That meant she had a very important
position. "Whatever happens, you must remember that as my daughter
you must uphold the honor of the chieftain, of the entire village." His
voice had been deep and almost laughing. But Mara had understood.
Everyone who lived in the northlands understood what honor was.

She turned back to where Brant lay and saw his bronze ax beside
him. "He will be dead, father," she said, trying to keep her voice as
strong as her father's had been. She picked up the handle, but she
couldn't raise the other end—the blade. Frustrated, she let it drop.

Then, she pushed Brant over enough to pull out the dagger he always kept in his belt. He had carved a boat for her with it once. She still had the boat.

She picked up the dagger and started toward the fighting, toward the man whose arrow had killed her father.

She was six years old that night.

"Mara!" came a voice from behind her.

She whirled around and leveled the dagger, as she had seen the boys of the village do in their games. It was slippery in her hands, which were wet from Brant's blood.

Elsa came running toward her. "Put that down, Mara. We must get away."

"My father is dead, and so is Brant, there." Mara pointed with the dagger.

Elsa's beauty was known throughout the island and farther, into the mainland whose pagan customs were only whispered of, and into the barbarian land across the sea. Mara's father, who was Elsa's brother, had killed several men who had tried to take Elsa. She was to marry when next the moon was round like the sun. Mara was very glad to see her.

Elsa had not had time to bind her hair, so it fell like a mantle around her tall body. Unlike Mara, she had not put on a tunic, and only her bronze belt-plate covered her bare belly. Elsa's cheeks, normally rosy, whitened as she looked at the body of her dead brother.

"We cannot avenge their deaths," she said after a moment. "Not now. We must get away from these savages, these barbarians." She spit the last word out like a curse. Elsa took Mara's hand and dragged her back up the hill to their hut.

Mara stared again at the bodies in the clearing near their hut.

"They must have killed the boy before my brothers heard them and woke. Likely, he was trying to protect us," Elsa said softly.

They ran into the house. While Elsa grabbed some food and their cloaks, Mara looked around the room, and then she went to the corner to get her beads of sea-gold.

"Hurry," Elsa urged, and pushed Mara out into the night again.

Elsa grabbed Mara's hand and they raced down the other side of the hill, toward the thick trees at the bottom. They had gotten almost halfway down when they stopped.

A man, brown-eyed and strangely clad, stood facing them with a sword. He was shaking his head and smiling. He was not dressed like the other strangers, in only a short cape. Mara saw the moon's light reflecting off his chest and realized that his chest was encased in bronze. She had never seen anything like that before.

Thinking quickly, Elsa pulled Mara behind her and wrapped Mara's arms around her waist. But her beautiful face was defiant, and Mara tried to match it with her own.

The man approached them, slowly. He grasped Elsa's chin and turned it to the side, gazing at her with astonished brown eyes. He tried to pull Mara away from her, but Elsa yanked free and picked Mara up in her strong arms. Mara winced as the sharp point on Elsa's belt-plate poked into her side. "Hold on tight," Elsa whispered.

"Where are you running to?" the man asked in their language, with an awkward accent.

It did not seem strange to Mara that the barbarian spoke their language. She knew their language was spoken on the mainland, and everyone knew what was rumored about mainlanders. All of the villages had lost their identities by uniting with each other under one rule. They sold not only their sea-gold, but also the skin of animals, and even their own people, to barbarian traders who then sold the furs or the slaves to strange desert kingdoms or madmen who danced with bulls. The mainlanders were said to live in houses of two levels and have members of their own villages work for them. Worst of all, they named the sun and reduced the sun's spirit to the image of a man. If people like the mainlanders spoke their language, Mara was not surprised that this barbarian did as well.

Elsa, however, was surprised. "Who are you? How do you speak in our language?"

The man snorted, in amusement Mara thought. "I am the chief of the Huntar, a tribe across the water. And it is helpful to be able to speak with one's allies."

Mara didn't understand, but Elsa did. "Who?" she breathed.

"An interesting question. You have so many enemies?"

Elsa refused to answer that.

"The villages on the mainland despise the people of this island. Surely you know that. You will not unite with them, and trade independently. Even if you did not live like ignorant peasants, you would be destroyed."

Mara could see the trees behind the man; she could see the needles and the thin branches swaying in the changing wind. If they had made it to the trees, she thought, it would have been all right. Her father was dead. Brant was dead. The village was burnt to the ground. But the trees were still there, even blacker than the sky. The trees would have hidden them.

Elsa closed her eyes. "May they burn in darkness . . ."

"Yes, yes, I know," the barbarian interrupted. "Until the sun is devoured and all that. You islanders are so predictable. You don't seem to understand that your entire village has been destroyed. Where were you planning on going?"

Elsa raised her head. "We have friends." Mara knew she was thinking of the man in the next village who she would marry.

"I hope they were not on this island for the entire island is being destroyed. Some of the villages by my tribe, and some by the mainlanders themselves."

Mara was proud that Elsa's face showed no hint of a reaction to this statement. She felt Elsa's hand against her side, and she knew what Elsa wanted. Mara pressed Brant's dagger, which she had held the whole time, into Elsa's fist.

Elsa was strong and quick, but she was hampered by Mara, and the stranger was apparently expecting an attack. He grabbed Elsa's wrist and squeezed until she dropped the dagger, with a cry of frustration. Mara fell to the ground as well, and she picked up the dagger and hid it in her tunic with her beads.

"You are very beautiful," the barbarian said.

Elsa spit in his face.

Mara had been taught how even the smallest occurrence could change the line of one's fate, how looking over one's shoulder might prolong a life for years. Had the chief of the Huntar sent one of his warriors to secure the boundaries of the village, Mara and Elsa would have been killed immediately. But he had not. He had gone himself, and he was the chief—a chief who appreciated courage and beauty and was not ashamed to change his mind.

And so Mara's fate line did not end on that hillside.

The barbarian was not angered by Elsa's action. He was, in fact, still amused. Chuckling, he wiped his face with the back of his hand. "Listen to me. I have ordered my warriors to kill every person in this village. We were not to take any captives. But I am the chief, and I think I will make an exception. I will swear not to harm you or the girl if you come with me quietly."

At once, Elsa nodded. Mara knew that Elsa only agreed so that she—Mara—would not be harmed. And, after all, it was the word of a warrior and could never be doubted.

Elsa and Mara were led away from the trees and back through the village, nothing but smoldering wood now, to the sea, where the scantily clad savages had left their boats.

Elsa hugged Mara and pointed to where the strangers were loading their boats. "The sea-gold," she said.

Mara tucked her own beads of sea-gold into a fold of her skirt. The sea-gold was a gift from the sea and the sun, and it washed up on the shore of their village. They used it for trading with those across the water—barbarians, but not these barbarians—for bronze and gold. They never wore the sea-gold themselves anymore. But Mara's father had given these beads to her because she was the daughter of the chieftain, and she should have something to set her apart from the others.

Mara tried not to cry.

By the time all the strangers had gathered at the boats, the sun had begun to rise. It cast its warmth and gracious light onto the people standing on the shore. It burnished the pale gold of Elsa's hair and the deeper gold of Mara's. It sparkled on the small waves of the sea, turning the gray of the water to star-white. It glinted off the swords of the strangers who had come across the sea to destroy them. Mara raised her face to the sun and felt its rays touch her cheeks. The sun was life-giver. The sun was comforter.

The sun, her father had said, was always a blessing to those who were worthy.

PART I

SOLOMON

"Remember your Creator
in the days of your youth,
before the days of trouble come
and the years approach when you will say,
'I find no pleasure in them'—
before the sun and the light
and the moon and the stars grow dark,
and the clouds return after the rain."

Ecclesiastes 12:1-2

Chapter 1

Israel

Mara pushed her tangled hair away from her burned face and wondered what the people of this land had done to deserve such a curse from the sun. She lowered herself onto a rock and laid her lyre beside her on the dirt, wincing as her leg muscles tightened when she bent her knees. She had been walking all day, since before sunrise when she had escaped from the caravan.

She could see the heat shimmering in the air, just above the rocky ground.

She closed her eyes. There had been a pond in the trees behind her home, and when the summer days were too warm, she had shed her clothes and jumped into it. But that was years ago and very far away from the dry, sun-cursed hills she was trapped in now.

She hadn't drunk any water all day.

She was always alone in the end. It had been years since she had any deceptive ideas about friends or family. Companionship, love, was just an illusion; eventually, everyone was torn violently away from her. And she had realized, long ago, that she was always alone in the end.

Which is why she was so startled to find out she wasn't. The voice broke the silence of the hills. Mara didn't understand all the words, for the language only seemed vaguely familiar to her, but the last word he spoke sounded like "Golden."

Mara's eyes snapped open, and she pulled a dagger from a fold in her tunic as she jerked to her feet.

"Don't touch me," she hissed at the young man standing in front of her in the language of Danel, the Tyrian merchant, leveling the dagger.

The boy's dark eyes, which had been filled with awe, widened in surprise, but he switched languages easily. "I wasn't planning on touching you."

The boy was several years older than she had thought at first, for he was tall and well-made, but he didn't have a full beard yet so Mara could not consider him a man. He was smiling now, and his eyes were kind. Mara didn't lower the dagger.

"You looked like you needed help, and I have never seen hair like yours before." The young man sat down on a rock next to the one Mara had just vacated and looked at her quizzically.

Mara didn't move for a minute. Then she, too, sat down. But she didn't put away the dagger.

"My name is Jedidiah," the boy said pleasantly. "Why are you alone in these hills?"

"I . . . I choose to be," Mara said stiffly.

Jedidiah frowned. "It is dangerous. I think . . ."

"I can take care of myself."

"So I see." He seemed to be hiding a smile. "But can I help you in any way?"

"Is there no water in this sun-cursed land?" The question came out as a wail rather than the polite inquiry Mara had intended it to be.

Jedidiah stood up quickly. "Oh, you are thirsty. Come, I'll take you to a stream." His face was no longer amused, and Mara was reassured by the consternation she saw in it.

She pulled herself to her feet, hiding the pain she felt as the open cuts on her bare feet touched the hot, dry ground. She followed him silently, wondering who he was. He wore only a short tunic of plain material and worn sandals. He was probably a shepherd boy who had wandered away by himself for the day.

The water was so near that Mara could have hit herself. Grass and weeds were growing around the stream, and the green comforted Mara. It wasn't more than a small trickle running down from the hills, but to Mara it was as assuaging as the sea.

Instead of kneeling down and drinking with her hands, Mara got into the stream and lay down on her face. It was just barely deep enough to cover her whole body.

After a few minutes, she got out and almost smiled at Jedidiah's astonished face. Her hair and clothes were dripping, and the cuts on her feet were stinging, but she felt wonderful. "Thank you for your help," she said. She hoped he would understand her meaning and leave.

His smile told her he understood her meaning, but he didn't leave. "Now that I have helped you, you have to help me."

Mara went stiff and her hand closed around her dagger.

". . . by telling me who you are and what you are doing by yourself," Jedidiah continued.

Mara relaxed, slightly. "It is a long story."

"Good," he said. "I have plenty of time, and I love stories."

"I will make it short. I was with a caravan to be given as a slave to a king, and I don't wish to be a slave anymore."

Jedidiah nodded, hiding the surprise he must have felt at her words. "I see. And which king were you to be given to?"

"King David in Jerusalem."

Mara saw Jedidiah's face go very still for just a moment; then he grinned. "Then you were to have the best of all masters."

Mara looked at him suspiciously. "Is he your king?"

Jedidiah nodded.

"Even so, I don't wish to be a slave."

"And how did you become a slave to begin with."

Mara sighed. "A Tyrian merchant bought us, over the sea."

"Us?" Jedidiah asked politely.

"Elsa and I." Mara fought back the memory but the images came, as they always came when she said Elsa's name.

Danel buys them in the barbarian land, but he takes them to the island of Caphtor on his ship. The kingdom on the island, Danel tells her, was once the greatest in the world, but the wealth has gradually died away and the earth has moved to bury many of the cities and all of the palaces. "But there is still plenty of money to be spared on slaves," he chuckles, the enormous dimples in his cheeks flashing above his dark beard. He leads Mara and Elsa and a few other slaves—one is a boy younger than she is—through the streets of a city. The wealth and power of the people may have waned but the enthusiasm certainly has not. The streets are crowded, and she hears more laughing than she ever has before.

Then she sees the dancers in the market square. She is fascinated. The dark, oiled skin of their lithe bodies glistens as they twirl and glide in synchronized motion. The crowds around them cheer, and Danel tugs Mara away. "Come, little one," he says. "This way." His smile is indulgent, as it always is when he looks at her.

She does not understand at first, when Elsa is made to stand in front of a crowd. Then the boy tells her. They are bidding on her; they want to buy her. The bidding goes on for a long time, and Mara can see by Danel's face that he is pleased with the result.

Elsa hugs her tightly and kisses her on the cheek. "May the sun always warm you, Mara." The words of good-bye.

Mara almost chokes, but she forces herself to say the rest. "And you, until the sun is devoured by the sea."

Elsa walks away from her then, with her back very straight and her beautiful head very high, to the man who has bid the highest for her.

Mara tries to run after her, but Danel catches her by the shoulder and gently restrains her as she struggles, sobbing.

It is then that Danel decides that she is not to be sold at Caphtor as he originally planned, but will be taken with him to his city, to Tyre. But it doesn't matter now at all. For she is alone.

Mara looked up at Jedidiah's bewildered face and, despite the pain—still raw after years—smiled a little. "Let me begin at the beginning. Elsa was my father's sister, and when the Huntar came to steal our sea-gold and destroy our village . . ." Mara paused for a moment to swallow. She should not have lived passed that night, she had decided years ago. Whoever it was that decided the fate of man made a mistake when he kept her alive. At the time, in her desperation and naiveté, she had been sure that time would stop, that nothing could go on after such a devastation; but somehow, time did go on, and for some reason, she went on with it.

"Sea-gold?" Jedidiah's voice broke her reverie.

Mara reluctantly pulled out the beads that she had taken, along with the dagger and her lyre, from the caravan when she had escaped. She had protected them for years. Symbols—not useful or precious, but all she had left. She held them so Jedidiah could see them.

"Amber," he breathed. "It is very rare here."

"Anyway, everyone in the village was supposed to be killed, but the chief, for reasons I have never understood, kept me and Elsa alive. I don't remember much of anything after we left the island until we were sold, with our sea-gold, to a Tyrian merchant, Danel. I learned his language, and he took me to Tyre. Danel grew to like me, so he arranged for me to be sent with other gifts to King David, whom he said would treat me kindly. He did not like me enough to give up his profit." Her tone was bitter.

"Well," Jedidiah said. "He was a Tyrian. You couldn't expect anything else. How long were you with him?"

Mara shrugged. "A few years. I do not know for sure."

Jedidiah reached down and pulled away the heavy wool that Mara used to cover her lyre. "Do you play?"

Mara nodded. "Danel thought it would increase my value, so he had someone teach me."

"Why do you suppose that the tribe that attacked your village—the Huntar?—did not keep more of your people alive as captives?"

"I do not know. Perhaps their sky god was hungry that day. And it was night, you know. So the sun was not there to protect us." Mara had said those words to herself over and over again throughout the years, hoping that one day she could believe them again.

Jedidiah's eyes were sad. "Your people worshipped the sun?"

Mara nodded. "Yes. It didn't do much good, did it?"

Jedidiah shook his head. "And do you still?"

Mara tried to retreat from the question inside herself, but in every place she tried to hide the question was there, with her father's furious face. She knew that she had abandoned everything her father and their village had lived and died for. She knew that if her father were alive to see what she had become, he would turn his back on her.

5

The sun was here as well as in her homeland, but it was not a gracious sun, and she wondered if it was even the same one. She lived her life, now, trying not to think of any power greater than herself.

She couldn't allow herself to think about worship. It left one too vulnerable. "I worship nothing. I try to survive."

"So why . . ."

Jedidiah never finished his question.

Mara recognized the man who stood before them as one of the guards from the caravan; she could not miss the huge gold ring in his nose. "Stand up," he growled.

Mara and Jedidiah stood up slowly. The man turned to Mara, "What did I tell you I would do to you if you tried to escape, you little . . ."

Mara never could remember exactly what happened, even when she relived the moment in her imagination, over and over again, during the following years. The man had been holding his sword tightly, but before she could see any movement, it went flying across the stream, and blood was dripping from a gash in the man's arm. He turned in astonishment and anger to Jedidiah, who held a knife to his throat.

"I think you want to go back to your caravan and pretend you never saw the girl." Jedidiah's dark eyes were ice, and Mara thought that maybe she had estimated his years too low. Surely, no boy could look so hard.

The guard ignored Jedidiah's words and made a grab for the knife. Jedidiah gracefully evaded his hand, and brought the hilt of the knife down—very hard—on the side of the guard's head.

The guard crumpled to the ground.

"How did you do that? He is so much bigger than you." Mara wondered.

Jedidiah turned back to her and gave her a rather breathless grin. "It is not hard when you know the right place to hit him. He is big but has never been trained to fight well. He was clumsy. Come, let's go."

"You aren't going to kill him?" Mara asked, incredulous.

"Of course not. I won't thoughtlessly take a life like that."

"But, Jedidiah, he won't . . . Jedidiah, duck!"

6

Jedidiah flattened himself on the ground as a dagger went whizzing past him to bury itself, harmlessly, in the dirt.

The guard wasted no time and threw himself on top of a prostrate Jedidiah. Mara hurried to where she had left her own dagger, snatched it up, and ran to the two men. She watched for a few moments, but when she saw Jedidiah miss two opportunities to kill the man, she moved forward. Waiting until the guard was on top of Jedidiah again, she thrust her dagger into the back of his throat. It took the man only seconds to die.

Jedidiah stood up, looking at the girl and her crimson-stained dagger in disbelief.

"You killed him," he stuttered.

Mara went over to wipe off her dagger in the grass, coldly glancing at the guard's body, half-covered now with blood. "I gave you the opportunity, but you would not take it. He is a man that would not be stopped until he is dead." She had not wanted to take his killing, but had she not they both would be dead.

"But you are just a girl," Jedidiah said, still staring.

Mara shrugged. "He deserved to die," she said. "He was an animal. My father used to say that when a good man dies, the wind comes to carry his spirit away. There is no wind."

Jedidiah shook his head. "I should not have let you kill him."

"He has no one who will come after us for vengeance. Everyone despised him. I had to kill him," Mara told him. "There was no other way."

"There is always another way."

Mara chose to ignore that and picked up the rest of her belongings. She had never killed anyone before, but she felt no regret. But if she allowed Jedidiah to continue talking, she would be forced to take the act more seriously than she wished. "I will leave you now. I have brought you enough trouble. Thank you for your help."

"Where will you go?" Jedidiah asked, shaking the dazed look out of his eyes.

Mara shrugged and turned to walk away. Jedidiah followed her.

"What do you want?" she asked, exasperated.

7

"What are my choices? I can take you back to the caravan and explain about the man we killed. That is probably what I should do . . . but, I think if I tried that I would not get to the caravan intact."

Mara narrowed her eyes.

"So, I can leave you, like you want, without any food or any place to go, to the mercy of the lions and bears that sometimes prowl around here."

Mara hadn't thought about that, and she shivered involuntarily.

"Or, I can take you with me to my father's house."

"And what would I do there?" Mara asked, stiffening.

"You could work for us," Jedidiah responded with a little smile.

"I will not be a slave."

Jedidiah threw up his hands, as if to defend himself. "Not as a slave. You would work, and we would feed you and give you a place to stay. We always need good musicians. You would be free to leave if ever you wanted."

Mara hesitated.

"What other choice do you have?"

"None. I have no other choice." Mara looked up at Jedidiah. He really was very handsome, but not in the way Brant or her father had been handsome. Jedidiah's face was finer cut, with a stronger nose and a sharper chin. He had been very kind. He had fought a man for her. And she really had no other choice. "Very well, I will go with you."

Jedidiah nodded, "Good, we will not make it back in one day, but we should get started."

Matching his stride, Mara sighed. She had reached another fork in the road of her life: a road, she had learned, that never ran straight.

Chapter 2

Mara followed her new companion in silence until just before sunset. "How far are we going to go today?" she asked at last, trying not to let the weariness into her voice.

"Oh," Jedidiah said, turning around. They had reached the top of a hill, but there was leveler ground in front of them. The stream had widened, and they were walking, Mara thought with pleasure, on grass. "We can stay at the foot of this hill for the night."

"Be careful," Jedidiah warned. "This hill is steep and the rocks are wet from the stream."

Mara nodded as she picked her way down the hill in front of Jedidiah. She was almost at the bottom when her foot slipped, and she would have fallen had Jedidiah not whipped his arm out and slammed her against his chest. Startled, but not entirely surprised, Mara jerked away from his touch. She managed to keep her footing, but Jedidiah was thrown forward and lost his balance. Mara looked down to see him sprawled, face down, in the mud.

"Are you all right?" she asked, hurrying down to join him, ashamed of her reaction that caused his fall.

"Yes I am," Jedidiah gritted through his teeth as he raised himself onto his elbows.

Mara couldn't remember the last time she had laughed, or if she had ever laughed in her short life. So she was vaguely surprised when, as she watched this young man spitting out mud, she laughed so hysterically she had to sit down.

"Stop laughing," Jedidiah ordered, trying, unsuccessfully, to stand up. His attempts only increased her hilarity. "How dare you! You dirty little peasant. I am the son of a king."

Mara stopped laughing abruptly. She raised her chin to a proud tilt. "And I am the daughter of a king." She paused a few seconds, "But I am not covered in mud."

Mara wondered if she would have to run away from Jedidiah's wrath at her response, for his young face twisted frighteningly as he tried to control his anger. But in a moment he started to chuckle. He went over to the stream and submerged himself like Mara had done a few hours before. "I was serious," he told her after he had wiped the mud from his face and arms.

Mara shrugged. Her father had been a chieftain, a king. Whoever Jedidiah's father was, he was no greater than her own had been.

Jedidiah looked at her curiously. He pulled himself out of the stream and wrung the water out of his dark hair. "You don't seem surprised that I am the son of a king."

"I'm not," Mara responded. "I thought you were a shepherd at first because of your clothes, but you couldn't be. Surely shepherds in this country don't know more than one language, or hire musicians, or fight in the way I saw you fight."

Jedidiah grinned. "You'd be surprised at how well a shepherd learns to fight. My father was a shepherd."

"I thought you said he was a king."

"Oh, he is *now*. He *was* a shepherd." Jedidiah looked around. "Are you hungry?"

Mara nodded. She watched as Jedidiah made his way gracefully up the hill they had just climbed and out of sight. He moved like the dancers she had seen in the streets of Caphtor, before Elsa was taken away from her. Mara rolled her eyes. She had certainly picked a peculiar companion. Who ever heard of a shepherd who was a king? But, then, her father had been a fisherman and a king, so maybe it wasn't so strange in this land.

Mara looked around her. The sky was growing darker, and the air cooler. It wasn't refreshing. In her village, the air was crisp and clean; here, when she took a deep breath, she felt like she was inhaling dust—dust and heat.

Shortly, Jedidiah reappeared and climbed—very cautiously this time—down the slope with a dead partridge, which he proceeded to pluck and roast over the fire he made.

"How did you kill that?" Mara asked as he worked. "You had no weapon but the knife."

Jedidiah gave her a half smile. "They can't fly, so it's easy enough to just chase them and hit them with a rock."

"So why are *you* by yourself in these hills?" Mara asked, changing the subject.

"I get tired of everyone sometimes, and I like to wander around by myself for a few days."

"What does your father, the king, think about that?"

Jedidiah evaded Mara's calm blue eyes. "He doesn't actually know about it."

Mara snorted. "You are saying that you disappear for a few days and your own father doesn't know about it?"

Jedidiah nodded.

"How is that possible?"

"Our house is . . . rather big," Jedidiah explained.

Mara didn't believe him. "It must be."

"Well," Jedidiah began, visibly offended by her transparent disbelief. "The palace of the king of Israel would naturally be so large."

Mara stared at him. "The king of Israel? Are you saying that King David is your father?"

Jedidiah nodded, wrinkling his brow. "Surely you knew that. There is only one king in Israel."

Mara jumped to her feet. "Knew that? How would I know that? You are taking me exactly where the caravan was taking me. To be a slave again." She started to gather her possessions, turning crimson in anger and embarrassment.

"Not a slave. Just a servant. I told you. You don't have to stay there if you don't like it. Where are you going?"

"Somewhere away from you," Mara said, mustering all the hauteur she could. She started to walk away. It was dusk, and the sky was pink and gold, spreading across the hills like a blanket. Part of her mind recognized its beauty, but another part dismissed it. The sky, the setting sun, the dusty hills, and the trickling stream were all a part of Jedidiah, who had been deceiving her the entire day.

"Don't leave. You will get yourself killed," Jedidiah hurried over to stand beside her. "I don't even know your name."

11

Mara looked up into his face. His expression was earnest, but she could glimpse a twinkling of amusement in his eyes. "You mock me," she whispered.

The amusement disappeared. "Never. I mock myself, maybe, for wanting you to stay so much."

Mara peered into his eyes, luminous and reflecting the setting sun, and was satisfied. She went back to the fire where the partridge was burning and sat down again. "My name is Mara."

"Mara," Jedidiah repeated, drawling her name out longer than Mara could allow.

"Not like that. Mara," she said again.

"In Israel, we have a similar name, but we pronounce it slightly differently. You had best get used to it as I say it. Oh, and my name is Solomon—my other name, that is."

Mara looked confused.

"My family calls me Jedidiah. But everyone else calls me Solomon."

"Solomon," Mara repeated, trying to drawl it the way he had her own name.

Solomon grinned at her, and Mara liked the way his face was transformed when he smiled.

Mara chewed on the piece of meat he gave her in silence. Then she asked idly, "Are you the oldest in your family?"

Solomon shook his head. "No, but I am to be the next king." His tone was defensive.

"How is that possible?" She swallowed the piece of meat. It was burnt and dry, but she was hungry, so she took another bite.

"That is the Lord's will."

Mara cocked her head to one side. "Your god is so clear about that kind of thing?"

"He is about this."

"What about your older brother?" Mara asked, trying to imagine a family where the oldest son did not inherit.

"I had several," Solomon's voice had grown tense, but Mara continued to question him.

"Several? And you are to be king instead of them?"

"Many of them died as children. One of them is mad. Of the three oldest sons—Amnon, Absalom, and Adonijah—only

12

Adonijah still lives. Amnon died when I was still young. Absalom killed him."

"Wait," Mara interrupted, sitting up straighter. "I thought you said that they were brothers."

"They were—half-brothers. They hated each other. Amnon probably deserved to die."

Mara's eyes seared Solomon, and he pushed a dark curl from his eyes impatiently. "Don't look at me like that. You know nothing at all of the matter," he said.

Mara turned her eyes from Solomon to the hill behind which the sun had just set. "Perhaps. But I do know that my father would have burned in darkness for eternity before he would have betrayed his brother as you have done with your words, no matter what Brant had done."

She turned her gaze back to Solomon. He had lowered his eyes, and she thought she saw his cheeks flush. She felt a little sad for him, for the tragedy of his family, but she had traveled too far and seen too much to spare the little pity she had on one who had never known need. "What happened to Absalom?"

"He was killed when he led a rebellion against my father."

Mara's mouth fell open; then she giggled. "Now I know that you are lying."

"I do not lie."

Mara couldn't comprehend it. "Then you are mistaken about them being brothers. No family would act that way. I mean, family is . . . family; there is no stronger bond."

"You were blessed with your family. But do not expect all families to behave that way. My father has many wives, and many children from each wife. And my own mother . . ."

Mara was startled by the bitterness she heard, "She is not his wife?"

"Oh, he married her." His voice was dripping with scorn.

Mara had to turn away from the look she saw in his eyes. His expression scared her. She knew instinctively—despite her life and her capture and the blood that she had seen—that his pain reached beyond bitterness to a place she did not know. It was, she decided, time to change the subject. "I never knew my mother," she commented.

Solomon eagerly took up the new subject. "She died?"

13

"When I was born. Elsa was the only mother that I knew, and she was very young." Elsa, with golden hair like a mantle and blue eyes with stars in their depths. For the first time since the market in Caphtor, her own eyes filled with tears at the thought of Elsa's beautiful face.

"What happened to her?" All signs of scorn had disappeared from Solomon's expression, and his face showed only sympathy and a tenderness that nearly broke her control.

But control was something Mara had learned in her life. She smiled a little. "I'm not quite sure. She was sold at a slave auction. On Caphtor. I try not to imagine what her life is . . ." She didn't finish.

"What was she like?" Solomon asked, handing her a jar of water.

Mara took a long sip of water before she responded. "Beautiful. So beautiful that men killed for her. And strong. She stabbed three of the strangers who tried to violate her. She was so brave."

"Much like you, I imagine."

Mara thought a long time before she responded to that. Such discussions, she had learned, could give too much away. "My father said that Elsa was just like me when she was a child. I wouldn't know."

Suddenly, she was very tired. She couldn't fight back a yawn.

"I think it is time to sleep." Solomon reached over and touched her arm, very gently. "You will not run away during the night?"

Mara thought for a moment. "I will not. I swear to you."

"No need to swear. I don't think you ever lie . . . about anything important."

Mara thought about that for a long time before she slept, and she concluded that Solomon was far too perceptive for her to be entirely comfortable.

"It was called Jebus, the capital of the Jebusites, before my father conquered it. Now it is Jerusalem, the city of David. We will be able to see it as soon as we reach the top of this hill." There was pride in Solomon's eyes as he explained.

Mara did her best to keep up with Solomon's long strides, eager to see the city that was to become her home—if she wanted it to. They reached the top, and Mara looked toward Jerusalem, still several miles away.

She sniffed a little. "It must be easily defended," she said, not particularly impressed. Caphtor had been towered by aging, brilliantly crafted buildings and the memory of faded glory. Tyre, built on a rocky coastline, had brightly painted villas and monuments, and above them, the masts of hundreds of ships had decorated the skyline. From what Mara could see, Jerusalem boasted no such glories.

"Yes," Solomon said, replying to her one comment. "This is the only direction an army can invade from, you see. The other directions are—"

Mara could see Solomon was about to embark on a tactical lecture in which she was not interested, so she interrupted him. "I wonder how David conquered Jerusalem to begin with."

Solomon chuckled. "Now that's a story. You'll hear it soon enough. People still talk of Joab's feat."

Though he smiled, Mara could see distaste in his eyes, so she didn't press the subject. The hills had gotten greener and greener as they had walked this morning. At one point, they had reached the top of a hill and looked out on a valley covered with tiny purple flowers. It didn't seem fair that there could be such beauties in a land she was determined to hate.

When they entered one of the gates to the city, Mara decided that Jerusalem was not that much different from any of the other cities she had seen. There were no dancers in the street like she had seen in Caphtor, and the air didn't smell of the sea as it had in Tyre, but the crowds, and the vendors, and the noise were all the same. Solomon led her through the narrow streets, and Mara kept her eyes down as much as possible.

When she looked up, she gasped. "That is your father's house?"

"His palace, yes," Solomon affirmed.

David's palace was four stories tall and was encircled entirely by balconies. "I am impressed. It looks like Tyrian buildings."

"That's because Tyrian craftsmen built it," Solomon explained.

Mara nodded, and started toward the main gate in the wall surrounding the palace grounds.

"No, not that way," Solomon stopped her.

15

"But that is the entrance."

Solomon shook his head. "Not the one I use. Here, around the back."

Solomon led her to a smaller gate in the back. The guard grinned at him. "It's about time you were back. I hear your father was looking for you."

"Oh no," Solomon groaned. The smile on his face faded. "When, Jacob?"

"Today. Not too long ago. You should hurry, though."

The guard looked curiously at Mara, but he refrained from asking any questions. Mara could well imagine what he thought of the situation. The same thing anyone would think.

The man Solomon took her to had a graying beard and the whitest smile Mara had ever seen. "Solomon, your father is looking for you." The man had a deep, throaty voice.

"So I hear." Solomon reached over and took the shawl from Mara's hair. "Can you find a place for her, Ahishar? She plays the lyre."

"Can I what?" Ahishar covered his face with his thick hands. "We don't need another musician in this palace. We are overflowing with them already."

Mara turned to Solomon, but he looked unabashed. "Ahishar doesn't appreciate music. He is in charge of all the servants. He will take care of you. If you have any problems, tell him, and he will talk to me."

Mara nodded and was suddenly very frightened. "And if I don't like it . . ."

"Tell me," Solomon finished for her. "I will do something about it."

Ahishar looked at the disheveled girl before him and sighed. "What is your name?"

Solomon answered for her, "Her name is Mara."

"I must go now and find my father. I will see you soon, I expect," Solomon said over his shoulder as he walked away.

"Come, Mara. I will take you to your quarters."

Mara followed Ahishar's portly figure and sighed. She wondered where the winds had taken her now.

16

Chapter 3

Jerusalem

Perfume. Strong and dense, sweet or musky, hanging in the air like a dying song. In the palace, it was unavoidable. Aloes and calami from the Far East, cassia and saffron from the islands, myrrh from Arabia. For Mara, the world of the palace was made up of perfume, and at this moment, she couldn't imagine any other world.

She walked quickly through the cedar-paneled halls of the palace of David of Israel, trying to look as if she had something to do. If she appeared idle, one of the ladies of the harem would ask her to braid hair or take a stain out of a robe, and Mara didn't feel like listening to court gossip this morning.

After two years in the palace as a musician, she had still done very little playing. Hadad, director of the musicians, thought she was too young to play at banquets and court functions, despite her adamant arguments to the contrary. And David played the lyre himself and had many very fine musicians, so she had never played for him. Often, one of David's wives or concubines would ask her to provide background music to their relaxation, but Mara was sure her soft music was never heard over the gossiping.

She sighed, then smiled shyly as one of David's special guard—a Pelethite she guessed from the braided hair—winked at her as he passed. She did not recognize him by name, but she knew that he and Benaiah, the captain of the king's bodyguard, were close friends; there was also an unconfirmed rumor going around that this man had saved Solomon's life somehow while hunting. Anyway, she was quite sure that he would support Solomon rather than Adonijah if it came to that, so it was safe to smile at him. Even the smallest gestures, even from a slave girl, had to be measured carefully at court.

If anything could be accepted as true in this palace and these times, it was that the smallest incident could upset the delicate balance of favor and power in the court.

The guard greeted her casually. Everyone at the palace knew who she was—the golden-haired slave girl who had eyes like the sky at night. She giggled as she remembered the musician who had said that to her last spring. Then she sobered. The man had died a few months later from a fever.

Mara had learned the language of Israel quickly, and she had also learned the ways of the palace. She grew accustomed to the manipulation and subtle maneuvering that went on, even among the slaves. And she had become adept at making herself pleasant, at flattering and cajoling her superiors and also at placing carefully measured words here and there, where the impact would be the greatest.

Everyone in the palace thought that she was a slave, for Solomon had not wanted to create more gossip by explaining their real arrangement. At least, that was what he had told her two years ago. Now she rarely saw Solomon, and she could count on her fingers the times they had spoken. But she was a slave girl and he was the son of a king, and she could hardly blame him if he wanted to avoid any sort of scandal, especially in his precarious situation.

Mara reached the end of the hall and stepped out onto the terrace that overlooked the stables. She had heard that a merchant had arrived this morning in a caravan from Egypt with horses, and he had brought one particularly for Solomon. Such favors were not strange in the palace these days, and Mara wondered if the merchant had brought a gift for Adonijah as well.

Mara glanced down and, as she had expected, Solomon was in the clearing next to the stables with his new mount.

Solomon was striving to calm the rearing horse, and Mara took a moment to admire the beautiful strength of the animal and the glossy, jet-black coat. Then she turned her eyes back to Solomon.

She couldn't remember when she had started thinking of him as a man, rather than a boy; but his dark beard was full now, and his wavy hair reached his shoulders. He was still as graceful as the dancers of

Caphtor, as graceful as the horse beside him. And as strong. He was wearing only a tunic, so Mara could see his bronzed arms and legs.

"Mara," came a lilting voice from behind her.

Mara whirled, reddening and feeling ridiculously guilty. The figure before her was delicately dressed in pure white linen, and Mara could smell the expensive Arabian perfume she wore. The girl's face was exquisite, with enormous dark eyes and perfect white teeth. Mara recognized her. Everyone recognized the Shunammite. Abishag, who cared for David in his decline. Mara had seen her often, but had never made any attempt to know her. Abishag was just too beautiful and her position on too many things was unknown. But everyone knew that Adonijah favored her, so Mara had done her best to avoid King David's personal attendant.

Abishag moved over to stand beside Mara and look down at the courtyard. "He is so handsome. More handsome now than was his brother, Absalom. But his mother would be furious if she knew he stands, before the eyes of the palace, in only his tunic."

Mara ignored the last comment. She had heard that Absalom had been considered the handsomest man in all Israel. "You knew Absalom?"

Abishag shook her head. "No, but I saw him once as a girl. I dreamed about him for months after."

Mara looked back down at Solomon, struggling to mount the horse. "Oh," was all she said.

"But Solomon now is more handsome than any of his brothers. And far more worthy to rule after David." Abishag's dusky eyes held Mara's, and the message in them was undeniable.

Mara gasped, and looked quickly around, but they were alone. She was shocked by Abishag's words, dangerous words around the palace now, but she hoped they were sincere. "You mean that?" she asked softly.

Abishag nodded. "Even if I didn't know David's wishes, I would still find Solomon better suited for kingship. I just wanted you to know that right off, so that it would not interfere with what I hope will be a friendship."

"Thank you," Mara responded. "For being so direct. I'm afraid I had thought you favored . . ."

19

Abishag nodded. "Yes. Adonijah, the jackal, has . . ." She paused as a group of soldiers clattered through the hall. "He apparently thought that it would do him good to have my support. Well, he doesn't have it. But he does have half the country convinced that he should be king."

"He is the oldest," Mara ventured, half-heartedly.

Abishag's full lips turned up in a smile. "You defend him. Perhaps I was mistaken. I had thought . . ." She turned her head suggestively back down to the stables.

Mara threw her chin up and was furious at the blush she felt staining her cheeks. "You thought what?" she asked coldly.

Abishag laughed. "Oh, how proud you are. Your fair hair and skin may be beautiful, but it must be very inconvenient to redden so obviously."

Mara studied her companion's laughing face and wondered how she should take that comment.

"And, here, I came to find you specifically so we could become friends."

Mara narrowed her eyes. "You did? Why?"

"Well, the king is in a humor to hear music, and he wanted to see— after two years—the golden-haired beauty Solomon has brought to the court. I volunteered to search for you, because I have been wanting to get to know you."

"Why is that?" Mara asked again.

"I have felt rather bad because I have never talked to you. You see, I have been jealous of how lovely you are. I am ashamed to admit it, but you have taken much of my admiration away from me." Abishag's eyes were open and earnest.

"I have?" Mara's mouth fell open. "But you are much more beautiful than I am."

Abishag laughed, and, this time, Mara joined her. "I will come with you to get your lyre. And along the way we will become friends."

Mara turned once more to look at Solomon. He had succeeded in calming the horse and had mounted it. She could hear his triumphant laugh from the terrace.

When she looked back at Abishag, she could see the young woman's eyes were full of such pity and understanding that she almost choked. "A fine man, is Solomon."

Mara was silent.

"Do not shut me out already," Abishag said, starting to glide through the shell-floored halls. "You see, I too know what it is to long for the dawn in the starless dark of night."

"Well, at last I get to see the great King David of Israel," Mara commented as she and Abishag climbed the wide stairs up to David's chambers.

"You have never even seen him?" Abishag asked, faintly incredulous.

Mara shook her head. "No, I haven't. I don't attend the banquets and court functions that he holds, and he has never wanted to hear my music before."

Abishag smiled. "You spend most of your time in the harem?"

Mara nodded.

"There was a time when that would have insured your sight of the king, but now . . ." Her voice faded away, and Mara saw sadness in her eyes. "Now he rarely leaves his chambers. Nothing is sadder than when a great king grows too old for greatness."

Mara's blue eyes widened. "You do not speak with the respect I would have expected from the king's . . . hand-maiden."

Abishag gave an amused snort. "Hand-maiden, indeed. All that I wish is to return home and marry my love, and instead I feed the king his soup and wipe his brow when he is warm."

"Then why don't you leave?"

"Can I leave? The king has asked, and I can hardly deny him. I am his subject in all things."

Mara studied Abishag's face. "In all things?"

Abishag stiffened. "Not in all things. I will keep myself pure for my love."

"Who is he?"

"A shepherd from Shunam. I have known him since childhood. He waits for me until I return." Abishag smiled softly, and her eyes were far away.

They reached the carved cedar doors of the king's chambers, and they paused while the guard noted them and opened the doors.

Mara felt her hands grow damp as she entered the cool of the room. More perfume, not sweet but raw and pungent. The rich decorating of the chamber also overwhelmed her. The walls were paneled in carved cedar and the candlesticks, vases, and legs of the chairs were gilded in gold. Mara had to look for several seconds before she saw the man smothered in vividly colored blankets on the couch next to the window.

Abishag approached him. "My king," she said. "The golden-haired musician is here."

David turned his head to face them, and Mara was disappointed.

This was the man who had killed a giant and claimed a kingdom? This was the man who had conquered nations and triumphed in battle? This was just a wrinkled old man with thinning gray hair.

He didn't look at all like Solomon.

"So you are the girl that my son has brought to the palace? He has spoken of you. Perhaps you will tell me how it really came about." Mara had to lean forward to catch the words.

She cleared her throat. "I am sure that whatever your son has told you is correct."

Then David smiled, and Mara could see that he was, after all, Solomon's father. The smile transformed his face, and Mara understood what had made him so attractive and charismatic to a nation. "Ah ha, you have left me no argument. My son, whatever his faults, is not a liar. But sometimes he does not care to tell me everything."

Mara didn't respond. She stood uncomfortably in front of the king and clutched her lyre.

"And she has nothing more to say. You must follow her example, Abishag, and not speak when you have nothing to say."

Abishag laughed softly at his joke and moved to block some of the light from David's eyes.

"Play for me . . . what was your name?"

"Mara," she replied. David nodded his acknowledgment, and Mara seated herself on one of the thick rugs that were scattered on the floor.

Mara had been playing for nearly an hour when the chamber doors were thrown open and a very large man barreled in.

David glanced over at him and shook his head. "You should have at least enough respect for your king that you allow yourself to be announced, Joab."

Mara continued playing, but she sat up straighter. She had seen Joab many times, the king's cousin, captain of the armies. He, at least, had met her expectations. He was nearly as tall as her father had been, and just as broad across the shoulders. He must have been almost as old as David was, but his hair was still mostly brown, and the lines on his forehead and around his mouth did nothing to mar the strong features.

In fact, Mara realized instinctively that Joab was more powerful now than when he had led the attack on Jerusalem as a young man.

Mara had heard the story several times. Joab had climbed in through the water shaft that led from the Spring of Gihon into Jerusalem, and had thus breached an unbreachable city.

Everyone knew that Joab did not favor Solomon as the next king, but his devotion to David was acknowledged by all, and no one doubted that he would support David's decision.

"Do not speak to me in that way, David. I am not one of your menials."

David sat up straighter. "That would indeed be a mistaken assumption on my part. Is there something that has bothered you?"

Joab snorted. "Bothered me? What have you done in the last two years that hasn't bothered me?"

"Perhaps you can be more specific." David's face showed no surprise or upset. He was, in fact, smiling.

"I would appreciate it if you would speak to me like a man, and not like a naughty child." Joab took a few steps closer to David. "David, please. If you will not think of your family, think of your nation, the nation you will leave behind when you die." There was history here, more than Mara could possibly understand.

For the first time, David's smile faded. "What have you heard?"

"Nathan has been talking about Yahweh's temple. And when he talks about it he assumes that Solomon will build it. David you must stop him. The word will get around and people will think the decision has been made."

"But Joab, cousin, the decision is not mine to make, and it was made long ago. It is Yahweh's will that . . ."

"Yahweh would not will for such a spineless whelp to become . . ."

David pushed himself up. "You are speaking of my son." His eyes were narrowed, and Mara could see his hands clenched at his side. There was anger in the eyes, but behind it, she could see sadness. The men, she knew, were best friends.

Joab was not intimidated by David's anger. "Adonijah is also your son, and much more fit to become king. He is older; by all rights he should be the next king. Think of the situation when you die; there will almost certainly be a rebellion against Solomon. David, think of Israel."

"The God of Israel has chosen, and you think I feel intrepid enough to defy him? Joab, you are my oldest friend. Do not forsake me on this."

A choking sound came from Joab, and he fell on his knees before the king. "Forsake you! David, everything that I have ever done has been for you!" Mara caught the look that the two men exchanged, and she learned something about the nature of bonding and about love.

She was barely playing anymore, but she was afraid to stop altogether; it might draw attention to her. She felt that she should not be hearing this. It was too private, went too deep.

David lowered himself back onto the couch. "I know how much you love me, Joab. I only wish you respected my judgment as much."

Joab rose to his feet. "David, listen to what I say, for once. I . . ."

David held up his hand. "The decision is made. You will not change my mind."

Joab whirled around, and Mara shrank from the fury in his face. He bent down toward her, and Mara bit her lip to keep from crying out. The captain of the armies of Israel grabbed the small table that was standing next to where Mara sat and slammed it onto the floor in front of the king. The guards placed outside the doors ran in, but David waved them away.

"You are wrong, cousin," Joab growled as he started toward the door. "You are wrong."

When he was gone, David turned his head toward the window and wept; Mara continued to play and stared steadily at the splinters of the table on the floor in front of the broken king of Israel.

It was a very strange thing, she thought, to have to struggle against feeling deep pity for both of these men. Men she shared nothing with. Men who would—without a second thought—use her for their own purposes. Men she didn't even really know.

Chapter 4

David's harem was located two stories below his own chambers, on the ground floor of his palace. Enormous doors opened into a wide hall, off of which were dozens of rooms for his wives and concubines. At the end of the hall, two more doors led to the women's garden, separated from the rest of the palace grounds by a stone wall; a wall high enough to block any inquisitive prier from a view of the king's women. Two weeks after the episode with David and Joab, Mara was summoned to the women's garden to relieve their troubled spirits with some music.

"Not that they have anything to be troubled about," Mara muttered as she hurried down the hall, assaulted by the waves of cloying perfume stronger in the harem than anywhere else in the palace.

David's concubines never left the harem, and his wives rarely did. Favored Bathsheba, Solomon's mother, was the only one who ever visited David in his chambers. This fact did little to improve feelings in the harem.

As Mara skipped down the hall, she gave a small cry of surprise when a horrible shriek came from the room beside her. She shook her head in annoyance. She had heard that bird squawk a hundred times, but it never ceased to startle her. It was such an unnatural sound for a bird to make. The birds at home had sung sweetly if they were small, or, if they were hunters, had called out defiantly. But they had never made such ungracious squawks. But the bird itself was unnatural. What kind of a bird had feathers of such incredible reds, blues, and greens? A parrot, it was called. A trader had brought it with him from the East, and Michal had taken a fancy to it. Mara hated the bird.

She entered the garden, and took a deep breath of flower-scented air, relatively mild after the stifling hall. Eglah and Abitar, two of David's younger wives, were bathing in the pool with the brown-skinned concubine whose name Mara could never remember. Michal, David's first wife and the only one without children, was lounging with Abigail and Maachah among the brilliant colors of the flowers. Mara approached them.

"Here is our musician," Maachah announced, sipping her drink. "Sit there and play for us."

Mara obeyed and began to play softly. She didn't concentrate very hard because she knew from experience that the women barely listened.

"Tell us more about the land you come from, Mara," Maachah said after a moment. "About the land filled with trees with leaves that are always green, even in winter."

This was a frequent request, so Mara was not surprised.

Israel knew little of the people of the land she had come from, or the lands she had traveled through during her life. Many of the desert armies hired barbarian warriors as mercenaries—from tribes like the Huntar—but little was known about their lives and beliefs. Mara, perhaps, knew more than anyone else, but no one thought to ask her except the women of the harem. Her own homeland, even farther away than the land of the barbarians, was looked on as almost a legend, a fable of a snow-covered land.

Mara wondered sometimes if people thought she had sprung, fully grown, out of the ground.

"In the winter sometimes it snows so that the snow on the ground reaches your waist."

This caused a stir, and the women in the pool moved closer to Mara. "It doesn't melt?" Eglah asked.

Mara nodded. "It is cold all winter. Much colder than it is here."

"And tell us about the men that live in this land," said the brown-skinned concubine in her throaty voice. "What are they like?"

Mara smiled. "They are all as large as Joab, and they have golden hair like mine."

This caused an even greater stir. "And do the women all look like you?" Maachah asked.

Mara shook her head. "I do not know. Some are beautiful, some are not. I don't know if they look like me."

Michal raised her graying head. "Have you never seen yourself in a mirror?"

Mara shook her head again. "I have never had the opportunity. I have seen myself in water, but, of course, the image is not very clear when one's mouth runs up the side of one's face."

"Abigail, take Mara and show her herself in a mirror," Michal ordered, with the authority of the first wife.

Abigail smiled kindly at Mara and rose. "Come, dear. I will show you."

Mara shrugged and followed Abigail into her chamber. Abigail pointed to the piece of polished silver on the wall. "There, you may see yourself."

Mara walked cautiously over to the mirror, and peered into it. She gasped. The face was oval. The eyes were long, and deep blue. The nose was straight and the lips and cheeks were red. The face was Elsa's face.

"What is it?" Abigail asked.

"I look just like Elsa," Mara stated. "She was so beautiful."

"So are you," Abigail responded with a smile. "Did you not expect to be beautiful?"

Mara shook her head. "I don't know. Everyone says that I am beautiful, but I thought it was because I look different. I did not expect to look like Elsa."

"Elsa was the one the men always fought over?" Abigail asked kindly.

Mara nodded.

"Come, we must return and report to Michal." Abigail chuckled. "We wouldn't want her to get angry and think we were revolting."

Mara tried to repress an answering smile. It was hard not to take sides in the quarrels of the harem. David must have been a fool to ignore such a wonderful woman as Abigail in favor of Bathsheba. Mara had never spoken with Bathsheba, but she had seen her from a distance. Startlingly beautiful, as glorious and sparkling as a diamond—and just as hard. Certainly not the mother Mara would have chosen for Solomon.

As Abigail and Mara started down the hall toward the garden, an agonized shriek echoed through the hall. Both Mara and Abigail jumped back instinctively. Abigail looked at Mara with a rueful grin, and murmured something about strangling a feathery neck. Mara would have laughed but the shrieks continued to come from Michal's room.

"What could be wrong with it?" Abigail asked.

Mara had to cover her ears because the shrieks were so loud. "You had better see what's wrong; I'll go get Michal," Abigail said, and scurried down the hall.

Mara took a deep breath so she wouldn't choke on the smell of perfume and entered Michal's chamber. The bird's cage was in the corner, and Mara shook her head at the cluster of scarlet, jade and azure feathers. "Miserable bird, what is wrong with you?" she asked aloud.

The bird continued to shriek.

Mara walked nearer, and then she saw what was wrong. The bird, apparently tired of being imprisoned in a solid gold cage, had tried to escape. He had thrust his head between the slender bars of the cage and was trying, unsuccessfully, to retrieve his head.

"Oh, you feathery fool," Mara muttered. She started to pull the bars apart farther when the bird, apparently thinking she was after something other than his release, nipped her finger with an indignant squawk.

"Ow!" Mara cried out. "I'm trying to help you."

She examined the situation for a moment, and then opened the door to the cage. She would come at the bars from behind, and thus evade his beak. She stuck one hand in the cage and managed to reach one of the bars holding the bird's neck in. Fortunately, the bar was, indeed, solid gold, and the bar bent easily under her pressure.

Her finger was beginning to bleed heavily, so she pulled her hand out to wipe the blood away. The bird, ungrateful to his rescuer, scolded her soundly as he removed his head from the bars. Then, noticing that the door remained obligingly open, he took that opportunity to escape.

Michal and Abigail, who had just entered, fell to the ground in panic as a scarlet arrow came flying straight toward them.

Michal quickly saw what had happened. "You let him out, you little fool. He will hurt himself. You must catch him."

Mara thought she sounded suspiciously like her pet, but she obediently ran down the hall in pursuit of the wayward bird. Fortunately, the bird had flown toward the doors that led into the rest of the palace and not toward the garden. "I'll catch him at the end of the hall," Mara thought to herself, changing her jog into a sprint, confident that she would not have to face Michal's wrath at the loss of the bird.

The next moment, she changed her mind. One of the guards outside the doors that led to the harem had heard the shouting and opened the door to investigate.

The bird flew out of the harem and into the halls of the palace.

"He's going to get hurt. You had better catch him, or I'll make sure you are sold to a brothel."

Mara winced as she heard Michal's angry shouts. She followed the bird into the halls of the palace, nearly trampling an astonished guard.

Mara caught a glimpse of scarlet feathers at the end of the hall, and she raced toward them. The bird came to roost on a copper candlestick attached to the wall. Mara pulled to a stop. She tiptoed closer to the bird, willing her breath to stop coming out in pants. She reached out her hand to grasp the bird, and it flew away with an indignant squawk.

She chased it again, colliding with a man in front of her. She did not even look up at his face; she just murmured her apologies, and kept on running. In the back of her mind, she heard the man's chuckle follow her down the hall.

"Oh, you miserable fowl. You did this on purpose," Mara cried as she followed the bird up the wide cedar stairs.

"You deliberately planned everything. It was all an ingenious plot that you cooked up in that tiny little head of yours." Mara's voice had risen to a wail, and she stopped abruptly when she turned to the next flight of stairs.

Adonijah, Solomon, and a number of other men—unknown to Mara—stood looking at her with their mouths open in astonishment.

She knew her face reddened as she gasped, "The bird, did you see it?"

The colorful bird flew down and perched innocently on Adonijah's shoulder. He grinned at her. "This bird? What was that about a plot against you?"

Mara covered her face with her hands. "He was trying to make an escape."

Adonijah nodded, as if enlightened. "I see. You'll find that birds are absolute fiends when it comes to thinking up schemes to escape."

Solomon, listening to this exchange with interest, could not quite restrain the snort of amusement.

29

Mara turned to him. "You can laugh and make fun of me. But it is not you who will get sent to a brothel if the bird gets away."

Adonijah turned to Solomon with raised eyebrows, and Solomon sobered immediately. "Who told you that?"

Mara did not answer.

Solomon stepped closer to Mara, and lifted her chin with his hand. "You know that no one will send you anywhere you don't want to go," he whispered. "I promised you."

Mara nodded mutely.

"Do you believe me?" Solomon asked, his eyes very dark and deep.

Mara shut her eyes so he couldn't read the expression in them. "I believe you."

Adonijah chuckled. "Well, now that is settled, will someone remove this appendage from off my shoulder?"

Mara walked over to Solomon's brother, trying to avoid his curious eyes. Only now did she wonder at the strange situation of the two brothers together.

Still chuckling, Adonijah reached out and ran his fingers down Mara's red cheek. "I didn't realize my brother was so fond of you. Interesting."

Mara schooled her face to show no expression, but she wanted to jerk away from his touch. She grabbed the bird with both hands and said over his shrieking. "Be quiet, or I will twist your scrawny neck."

"I hope you are speaking to the bird," Adonijah said, feigning shock.

Solomon smiled, apparently unaware of Adonijah's preoccupation, and shook his head. "You had better return the bird to its owner."

Mara, firmly grasping the bird, hurried away from Solomon's kind eyes and Adonijah's broad grin.

Chapter 5

A few weeks later, Mara hurried down the same hall, trying to keep from laughing. Abishag had just rescued her from the chatter of the harem by requesting her presence in the king's chambers.

"I am sorry for pulling you away, just at the exciting part in the story. Now you will never know *who* Michal's dresser was found with yesterday afternoon." The dimple beside Abishag's mouth flickered.

"Perhaps I will be filled in later," Mara responded, with a matching twinkle in her eyes. "Why does the king want me?"

Abishag shrugged dramatically. "I suppose he was so taken with your music last time that . . ."

Mara snorted, something she had never done before she met Abishag. "He didn't even hear me last time."

"Maybe that is why he wants you back."

"Any more intrigue lately?" Mara asked. Abishag was one of her surest sources of palace news.

Abishag shook her head. "Nothing new. Same old stuff. Support for Adonijah. Support for Solomon. People switching sides. People playing both sides."

"Why doesn't David just announce that he will be the next king and stop all of this intrigue? Why does he just sit there and wait to see what happens?"

"He probably could not stop it. And anyway, he is afraid."

Mara looked at Abishag sharply. "Afraid? Of what?"

"Appointing Solomon as his successor instead of Adonijah is against all the rules of succession. David is afraid that Israel would not accept it, and he doesn't want to face another uprising. Would you?"

"I suppose not," Mara said slowly. "But surely he knows that Adonijah is going to try something anyway. The whole palace knows."

Abishag smiled slowly. "David has always been blind to his sons' feelings—their pains and their ambitions."

"I would think that if he really believed that Solomon was Yahweh's choice to be king, he would do something about it."

"But that is part of the problem. He thinks that if he just waits around, Yahweh will show him the way it should be carried out. He is probably right."

Mara shook her head. "Hmmm. I'm not sure Adonijah will wait around for your God to throw down lightening from heaven."

Abishag laughed. "Don't worry. Bathsheba won't wait, either."

They reached the stairs and began to ascend. Mara thought it was a good time to change the subject. "Have you heard from your shepherd recently," Mara asked, noticing a particular exuberance in Abishag's mood.

Abishag nodded, "I was hoping you would ask me. I didn't want to bring it up myself. You know I am not the kind of person to talk incessantly about myself."

"Of course not," Mara affirmed. "But do strain yourself just now and inform me."

"He got one of the stable boys to give a message to one of the cooks, who gave the message to a serving girl, who gave it to me."

"Impressive," Mara murmured. "Are you sure it is still the same message?"

"He says he is doing well, enjoying the company of endless sheep, and is missing me with every breath he takes. He says he will come for me as soon as the king dies." Abishag lowered her voice to a whisper when she heard someone on the stairs behind them.

"But what if you are not allowed to leave?" Mara asked, hoping this question was vague enough not to trouble Abishag.

"It will not matter. I will do my duty to King David, but I will not stay any longer than his life."

"Then I will pray to your God that the king will live forever," Mara said earnestly.

Abishag laughed joyfully and reached to squeeze her friend's hand. "You are welcome to join us. I will not want to leave you behind. You are the best friend I have."

Mara felt a warmth flood through her chest at Abishag's words—the first real friend she had ever made—but she twisted her lips slyly. "Oh yes, and I can watch all of the children that you will be having while you . . . tend to other business."

Abishag reached to give Mara a friendly shove, but it was ill-timed because Mara had just missed a step on the spiral staircase. Mara felt herself falling backward and she tried to brace herself for the impact of the hard cedar at the bottom.

To her surprise, instead of hard wood she felt herself being caught by very strong hands. She looked up into very brown eyes.

The man smiled. "Yahweh be thanked that I was here. You could have been hurt."

"Yes," Mara managed to gasp, still breathless from her fright. "Thank you."

"I will be glad to catch you anytime you wish," the man responded. When he smiled, the corners of his eyes crinkled up in little lines.

Abishag came running down the stairs to join them. "I am so sorry, Mara. Are you hurt?"

Mara shook her head.

The man turned amused eyes to Abishag. "And what has this golden-haired one done to deserve such violent treatment?"

Abishag gasped, "Of course I did not mean to push her down the stairs. Mara will tell you so."

Mara, having caught her breath, was beginning to find the situation a little funny. So many things were funny now that she had met Abishag. Abishag had taught her how to laugh. "I don't know, Abishag. That was quite a push. Could it be that you know that I am also corresponding with your sh——" She stopped abruptly, realizing that the stranger was still standing there, smiling.

Abishag giggled nervously. "Liar."

Mara looked at the man—he was dressed like a soldier—and cleared her throat. "Again, I thank you."

The man nodded. "I see. I will leave so you can continue your discussion. Do be more careful next time." He climbed with sure strides up the stairs.

"Who was that?" Mara whispered. "He must think me a fool."

Abishag shook her head. "His name is Joel, the son of Eleazar—you know, Eleazar, one of the Three, the mightiest of David's mighty

33

men. I have heard that Joel is becoming as great a warrior as his father."

"Oh," Mara responded, watching Joel's retreating figure with more respect. A warrior—like her father.

"Don't you think he is handsome? All of the young women are praying that he will choose them to wed. He is taking a very long time with it."

Mara looked a little surprised, but studied Joel's back. He was very tall and strong. And perhaps if girls had not known someone so much better . . .

"What tribe is he of?" Mara asked.

"Benjamin," Abishag replied with a rueful look. The king before David—Saul—had been of the tribe of Benjamin, and there was still much discontent, Mara had heard, among that tribe with the present king.

Joel turned just then and looked back at her. Their eyes met, and Mara blushed. The right side of Joel's mouth quirked. "Did you ever catch that ridiculous bird?" he called down to her.

"What?" Mara said, startled. "Oh yes, yes I did." She found herself smiling at him fatuously.

He returned her smile and turned away.

Mara groaned. "Why am I so stupid? Now he will think I am one of those girls."

Abishag's smiling face sobered. "He would not be so foolish."

Mara didn't know what to make of this statement, so she didn't speak the rest of the way to the King David's chambers.

Mara had been playing for David most of the afternoon when a servant came in to announce Bathsheba, the king's wife. Mara knew, from more than two years in the palace, that it was a sign of Bathsheba's favored station that she was allowed to visit the king in his chambers.

Mara continued playing, but she went very stiff; she did not like Solomon's mother at all.

Bathsheba was beautiful and hard—like a diamond, Mara could not help thinking. The dark hair and eyes were like Solomon's, as was the unconscious grace of her movements. But her smile was empty, and her voice brittle.

"My king," she said as she entered. "I thank you for seeing me." Mara opened her eyes wider as she watched, for there seemed to be real affection—even love?—in Bathsheba's eyes.

David shook a tired, graying head. "As if I wouldn't, my love." He was in better health today than when Mara had last seen him, for he was fully dressed and sitting in a low lounge.

Bathsheba looked idly at Mara, seated on a brightly colored rug in a corner of the room, then turned away, disinterested. It was amazing, Mara thought, how her expression changed when she was not focused on the king.

Mara turned her eyes away when the king rose and embraced his wife. They murmured things that she could not hear—that she was glad she could not hear—and she wished she was no longer in the room. Apparently, cold as she was in all other things, Bathsheba really loved the king.

"I have been hearing things that bother me," Bathsheba began after a time, still hypnotized by the king.

David raised a ringed hand. "Nothing unpleasant today, please. I only wish to talk of enjoyable things. I have asked our son to join me. I'm sure you will be glad to see him. I have been planning the temple for Yahweh, and there is much we need to discuss."

"Oh yes," Bathsheba said, forcing a smile. "Your temple. Sometimes I am jealous of your temple."

The chamber doors opened again, and Solomon strode in, obviously delighted to see his mother.

"What a joy to see you here, mother. How have you been?" he asked, reaching to grasp her hands.

She smiled indulgently, but Mara noticed her eyes did not light up the way they did when she looked at the king. Mara felt herself grow cold, because she knew—even from the few times she had spoken with Solomon—that he adored his mother more than anyone on earth.

The king and his son began to talk about the temple that Solomon was to build for the God of this land. Mara knew him by now, and she no longer wondered that this nation could worship only one god. Yahweh was not a spirit of the sun or the sea, the kind of spirit that Mara's father had taught her about. Nor was he one of a congregation of gods like the Tyrian merchant had explained to her. From what Mara had been told by other slaves and servants, this God was the only one in the nation—maybe the only one in the world. Mara had heard all the stories by now—about Abraham, and Isaac, and Jacob, the fathers of this people, and she had heard about all the great things this God had done for them. She was not surprised that the king was at last building a house for Yahweh; she was surprised it had taken them so long.

Mara, wrapped in her own thoughts, plucked the wrong string when she heard Bathsheba say, "My love, I still do not understand why you do not just announce to the nation that Jedidiah will be king after you." Mara met Abishag's eyes over the king's couch, but she continued to play.

David yawned. "Yahweh will work things out in his time. There is no need to rush things."

"If we do not rush things," Bathsheba began, exasperated, "Adonijah will claim the kingdom before we have a chance to do anything."

The king chuckled. "He will at least wait until I am dead."

"Your other son did not," Bathsheba muttered, loud enough for everyone in the room to hear.

Mara tried not to gasp.

David sat up very strait. "Do not," he warned, "Even say his name."

Bathsheba looked contrite. Mara thought that she sincerely did not want to upset her husband. "But still, you should do something definitive about your successor."

David sighed. "Jedidiah will be king, never fear. And he will be a great king—better than Adonijah." He paused a minute than said, "Jedidiah, what have I said that makes you frown?"

Solomon's eyes hardened in the way they only did when he was hiding his pain. "I do not wish to show disrespect, but you were speaking in a way that implied that I was going to become king because of what I was rather than who I was. We both know that is not true."

There was something about Solomon's voice just then that made Mara's stomach tighten. She studied him carefully. He was a picture of calm and casual indifference. His shoulders straight, his chin raised, even his hands, she noticed, were relaxed, hung loosely at his sides. But something was wrong.

"What do you mean by that?" David asked. "Of course you are becoming king because of who you are. You are Yahweh's choice to succeed me."

"Yes," Solomon responded, perfectly polite. "I know that. But you were talking as if Yahweh's choice had something to do with my own nature, my merits. The person I am has nothing to do with his choice."

Mara was scared now. There was still no hint of strong emotion on Solomon's finely chiseled face, and his hands, beautiful and delicately tapered, were still relaxed at his sides. But she could feel something, a coiled energy, a force of raw emotion, building inside of Solomon, held back only by his unnatural control. She could feel it, even from halfway across the room. She wished, suddenly, that David would have one of his weak spells and demand that everyone leave.

David didn't. She could see the brash charisma and active nature that characterized the old king clearly as he paced the room. She looked at his hands, and he was clenching and releasing them, over and over again. "I don't really understand what is bothering you. You have all the strengths and talents that this country needs to turn it into something more than a collection of tribes constantly fighting to keep its land. You can turn Israel into a great country, a power in this world."

"That may be true, and, honestly, I think that it is true," Solomon admitted, his voice never wavering. "But that is not why I am chosen to be king."

David shrugged casually, revealing how little he understood his own son. "You will be king because that is Yahweh's will." His voice began to sound impatient, and his pacing became quicker. "And he will choose the best man for the kingship. That is you. Why does it matter why he chose you?"

Solomon pushed his hair away from his face in a swift, frustrated gesture. Something Mara had never seen him do before. And it was that minor thing—that small break in his habitual composure—that revealed to Mara how deep this issue went in Solomon. "But Adonijah is older, and stronger, and has more support. I do not doubt Yahweh's power to work through these circumstances, but aside from Yahweh's will, Adonijah is a much better choice. It just bothers me to hear you talk about my worthiness for the crown." Solomon stood absolutely still before his pacing father, and the light from the large windows burnished his dark hair. In the light, it looked almost reddish. David's hair had been auburn, before it had turned gray.

But Solomon looked nothing like his father.

"There is no situation apart from Yahweh's will; you know that as well as I do. And you certainly know your own worth. Yahweh will work it out so that the nation will see the justice of his choice."

One word. Sometimes all it took was one word to break down barriers that had been built up for years. "Justice," Solomon repeated, his voice no longer perfectly calm. "Justice!" The words, Mara could see, were forced out of him. "Had justice been done, I would never be king. I would never have been born."

The words had been said—could not be unsaid—and the silence seemed to close in around them.

Mara smothered a cry of pity at the pain she heard beneath the hard edge of his voice, but in the corner of her mind that could still note these things, she saw Bathsheba's eyes narrow at the implications of Solomon's words. And Abishag, she saw, had turned her back to the royal family and was now gazing out at the gardens.

Mara had heard the story before, many times, whispered throughout the harem in spite and secret pleasure, of a wife desired and a good man killed.

Finally, David, who had been taking ragged breaths, gasped, "No! Never believe that. Jedidiah, Yahweh's plan works through the sin of mankind."

Solomon's breathing had been as harsh as his father's, but Solomon was who he was, and the next words he spoke had no trace of pain, his voice had no hint of breaking. "I am sure that is of great comfort to Uriah." Solomon's mouth was a tight line. Uriah—the good man who never should have died.

Mara could imagine what Bathsheba's face would look like at those words, but she couldn't turn away from these two men. She was no longer even pretending to play her lyre.

"Jedidiah, don't do this! Yahweh has forgiven me my sin. It has nothing to do with you." David looked older now than he had just an hour before, the creases on his face were deeper, the exhaustion even more apparent in the hunching of his shoulders. Mara would have given him her pity had she any left to give. It was all with Solomon.

"Nothing to do with me?" Solomon was again in control, but barely. Something was driving him that he could no more control than the rising of the sun. "My birth was only a sign of the remarkable strength of Yahweh's forgiveness; and the only reason I will become king is to prove to you that you are forgiven. Yahweh has destined my whole life through your sin. My life is not even my own."

David had stopped pacing and his mouth opened, as if he was going to speak, but no words came out. Solomon stood before him, still breathing heavily, his hands still loose at his sides. He was silent, waiting for his father to speak.

Mara waited too, holding her breath. At this moment and in this room, there were only two men in the world, only these two. And nothing of her own—not her memories, or her losses, or her pride—mattered in the smallest way. Nothing mattered but these two men, and the words they were about to speak.

David finally spoke. "Jedidiah, you must trust that Yahweh's plan goes beyond our own lives. Whatever I might have done in the past . . ."

"Whatever you might have done?" Solomon repeated, interrupting his father in his distress, another thing he had never done before. "You sent a man out to die. You are the king of Israel, a man the whole nation looks up to, a man after Yahweh's heart—and you stole a man's wife and then you murdered him."

The sound that came from David must have been a sob, and he covered his face with his hands as he pleaded, "Jedidiah, you cannot think that. You cannot hate me so much."

Mara saw the frozen composure of Solomon's face thaw slightly at the king's words. "Oh, father, . . ." he began.

It was one of the sharpest regrets of Mara's life that she was not able to hear how Solomon would respond to his father's words. A thing she would never be able to know.

Because the two men were not alone in the world, or even in this room. Mara herself had forgotten about Bathsheba, who had been seated behind the two men. The woman, however, had been listening, and growing angrier at every word.

She did not let Solomon finish. She stood up and walked over to him. In her beauty and the sparkling glory of her eyes, she stared at her son. "You dare to stand here, in front of the king, and reproach him for his behavior!" Her voice was shrill, and Solomon took a few steps away from her.

"Mother, I . . ."

Again, she interrupted him. "You speak of things you know nothing about, and you have no right to speak of them."

39

Mara saw Solomon clench his fists; it was not a thing she was likely to overlook.

Bathsheba continued, her voice thin and cutting, like a blade. "Our love was so strong that it defied all earthly laws. You will never love as strongly. This man is greater than you can ever hope to be."

"Bathsheba, do not," David insisted, laying a hand on his wife's arm, but Bathsheba pulled away.

Mara tried to hide in her corner. She silently prayed to Solomon's God that he would stop the words in Bathsheba's mouth, stop her from cutting the thin string that held Solomon's pain in check. But she did not stop, and Mara saw it rush, like melting snows down a river, into Solomon's eyes.

"You are right," Bathsheba grated, still beautiful, still bright as a diamond. "You should not be king after David. The child that died should have been king. He was the child of our love, but he was taken from us as punishment."

There were so many conflicting and variously textured layers of pain in this room that Mara could not sort them out. She could only get lost in them.

Bathsheba was screaming and frantic now. "You may be king after David—I will make sure that you are—but you will never be worthy. Never be worthy!"

And with Solomon's reaction to those words, Mara felt something she had not felt in many years. Certainly, at this moment, she felt anger, hate, helplessness, frustration, pain, infinite pity. But there was something more. What she felt was astonishment. Mara was rarely surprised by anything—both the turnings of her life and her own nature prevented her from ever letting things catch her off guard. But Mara was genuinely, heart-stoppingly astonished by Solomon's reaction to his mother's words.

She had thought she knew Solomon by now. They had not had a multitude of conversations, but she was in a position to see a lot. And two years of careful observation can teach a perceptive person quite a bit.

But everything Mara had known about Solomon, all of the things that characterized him—his self-containment, his pride, his control over the passions that drove him—deserted him at that moment. He fell on his knees before his mother, and reached his arms out to her. "Mother," he gasped, "You don't really mean it?"

"No, of course she doesn't," David put in firmly, but far too late. The king placed a hand on Bathsheba's shoulder.

"Yes, I do!" Bathsheba screamed, hysterically, weeping. "My child should never have been killed. He should be king."

David dragged his wife from the room and into the smaller room that connected to his chamber. Before he shut the door, he turned to his son. "She is not rational. She still mourns our first child. Do not believe any of what she said. You are my most loved son."

Mara turned her eyes to Solomon and saw that he had crumpled to the ground and was weeping. She wanted to go and comfort him, but what could she say? And what would give her the right to comfort him? She wondered when she had started to cry.

After a few minutes, Mara was sure that Solomon had forgotten she was even in the room. So she blinked when he raised his raw eyes and smiled at her wryly. "I suppose your family would never behave like this."

"No," she said seriously. "They would never have dreamed of it."

Solomon winced. "I was terrible," he admitted. "I deserved everything she said to me." His voice cracked at the last word.

Mara could not allow that. "No," she said, shaking away her own tears and running over to crouch beside him on the polished shell floor. "You did not. What she said was unforgivable, inexcusable. It was not true."

Solomon shook his head. "It was. I will never be the man my father was; I know it. That is probably why I was so angry at him, still so angry at him. But how could I possibly live up to his reputation? How could anyone?"

"You will, Solomon. Of course you will." Mara's hands trembled, but she reached to grasp his hands in hers. "You will be the greatest king Israel will ever have. But forgive your father; despite what people have said about him, he is only a man."

It seemed to Mara, in the silence of the king's chambers, that something very important was being decided, but she could not understand what it was or why it was important. She watched Solomon's face intensely, waiting for his response.

But Solomon had hurt too deeply for too many years to forgive so easily. "If you only knew how much I despised him for his sin. How much I blamed him for it." Solomon twisted his hands, so that her hands were in his clasp now. "How I wished, sometimes, that Uriah was still alive and I had never been born."

"You must not think that, Solomon," she said. "How could that woman say such terrible things to you? She had no right. I hate her. I hate her."

Solomon made an attempt at a smile. "I don't."

And from that moment Mara truly knew Solomon. She understood the two truths that made up his existence. She understood the innate, constant, unshakable love—for his family, his history, his country, and for Yahweh himself. And she also understood the raw, bleeding pain he felt at the sundry ways this love had been torn.

She looked in his eyes, his mother's eyes, dark yet reflecting all the light around them, and she saw how these two things—the love and the pain, his twin truths—were vying with each other for control of the man.

She began to cry again, because she saw that, and she also saw that it was intimate knowledge of a man's soul that she had no right to possess.

Solomon shrugged his shoulders and ran a hand across his eyes. "Well, that is the way Yahweh has worked things out, and who am I to question him? I just wish that the world would stop right now, that the sun would not rise tomorrow, that I would not really have to live this life I've been given." He really looked at her for the first time. "Little Mara," he whispered. "Are those tears for me?"

Mara brushed her tears away and didn't answer.

"Thank you," he said, his voice a breath. And he forced himself to stand up to face the world that would not stop for his private pain and the sun that always rises, no matter what man makes of the world under it.

PART II

THE SUCCESSION

"Obey the king's command, I say,
because you took an oath before God.
Do not be in a hurry
to leave the king's presence.
Do not stand up for a bad cause,
for he will do
whatever he pleases."

Ecclesiastes 8: 2-3

Chapter 6

Mara hesitated only momentarily when she recognized Adonijah coming toward her in the hall that connected the servants' quarters to the rest of the palace. He was alone, and he had a scowl on his face, so Mara lowered her eyes and tried to pass him unnoticed. She wondered vaguely what he was doing in this part of the palace, but she would be just as happy not to know.

"Well, have you been chasing any more birds recently?"

He *would* have to remember that episode from six months ago. Mara had been trying her best to forget. She smiled politely—carefully keeping her eyes cold—and tried to walk past him.

"Why are you running away from me?" Adonijah asked, grabbing her arm and pulling her toward him.

"Please, I am needed elsewhere in the palace," Mara said, but her voice wasn't pleading; it was angry. Even if Adonijah had not been competing with Solomon for the throne, Mara would be wary of him. Under all of his attractive and good-natured charm, there was something unstable about his personality. As if one snap would break his composure, even his sanity.

"You wouldn't run away from my dear brother, would you?"

Mara narrowed her eyes. "I am not running away from you. I have work to do here."

"Yes, I have noticed the enormous amount of work you musicians do. I've wondered what you do for the other twenty-two hours of the day."

The truth of this observation did nothing to alleviate Mara's irritation. "Well, you should speak to your father about it."

Adonijah's face was not as handsome as Solomon's, but he had his father's air of strength and confidence. His grin lit up his face. "Maybe

I will. I can probably suggest another . . . occupation to take up some of your free time. I might even be able to help with it." His rough finger traced the smooth line of her cheek.

Mara had to force herself not to wince, and not to bite his finger. She kept very still, her face free from expression but her eyes like ice.

"That doesn't appeal to you?" Adonijah asked, leaning his face close enough to hers that she could feel his warm breath on her neck.

Mara knew it was somewhat miraculous that she had made it this far in her life without being violated. The fact that she was still pure, still a virgin, was nearly unexplainable. Even in the palace, slave girls were completely vulnerable to whomever might desire them. She often wondered if Solomon had something to do with her safety, but Solomon would have no power over Adonijah.

"No."

The one word, in a tone as proud as royalty, seemed to surprise Adonijah, and he took a step back.

"One would think that you were an heir to a kingdom, slave girl."

Mara tilted her chin up. "I am."

Adonijah gave a half smile. "Indeed? Well, I wouldn't let the news get around the palace. Someone might get jealous."

Mara's forehead wrinkled a little as she tried to decipher his words. "So Solomon is hiding a princess, is he?"

"Solomon is not hiding me at all."

Adonijah shrugged. "Well, he is doing his best. I agree that you are difficult to conceal. Who has ever seen such hair? Like spun gold. My father's hair was reddish, you know, like bronze, and everyone thought that was a rarity."

"May I leave now?"

Adonijah chuckled. "So proud, you are. I just hope you are also aware that if Solomon ever becomes king—which, please Yahweh, will never happen—and I am still alive—which is even more unlikely—I shall see you humbled. Because Solomon will make you the pride of his harem."

Mara gasped, "You lie."

"Oh, often," Adonijah admitted. "But not in this."

"He would not dare . . ."

At this, Adonijah laughed out loud. "Wouldn't he? You underestimate your own desirability. And, in case you are worried, let me assure you. When I become king you will achieve the same status."

Mara wanted to run away from his laughing eyes, but she thought of her father backed against a burning hut, and she pulled herself up to her full height. "We shall see."

"Yes, we will, and it won't be long," Adonijah agreed, and turned around to walk back the way he had come. "You have given me an idea," he said, turning back. "Why didn't I think of it before?"

"Well, believe me, it was completely unintentional."

Adonijah only laughed, and Mara stood like a statue, struggling not to be sick, until Solomon's brother was out of sight.

Mara pulled her veil closer around her face as she dodged two small, dirty boys and a cart pulled by a mule. This was the first time she had left the palace grounds since she had come to David's palace almost three years ago.

The first thing she had thought of after her interview with Adonijah was getting away from the palace. The perfume, the cedar-carved walls and the crushed-shell floors started to close in around her, and she had trouble breathing. She had not been thinking of any plan or idea; she just wanted to get away. So she had put on an outer tunic over the near-transparent white linen she always wore in the palace, pulled a veil over her head, and stole out of the palace. It really had not been hard at all.

She breathed the pungent air of the street, a far cry from the scented air of the palace, and sighed. She had not been really happy since the night her village had been destroyed. She was comfortable at the palace; she had fallen into the routine and the petty world of minor tensions, and she was glad of it. She had not had to think too much or feel too much, and only Solomon and her friendship with Abishag had broken the quiet sterility of her days. But she wasn't happy. She wondered if she would ever be again.

"I don't think you should be out here," a quiet voice said, from right behind her, and a hand grasped her on the shoulder.

Reacting instinctively, she whirled around and kicked out at the man standing there, hitting him on the shin. She stopped suddenly. It was Joel, the warrior Abishag had pointed out to her a few months ago, the one who had caught her when she fell. She had seen him in the gardens once with Solomon, and, although he was several years older than the prince was, he had clapped the young man on the back in a way that spoke of long friendship. Mara's instinctive mistrust of his Benjaminite heritage dulled under that impression and his friendly grin.

47

"Should you?" Joel asked in a strained voice, standing on one leg, rubbing his shin with his hand.

Mara shook her head. "I am so sorry. I wasn't thinking."

Joel smiled. "It's okay. I shouldn't have grabbed you. Are you leaving the palace?" he asked, his expression genuinely concerned.

Mara shut her eyes and thought for a moment. Was she? "No, I am not leaving."

Joel looked relieved. "I am glad. Can I help you with anything? If I remember correctly, I helped you once before."

"Yes, you did help me, and I appreciated it. But I don't think you can do anything for me now." A cart came perilously close to her, and Joel gently pulled her out of its path. Mara looked up at him, startled by the gentleness of his touch; he looked so strong.

Joel, misinterpreting her surprise, quickly removed his hand from her arm. "You're sure? I don't want to force my presence on you if it would be unpleasant, but I would like to help."

Mara smiled up at him, touched by his modesty and his sweetness. "Thank you, but I was just feeling . . . stifled in the palace, and I panicked."

"What scared you?" Joel asked, his brow wrinkling and his warm brown eyes darkening ominously.

"Nothing," Mara said quickly. "It was just . . . nothing."

Joel sighed. "Of course, you do not have to tell me. You do not know me and have no reason to trust me."

The fact that he was Solomon's friend would be reason enough for Mara to trust him, but she did not tell him that.

Mara started to walk down the street, and Joel fell in step with her. "You are a warrior?" she asked the man beside her.

Joel nodded. "Yes, I am a soldier. But there haven't been many wars to fight lately."

"Does that bother you?"

Joel looked confused, so Mara continued. "My father and his brother were also warriors, and they were always restless when they had no enemies to fight."

Joel pushed his hand through his shoulder-length brown hair. "I am not like that. I fight well, and that is my occupation. But I prefer peace. My father was like your father, though."

Mara remembered something. "Your father was Eleazar, isn't that right? He was with the king at . . . Pas Dammim, and when the men retreated from the Philistines he stood his ground, until Israel was victorious."

Joel grinned. "Yes, that was my father. A brave man, but a little foolhardy."

"And do you try to live up to your father's reputation?" Mara asked, revealing the course her thoughts had taken over the last few months.

"At times, I feel weighed down by it. Who doesn't live in the shadow of their ancestors? But we are different men, and I have made my own reputation. I hope to serve our next king as faithfully as my father served David."

Mara wondered if he meant Solomon, but she didn't ask him. "How did you recognize me? I was hiding my hair."

Joel chuckled at the sudden change in conversation. "Your hair is not the only way one can recognize you."

Mara smiled wryly. "Sometimes I feel like it is. It is like no one ever sees me, but only my hair, and maybe my eyes."

"You don't really believe that do you? Even with dark hair and eyes, your beauty would set you apart in the palace."

"But isn't there more than beauty?" Mara asked, looking up him.

"Of course there is," Joel responded. "Beauty rarely lasts for long. I'm sure there must be more to you than beauty."

"Thank you," Mara whispered. "That is nice to hear, although, of course, I have always known it."

Joel laughed aloud. "You are something different, Mara. Indeed you are. What was your home like?"

Memory rushed upon Mara like the tide on the shore of her village. And she told him about her father and the village he was chieftain over. About the sea-gold and the oysters. And the forest filled with evergreen trees and the snow that could cover the huts. She told him about the way the sun would rise over the water and turn the gray to starwhite. Then she told him about the night it all was destroyed.

"What horrors you have seen," Joel murmured. "It's a wonder you survived."

Mara smiled up at him, a little stiffly. She didn't respond.

After a moment, Mara stopped walking. "Where are we going?" she asked.

Joel looked around him, as if noticing for the first time. "We were just walking. These are the houses of the wealthy citizens of Jerusalem. You can tell by their size."

Mara looked at the houses and sighed. "How different it would be to live in a real house instead of the palace. It would be like the home was truly my own."

Joel watched her face from the corner of his eye. "Perhaps you will someday."

Mara chuckled. "I don't see how that could be possible."

Joel didn't comment further on the subject, but he looked at her speculatively. "Shall we go back to the palace now?"

Mara looked up. "Were you planning to go back to the palace today?"

Joel shook his head, "No, but I don't want you to run around Jerusalem by yourself."

"Do you think I would be in danger?"

Joel laughed through his nose. "Not in Jerusalem. It is really quite safe, but I would feel better if I could escort you."

Mara nodded her assent. She was feeling better now, herself, and she didn't mind Joel's quiet company. "In Tyre, Danel told me never to go anywhere by myself, or I would likely be taken to serve in a temple, as a prostitute."

Joel shivered, "Don't even say such a thing. We don't do things like that here. That is not how Yahweh deserves to be worshipped."

"And how do you worship him?" Mara asked, though she knew part of the answer.

"With our lives."

Mara gasped slightly.

Joel continued, "He has done great things for us; He deserves nothing less than our lives."

She closed her eyes, and it was dark. She smelled pine.

She smells pine. It is distinct and unusual because as they travel farther south, there are fewer and fewer pine trees. It is still a few hours before dawn, and she lays next to Elsa in the dark and smells pine.

Eventually, Elsa shakes her awake, although she hasn't been asleep. While the camp prepares for the day and begins to pack up to travel again, Mara looks for Anvar. Anvar is her friend. He is a captive of the Huntar too, and he is just her age. He gives her sweet red berries sometimes, and they discuss how they will revenge themselves on their captors when they grow old enough to do so.

But today, Mara can't find Anvar.

The Huntar are a wandering tribe, traders. Their pattern is to go north to loot and capture furs, or gems, or slaves. Then they travel south to trade them for gold. Sometimes they fight for gold. Sometimes they just kill for pleasure. But mostly, they trade.

The chief of the Huntar is always kind to Mara and Elsa. He promises to protect them from harm. Mara sees him, washing himself in a stream. But he doesn't see her, so she keeps looking for Anvar.

No one cares very much if Mara wanders around. She is just a girl and would never run away without Elsa.

She is about to turn around and go back to the camp when she hears a muffled sound. The sound of voices. But it is not a conversation—it sounds more like a song. She follows the voices.

They are louder now—the same words spoken over and over again—and Mara stays hidden behind the pine trees. When she peeks around one, she can see who is chanting. The holy man of the Huntar and his two apprentices. They are in a space between the trees, and their arms are waving toward the sky.

This is very strange, so Mara keeps watching. She sees a large rock between them, and there is something brown on the rock.

She just can't see very well.

The chanting is getting louder and louder, and Mara puts her hands over her ears to block it out. She can't. She moves to a closer tree and looks out again.

Now she can see what is on the rock. It is a boy. It is Anvar.

Everything is turning now, to the rhythm of the chanting, and she has to hold onto the tree for support. She sees a knife, in the hand of the holy man.

She knows what he is going to do.

She has to turn away, and she hates herself for doing it. As she turns, she hears Anvar cry out momentarily. Then there is nothing.

She runs back to the camp. She shouldn't have turned away. She shouldn't have been so weak. Elsa is next to the fire, and Mara hurries over to her.

"Did you find Anvar?" asks Elsa.

Mara shakes her head. Her whole body is shaking now.

Elsa understands a lot, and so she doesn't say anything else. She just pulls Mara into her arms.

But Mara doesn't cry.

51

"Human sacrifice?" Mara breathed, staring up at Joel. She forced herself to take a deep breath and keep her composure. She had completely forgotten about Anvar, until this moment.

"No," Joel explained, amused, although there was nothing amusing about it. "That would be worshipping him with death. I mean how we live our lives."

She could breathe normally now, and she was no longer shaking. The memory drifted back into the shadows of her mind. There was safety in shadows.

By the strength of her will, she responded to Joel's comment intelligently. "Yours is a strange God, but I have heard about the great things he has done. Rivers parted and food falling from the sky. I think you are honored to serve such a God." Mara was speaking aloud, but not really to Joel.

Joel seemed to understand, and he didn't say anything else until they had reached the palace grounds.

"Thank you for helping me again," Mara said, turning to face the man beside her.

"It was a pleasure, both times." Joel started to walk away, but he grinned at her over his shoulder. Despite the memory of Anvar and without really knowing why, Mara found herself grinning back.

Chapter 7

Mara was startled awake by a hand clasped over her mouth. She opened her eyes to see a man she didn't recognize. He was dressed like a soldier, but he was not one of the palace guards. His hand was rough on her mouth, and before she could struggle he placed a strange smelling cloth over her nose and mouth.

Within moments, Mara lost consciousness.

When she awoke, she was in a small, windowless room. She was lying on a straw pallet, but her hands and feet were tied. She shifted slightly; her right arm was completely numb. She tried to shake some feeling into it, but she could not manage much with her hands tied.

The room was lit only by an oil lamp on a stool in one corner, and the heavy, wooden door was shut.

She wondered where she could be. No one would have any reason for taking her. She was just a slave girl to everyone in the world. Except Solomon, and Solomon would certainly not capture her.

She was not particularly frightened. She had been in much worse predicaments, and she had always managed to extract herself.

But she was very curious.

She had to wait for several hours before her curiosity could be satisfied. She tried to doze some, but the attempt was futile. It was too strange a situation to sleep through.

Finally, the door opened and the same unknown man who had captured her came in.

"What am I doing here?" she asked him sharply.

The man looked at her. "I am not at leave to tell you. I hope you are not injured in any way."

"No," she said. "But I am very uncomfortable, and I am extremely hungry. Why have you taken me?"

"I just follow my orders," the man grumbled. "Though why I need to kidnap innocent girls is beyond me."

"Well," Mara began, seeing his disgust. "Why don't you help me?"

The man shook his head. "Oh, no. That would not be a good idea at all. You just stay put, and I'll see if I can get you something to eat and drink."

With that, the man left the room.

Mara sighed. That hadn't been very productive.

She decided to think it through logically. She had no enemies that she knew of. Many of the other servants did not like her for one reason or another, but they would be in no position to harm her. So her capture must not be because of anything she had done or who she was.

There had to be some other purpose to it.

Before she could follow that train of thought, the door opened again, and things started to become clear.

Adonijah walked in, carrying a dish and a cup.

"I heard you were uncomfortable," he said pleasantly, pulling up a stool beside the straw pallet. "I am sorry that I had to tie you, but I imagine that you are more resourceful than you look, and I couldn't take any chances."

"Why have you taken me?" she asked. "I have done nothing to you."

"That is true," Adonijah agreed. "I guess I will have to untie you while you eat. But I will stay here, and there are two guards outside of the door, so I suggest you don't try anything stupid."

Mara hesitated, and then nodded. She was very hungry, and perhaps if she were docile, Adonijah would tell her what his plans were. It must have something to do with Solomon.

Adonijah untied her wrists, and handed her the dish of stew and a piece of bread. She used the bread to dip out the stew. It was quite tasty.

"Can't you tell me why you have taken me?" Mara asked, when she had swallowed.

"For the kingship, of course."

Mara snorted. "All is now clear," she quipped, sarcastically.

"After you are discovered to be missing, Solomon will be frantic. He will certainly come looking for you, and it will be very tragic when the young prince is killed in the attempt." Adonijah beamed at her.

Mara rolled her eyes. "He will hardly come here to look for me. He doesn't trust you, but he certainly doesn't think you are capable of something so despicable."

"That is why it is so brilliant. I've set it all up perfectly. He will not come here to find you, but in search of information. I have had clues planted throughout the palace leading to the conclusion that I know something of the matter of your disappearance. Solomon, proud of his own powers of deduction, will come to ask me about you, never suspecting that I was the one who kidnapped you."

Adonijah's plan did not seem to be very reasonable, and the slightly wild look in his eyes supported this feeling. She decided her best course of action would be to play on his state of mind.

"That is the plan of a coward," Mara said. "To kill a man when he does not expect it. I suppose you will even stab him in the back." She pulled her knees toward her chest, hiding her feet under the blanket.

This angered Adonijah, which pleased Mara. When men are angry, they are more vulnerable.

"Silence! He is attempting to take a throne that is rightfully mine, and he deserves to die the death of a traitor."

"He will not come alone," Mara told him, reaching one hand under the blanket to work at the knots binding her feet. "Solomon would not be so foolish. He knows he cannot trust you." The fact that this statement seemed to contradict her earlier one made Mara shiver with worry.

What if Solomon did come? What if Adonijah's plan was not as illogical as it sounded? Would Solomon have to die, because he was worried about her?

"And anyway," she continued. "He hardly ever sees me. What makes you think he would go through so much trouble for me?"

Adonijah laughed. "Don't be naive. You know how much he cares for you. It is quite obvious when he looks at you. Not that I blame him." Adonijah ran his hand up Mara's arm, and Mara instinctively jerked away from him, spilling some of the water she had been drinking.

Adonijah turned when he heard some commotion outside the room. Mara realized that this was her chance. And she threw the remaining contents of the bowl into Adonijah's face, and pulled the remaining ropes off her feet. She ran from the room and onto what she discovered was the roof of a house. Probably Adonijah's house. He, unlike Solomon, did not live in the palace but had his own quarters in Jerusalem.

Running toward what she assumed were the stairs leading to the street, she collided fully with a man who had just climbed them. The man caught her by the arms, and she kicked at him. But she could not get away.

Adonijah had reached her by now, and he raised his hand to strike her.

"Do not," Joab said. "You have been craven enough for one day."

Adonijah gave him a menacing look, and wiped the stew from his beard. "She almost got away."

Joab shook his head and carried Mara ungraciously back to the little room.

When Adonijah had retied both her arms and her legs—much tighter than was necessary—he turned to Joab. "What are you doing here?"

"What are *you* doing?" Joab repeated. "Kidnapping a girl? Pathetic. Surely you can find a more honorable way to claim your rights? What will you do? Lure Solomon here and slit his throat?"

Adonijah looked a little guilty. "If Solomon is dead, there will be no other obstacle to the throne."

Joab's face showed disgust. "The throne may be yours by right, but this is hardly the way to get it. At least prove that you are worthy of kingship and act like a man."

"Solomon is a traitor," Adonijah said, as if he were persuading himself of the fact. "He deserves to die. You can help me. You are trusted at the palace."

Mara restrained a gasp, and looked at Joab sharply. Surely he would not betray David like that. He loved David.

"I will not have any part in Solomon's murder. It would break the king's heart, though why he cares for the whelp is beyond me. No, I will not help."

Adonijah sighed, his attractive face twisted into a pout.

"But, because I believe the law is on your side in the issue of kingship, I will not tell anyone of your plan," Joab continued, causing Mara's heart to sink. "You must decide for yourself if the action is worthy of a future king."

Joab stalked out of the room, taking Mara's hope with him. She had been sure he would help her.

Adonijah called a farewell to the commander of Israel's army, and turned back to Mara. "Do not try to get away again. There will be two guards outside the door. If my plants in the palace work properly, Solomon should arrive sometime tonight."

He left the room, leaving Mara alone.

Mara thought for a long time. She could always get out of trouble by herself. She always had before. Elsa had taught her that she must. And then, instead of thinking of a way to get out of the situation, Mara remembered something.

Elsa is asleep beside her, but Mara always has trouble falling asleep. She and Elsa have lived now with the Huntar for many months. Mara has completely lost track of time. Soon, she realizes, they will be in the south, where the Huntar will trade them for gold. At least, that is what Elsa tells her.

She listens to Elsa's steady breathing, the breathing of the other captives in their tent, and to the night bugs humming outside. Then she hears something else from outside, uneven footsteps and deep muttering. She sits up sharply.

Her movement wakes Elsa, who also hears the noise from outside. And so, Elsa is prepared when a brown hand pulls open the flap of their tent. He is a warrior and one of the guards for the night.

After living so long with the Huntar, Mara can understand much of their language. But the man's voice is slurred, and Mara can't make out many of the words.

But his intentions are clear.

He reaches for Elsa, who silently dodges out of his grasp. The man loses his balance and falls to his knees in the low tent. Elsa, always quick, grabs the man's sword and plunges it into his chest, pulling it out as he falls.

The other captives must have heard the noise, but they remain perfectly still under their blankets. Elsa looks at Mara.

"Help me pull him outside," she says softly.

So Elsa takes his shoulders and Mara takes his legs, and they drag him outside the tent, where they leave him in the dirt.

Elsa gently lays his sword on the ground next to him.

In the tent, there is blood on Elsa's blanket, so she curls up under Mara's.

"Do you understand Mara?" Elsa asks. "We have to watch out for ourselves. No one is going to protect us. Your father and Brant tried to, but they couldn't. The chief here promised that he would, but he couldn't either. We have to take care of ourselves. We are alone."

"When the sun is set," Mara adds, somehow still believing her father's teachings.

"No!" Elsa cries. "We are always alone. The sun is always set, and it is always night for us."

She hugs Mara tightly, and Mara nods her head. This is something that she can understand.

Mara shook herself out of her memory. She didn't understand why all these memories kept coming back to her. This was hardly the time for it. She had to think of a way out of this situation.

She had always done things with her own strength. But now, not only her own life was in danger, but the life of Solomon as well. And she could do absolutely nothing.

She hated the feeling of hopelessness, and she realized with a twinge that she was completely helpless.

Involuntarily, she thought of Yahweh, Solomon's God. She had heard of all he had done. He had brought Israel out of captivity in Egypt. He had parted a sea so they could pass through safely. He had made Israel invincible in battle. Surely, if he wanted, he could spare the time to help one small girl, even if she wasn't of his people.

Hating the situation that led her to it, Mara began to pray. After all, it was not just herself that was in danger, but Solomon as well. And Yahweh must love Solomon, even if he did not love her.

She did not know how long she prayed, but help did not come. Hours must have passed, and still nothing happened. She could not stand having to depend on someone else, but she had no choice. She could not let Solomon die.

The light from the oil lamp had almost flickered out when the door opened again. Mara's heart sank, sure that Adonijah had come to gloat over Solomon's death.

But it wasn't Adonijah. It was Joab.

He hurried over to the pallet and drew out a sharp knife. Mara gasped when she saw it, but he used it to cut the ropes that bound her.

"I found I could not let this happen," he said as he worked. "When you are free, run down the stairs to the right of the room. They lead to the street. The others lead to the courtyard. If you take the right stairs, Adonijah will never know you are gone, until it is too late."

"But the guards?" Mara queried, hardly believing what was happening.

"I have taken care of them," Joab told her, pulling her to her feet. "Now go."

She started toward the door, but turned back. "Thank you," she whispered, looking up at the aging man in front of her.

Joab shrugged. "Your life was not in danger."

"It was not my life for which I feared."

"I did what I did for King David," Joab said. "My best friend since childhood. And because I am a soldier and not an accomplice to murder."

Mara nodded her understanding and ran out of the room. It was night already, and she had to walk carefully down the stairs so she wouldn't fall. When she had descended the stairs, she raced down the street, putting as much distance between herself and the house as possible.

She had no idea how to get back to the palace.

She had not gone far when she saw a cloaked figure approaching. She recognized the cloak.

"Solomon," she hissed, not daring to speak louder. "Solomon."

The cloaked figure turned, saw her, and hurried toward her, drawing her into the shadows.

He lifted the hood of the cloak. It was not Solomon.

"Joel," Mara gasped. "But I thought . . ."

"Yahweh be praised that you are safe," Joel whispered. "Solomon has been frantic. He was sure you would not run away without speaking to him first. I was not so sure."

"I did not run away," Mara explained.

Joel nodded. "Adonijah? I thought the whole thing sounded strange when Solomon told me, so I refused to let him go. That way, if something was wrong, I would face the danger and not him. But I am glad that neither of us will have to face it."

Mara looked up at the man, open-mouthed.

Joel gave a quirky smile. "Come. Solomon is waiting at the barracks. Let us hurry back and tell him all is well."

When they reached the barracks, Joel herded her into a small room. Solomon whirled around and let out cry of relief. "Mara," he exclaimed. "Thank Yahweh you are safe."

Mara explained the whole story to the two men, and they listened with grave faces.

"I had not thought he would stoop to this," Solomon muttered. "Murdering his own brother!"

"I don't think he is quite sane," Mara ventured softly. "Whatever reason he had before is deserting him under the onslaught of his anger." She paused. "What will you do?" she asked Solomon.

Solomon shrugged. "What is there to do? Shall I bring the whole thing out in the open? Nothing would be worse for the nation. I will have to ignore the whole episode. And watch Adonijah like a hawk from now on."

Joel nodded, and turned to Mara. "You needn't worry. He will not try to hurt you anymore. He knows now that we would suspect him immediately. He will not risk it again."

Solomon returned with her to the palace, and Mara went gratefully to bed.

But she found she could not sleep. The idea that she had tried to repress since she had been rescued kept forcing its way into her thoughts.

She had been rescued. She had thought it was hopeless, but she had been rescued.

Yahweh had saved both her and Solomon. He had answered her prayers.

She tried to hide from the fact, but she couldn't, and she knew that someday she would have to face it.

Yahweh was a god unlike anything she had yet encountered. He had heard her prayer and answered, even though she was not one of his people, even though she had worshipped gods which must have been appalling to him.

Even though the sun had already set for the night.

Chapter 8

Something was going to happen. Mara had lived long enough in the palace to feel the changes in mood, and she had never felt so much tension in the air before.

One evening, she was sitting with a few other musicians, idling away the hours until it was time to sleep. There had been few banquets of any kind lately, and the musicians had very little work. Not all of the musicians who played in the palace were slaves. Many were upstanding citizens of Israel. But the professional musicians lived lives that were worlds apart from Mara's life.

None of Mara's fellow slaves knew where she had gone the day she had been missing. Many supposed she had tried to run away but had been found and brought back. Mara remained silent on the issue, however, and none of the speculations was ever verified.

One of the palace dancers, Kala, very young and brown and lithe, came over to join them. Mara had never socialized with Kala. Everyone knew that she kept Adonijah company, and, although slaves didn't really have a choice about that kind of thing, it was obvious to all that Kala enjoyed it.

Besides, Kala had always been very rude to Mara.

Mara was plucking out a tune on her lyre, a tune she had been working on for quite a while. Kala screwed up her beautiful face in distaste. "Something will have to be done about musicians who cannot keep a tune."

Mara's companions gave the predictable sounds of resigned exasperation, but Mara ignored the girl.

"And you are certainly in the position to do such a thing," quipped Shelomith, a flute player, who had always liked Mara.

"Oh, soon I will be. Very soon," Kala boasted. Mara saw that Kala was brimming over with some excitement, and she knew that Kala wanted more than anything to brag about it to those who looked on her with amused contempt.

Still, Mara said nothing; she knew how people like Kala should be handled. The others took their cue from Mara and remained silent as well.

Kala, getting no response, continued. "In fact, within the week. You will be sorry you did not try to be friends with me."

The little flute player was unable to contain an amused snort, and this angered Kala. "Ha! When Adonijah becomes king, I will no longer be forced to remain with the likes of you." Then she stormed away.

Mara felt a little sorry for the girl. Kala actually thought that being a king's concubine would be better than what she was now. Maybe he had promised to marry her. Kala should know better.

She was so naive, Mara thought. Mara could not remember ever being naive.

"Adonijah's up to something," said Shelomith. "I wonder what it is. Has anyone heard anything?"

Mara shook her head. "Whatever he is planning, he has been very secretive about it. If the servants knew something, I would have heard. We may have to move beyond the servants."

"What do you mean?"

Mara smiled at her companions. "The guards tend to know a lot more about Adonijah's movement. And there is one guard who fancies himself in love with me."

Shelomith gasped, although it was evident she was repressing a giggle. "You wouldn't!"

Mara's grin was mischievous. "One might as well make use of one's advantages."

Mara walked away from the giggling musicians. Kelub had admired her for more than a year, and she had never encouraged him. She hated to do so now, but she was willing to do a lot more than that to help Solomon. Adonijah was going to do something about his claim to the throne within the week, and she had to know what he was planning this time.

Later that night, she crept out of her chamber. Wandering around the palace at night was not a good idea, she had learned. The miscellaneous men one encountered tended to think her presence was an invitation. But she knew that Kelub was posted in the palace at night, and, if she remembered the schedule correctly, tonight he should be alone.

She tiptoed through the halls and down the stairs, and, just as she had expected, Kelub was at the door of the harem. He was leaning against the wall with his eyes closed. When he heard her approach, he straightened up hastily, and, when he saw who it was, he couldn't hide a grin.

"What are you doing up this late?" he asked softly.

Mara smiled at him blindingly. "I couldn't sleep so I thought I would take a walk."

He frowned his disapproval, but she could see that he was very glad to see her.

"It's all this tension in the palace. Can you feel it?"

Kelub nodded solemnly. "Who doesn't? Soon, it will all . . ." He didn't finish his sentence.

Mara didn't press him; she just leaned against the wall next to him, her shoulder brushing against his. "I would feel better if I just knew what was going to happen, what Adonijah was up to."

Kelub had been staring at her happily, but he nodded at her words. "If it makes you feel any better, it will not happen here, at the palace."

This is what Mara had been waiting for. Careful not to show too much interest, she asked. "Oh, where will it take place?"

Kelub, seeing no harm in chatting with a slave girl, was not concerned about telling her what he knew. "Near En Rogel. Adonijah has been getting together chariots and horses, and he is planning to take about fifty of the soldiers who are loyal to him. He will invite all the princes—except Solomon, of course—and all the royal officials, and declare himself king."

"But many of the officials are loyal to Solomon," Mara protested.

Kelub looked down on her with his superior knowledge. "True, but they will go along with it when everyone else does. It is too bad, really. But it looks like Adonijah will be the next king."

"Will you be going?" Mara asked carefully.

Kelub looked offended. "My duty is to the king, who, at this moment, is David."

Mara smiled at him. "When will he do this?"

"Within the next few days, supposedly."

"I still don't think that the army will follow him. If they are not loyal to David, they are loyal to Joab." This seemed to Mara to be an indisputable fact, and, without the loyalty of the army, a declaration of kingship was worthless.

Kelub apparently didn't have an answer for this one. "I don't know. But none of Adonijah's friends I have talked to seem to think that the army will be a problem. I don't know what they have in mind."

"Hmmm," Mara mused. "Oh well, I am not as worried now. Thanks for talking to me. I had better be getting back." Whether or not Adonijah's plan had a possibility of succeeding, he was going to try something open and public, and it would bring the whole succession issue to a conclusion.

Kelub looked disappointed. "Listen, this is not supposed to get around."

"Of course it is not," Mara agreed, which, she told herself, was saying little enough.

Mara thought about the situation all night. She couldn't decide who she should tell. She would not be able to see Solomon; he wasn't even at the palace now. And she didn't know who she could trust.

She finally decided to talk to Ahishar, the man in charge of the slaves and servants. She knew that he was loyal to David and that he favored Solomon as the next king. And she was sure that he would be able to let someone else know what was going to happen.

She went to him early the next morning. She did not even start with small talk. She explained the situation to Ahishar and watched his huge, white grin fade as she spoke.

"I hope it was right to tell you. Perhaps most of the officials already know. But the servants didn't, and that is always a good clue about how far things have spread," Mara finished.

Ahishar looked worried. "I am invited to this 'feast' at En Rogel tomorrow, but I had no idea what it was about. Adonijah has been very sly. You were right to tell me. I won't even ask how you found out."

Mara giggled nervously. "What will you do?"

"I will let the word get around, and make sure that the right people find out. The king will have to do something. He can no longer just wait around."

Mara agreed.

"You had better go about your business," Ahishar told Mara. As Mara walked away, she felt that she had made the right decision, but she needed to know what would happen next.

The next day she found Abishag in the morning, and urged the girl to suggest to David that he needed to hear the music of the lyre. Abishag looked at her suspiciously but agreed to try.

Shortly, Abishag came looking for her. "The king happens to be in the mood for some music. Who would have thought?"

Mara smiled her appreciation and fiddled nervously with her thick, blond braid.

"Today is the day that things will happen," Abishag commented.

"Yes, you are right," Mara affirmed, surprised, as always, by Abishag's perception. She had not yet told Abishag of Adonijah's plot, but she did so as they climbed up the stairs.

Mara had to play the lyre for five hours before anything happened. Fortunately, David was weaker than usual, and he kept dozing off. When he did, she stopped playing and exchanged worried looks with Abishag.

Why didn't anything happen?

It was mid-afternoon when a guard announced the unexpected arrival of Bathsheba. David looked surprised, but pleased, and he sat up to greet his favorite wife.

Mara wished it had been someone other than Bathsheba who would help Solomon to his throne, but she would accept anyone right now.

Bathsheba almost prostrated herself on the floor with her bow. That was not something she did often.

"What would you like?" David asked.

"My lord the king," she began, her voice carefully modulated to sound upset. "You swore to me by your God that Solomon would be king after you and sit on your throne. But now Adonijah has become king, and you do not even know about it."

David sat up sharply. "What are you talking about? What has he done?"

Bathsheba had carefully rehearsed her part. "He has sacrificed great numbers of cattle, fattened calves, and sheep, and has invited all of your sons, Abiathar the priest, Joab, but not Solomon. My lord, the eyes of all Israel are on you, to learn who will sit on the throne after you. Otherwise, as soon as you are laid to rest with your fathers, I and my son Solomon will be treated like criminals."

At the end of her speech, a guard entered to announce Nathan, the prophet. Mara thought, cynically, that they had planned the scenario perfectly. Bathsheba left the room while Nathan spoke.

Nathan, too, bowed his face before the king. Then he said, in reasonable tones very different from Bathsheba's melodramatics, "Have you, my lord my king, declared that Adonijah shall be king after you, and that he will sit on your throne?"

David stared at the priest. His lined face was frozen.

Nathan did not wait for a response, but continued, "Today Adonijah has gone down and sacrificed cattle, fattened calves, and sheep. He has invited all the king's sons, the commanders of the army and Abiathar the priest. Right now they are eating and drinking with him and saying, 'Long live King Adonijah!'" Nathan raised an imaginary glass to illustrate his point, and went on, "But he did not invite me, Zadok the priest, Benaiah, or your son Solomon. Is this something my lord has done without letting his servants know who should sit on the throne after you?"

David's old face looked bewildered. "But Joab will stop them. He knows my opinion of the matter."

Nathan shook his head. "He will not."

"Yes," David insisted, raising his voice. "He will. He is my best friend. He will not be disloyal to me."

Nathan took a step nearer to the king, his face full of pity. "My lord the king, he has betrayed you. He was the one who came up with this plan." Nathan's voice was very gentle, but it could not keep the daggers out of the words. Mara wondered how Nathan had learned that. She must not have been his only source.

David did not seem to comprehend the words immediately. When they finally sank in, he leaned back against his couch and wept.

Mara ached for the old king, remembering the look she had intercepted between Joab and David and realizing that she had never known such a friendship.

And Joab had saved her, Mara remembered; she could hardly forget.

After a while, the king recovered and called Bathsheba back in. He struggled to his feet and Mara could see Abishag resisting the urge to help him. When he was standing he said, "As surely as the Lord lives, who has delivered me out of every trouble, I will surely carry out today what I swore to you by the Lord, the God of Israel: Solomon your son shall be king after me, and he will sit on my throne."

Mara saw the satisfaction in Bathsheba's face as the woman bowed to the ground again. Bathsheba said, "May my lord the King David live forever!"

Mara could almost believe that she really meant it.

Then David ordered Zadok the priest and Benaiah, who had been the captain of the king's bodyguard, to come to him. He told them to find Solomon, and put him on the king's mule and go with the king's bodyguard to Gihon, where Solomon was to be anointed by Zadok and Nathan, and then proclaimed king.

Benaiah was a large man with a plain face, but Mara had always liked him. She could see the relief on his face as he said, in response to the king's words, "Amen! May the Lord, the God of my lord the king, so declare it. As the Lord was with my lord the

67

king, so may he be with Solomon to make his throne even greater than the throne of my lord King David!"

Mara echoed the sentiment in her heart.

Everything occurred as David had ordered it. And Mara, later that evening, could hear the people cheering for Solomon, their new king. Abishag had explained to her that it would be a kind of joint rule until David died.

"What about Adonijah," Mara asked her friend.

Abishag shook her head. "Solomon should kill him right away. Adonijah will not give up so easily."

Mara agreed but she thought about Solomon and the caravan guard, whom he had refused to kill. Solomon would not kill his brother until he had to.

Mara was running an errand for Abigail a few months later, when she ran into Solomon. She literally ran into him, for she had been looking behind her at the soldiers clattering down the stairs. Everything happened as Abishag had predicted—Solomon was king when he returned from Gihon. But Adonijah had not been killed.

Solomon smiled at her, a little nervously. "Mara, I haven't seen you in a long time."

"Not since you became king." Mara's forehead reached Solomon's chin, so she had to look up into his eyes. "How are you enjoying it?"

Solomon responded, "I haven't done anything but talk to my father about the temple I am to build. But it will be the greatest temple ever built."

"So I hear." Mara reached her hands behind her back to play with her thick braid. "How is your father?"

"He will not last much longer."

Mara nodded, her eyes sympathetic. "You will be lost without him."

Solomon tossed his head back, "Why do you say that? I may be young, but I am well-prepared for kingship."

"Of course you are," Mara said hurriedly, appalled at her lack of tact. She wondered where her well-practiced polish had disappeared. "That is not what I meant."

Solomon looked at her anguished face and smiled. "I know. Please forgive me for snapping at you. You are right. I do not know what I will do when he dies."

"You will be a great king," Mara told him.

"I don't know. My father was a great king, and I am supposed to be greater than him. Do you think I could ever be? Could anyone?"

Mara nodded her confidence. "You will be greater."

"I may be as great a king, but I will never be as great a man. I know. Sometimes, I feel like a puppet in a child's play."

Mara had to turn away from the hopelessness in Solomon's eyes. She didn't know what to say.

"Yahweh can make you great," she said at last. "I have never seen a god with such power."

Solomon nodded. "You shame me, truly you do. I often forget that I am not alone in the world."

Mara looked up into his eyes, and she felt herself falling. "You will never be alone as long as I am living," she whispered. Then she caught herself. Had she really said that aloud?

Solomon's eyes held hers for a moment. He shook his head, as if he were waking himself. "Have you heard? I am to marry the daughter of the Pharaoh in Egypt. It will be a great thing for Israel, to have such an ally. I have been arranging it for some time."

"Marry?" Mara repeated. "When?"

"She will be leaving Egypt shortly." Solomon looked proud at his accomplishment, and Mara wondered if he were happy about the marriage or the alliance. She felt her heart contracting. Solomon was to be married?

"You don't seem excited about this," Solomon commented, pushing a stray piece of dark hair behind his ear. "Who would have thought the day would come when Egypt would make a marriage alliance with Israel? Think of the resources they have. Think of the builders. They build incredible things in Egypt."

69

Mara closed her eyes, trying to shut out his words. She did not care about buildings. Solomon was to be married.

"Mara, what is wrong? Something has hurt you." Mara opened her eyes to see Solomon's face very close to her own. "Mara, tell me. I know you too well for you to hide anything."

Mara's eyes blazed. How dare he speak to her so intimately when he was to be married? "You know me? How can you possibly know me? You don't know that much about me at all. Can you tell me what I think about when I lie awake at night? What makes me smile when I am alone? You can't, can you? We have only spoken with each other fifteen times in our whole lives."

Mara broke off. She knew she had made a mistake, and she couldn't bring the words back. She gave a little cry and tried to run away, but Solomon caught her shoulder and trapped her against the wall.

He would know how she felt now. He would have to know. How else would she know exactly how many times they had spoken? Only if she had rehearsed them in her head, over and over again, reliving every detail of the scenes. As she had.

"I don't understand," Solomon stammered.

Mara shook her head, trying to free herself from the king's grasp.

Solomon's brow wrinkled, and Mara relaxed. She would face it bravely. Face his scorn and shock as he realized that a slave girl had presumed to love the king of Israel.

"I don't understand," Solomon repeated. "You said we had spoken fifteen times." Mara winced at the incredulity in his voice. "I had only counted fourteen."

The world stopped for Mara, as it had not stopped since a star-lit, fire-lit night in a village next to a northern sea.

Solomon had counted fourteen.

She looked up into his eyes, and they were pools of tenderness. She was falling again. Dazed, she stammered, "You probably did not count that time the ambassador from Sidon visited, and you whispered to me about his garish clothes." She wondered if she were speaking discernibly.

70

Solomon nodded, smiling slowly. "No, I didn't count that because you didn't speak to me." Solomon lowered his head. "Can it be that each time meant as much to you as it has to me?"

Mara smiled a little. "It must have. For they have meant everything to me. You have been my breath."

Solomon drew in a quick gasp. "And, little Mara, you have been my dawn."

Mara closed her eyes, and she knew she was going to be kissed by the king of Israel, and she knew that she had longed for this all her life, before she had even met him.

"Do you know that I love you?" Solomon whispered, against her cheek.

"Not until this moment," Mara responded, reaching for his kiss.

After a minute, Mara pulled away. "But you are to marry the Pharaoh's daughter."

Solomon shook the dazed look out of his eyes. "Yes, I am. So what are we to do?"

"You can't call the marriage off." It was a statement, not a question, for Mara knew enough to know that such an action could not be reversed.

Solomon shook his head. "I will marry you as well." His voice was faintly hopeful.

Mara had imagined this moment so many times, in fantasies and dreams. But she had never actually expected it to happen. It was a scene from a tale or a song, never to be envisioned in real life. In her dreams, she always knew what her answer would be.

But this was not a dream—this was reality. And so she was unprepared.

Two paths stretched out before her. She could see them both clearly. One of security, of luxury, of nights in Solomon's arms. And one without those things, faced all alone.

Mara shook her head. "No. I will never submit to being one of many wives." The decision was made before she fully thought it through.

"If you love me . . ." Solomon began.

"Because I love you, I could never share you." Mara discovered that she was certain about this one thing. She would not be a part of a family such as David's. She had seen what could happen.

"So it is hopeless." The joy that had been shining in Solomon's dark eyes faded, and he shrugged as he did when he resigned himself to circumstances, adding another burden to his load.

"A life together is hopeless, yes," Mara agreed, aching more for him than for herself. She had learned to anticipate disappointment. "Did you really expect anything different?"

Solomon shook his head. "That you love me surpasses all my expectations."

The words covered Mara's spirit like a blanket. "And you can live with the knowledge that there is one who will always love you."

Solomon smiled. "I wish I had known earlier."

He kissed her again, and she savored it because she knew it would be the last time. She would make it the last time. It would be better that way.

She pulled away. "You will never know," she murmured, rubbing the back of her hand against his neatly-trimmed beard, "How unspeakably dark my life was . . . before I met you."

She hurried out of the curtained alcove they had been standing in, and turned back to see Solomon slouched against the wall, watching her glide away from him.

Chapter 9

"Please," Mara begged. "I have been playing at the palace for more than three years now. I am as good as any of the lyre players here except Seth."

Hadad, in charge of the palace musicians, looked at Mara speculatively. "I don't know. This is a very important banquet. Envoys from King Hiram in Tyre have arrived today, you know."

"I know," Mara said. "But I won't disgrace the king. You know how well I play. You have taught me so much."

Mara added that last sentence because she had learned that flattery accomplished a lot with Hadad.

She could see that he was yielding, so she threw in her final stroke. "King David himself told me after I played for him that my music would charm the coldest listener." The situation with David and Solomon both being kings was very confusing to her, and Mara never knew whom she should speak of as king.

Hadad chuckled. "I'm not sure he was influenced only by your music. No one should have such blue eyes. It isn't fair." He threw up his hands. "Very well. You may play at the banquet tonight. But if I hear one mistake you will be back to playing in the harem."

"Oh, thank you. I will astonish you with the perfection of my music," Mara assured him, grinning at her success.

She had wanted to play for the royal banquets for as long as she had been at the palace, and finally—it seemed—she was going to be able to do so. She was sure that Hadad's change of mind had a lot to do with David summoning her to play for him in his chambers, four times now, in as many months.

The envoys who had arrived from Tyre were very important. They proved that Hiram acknowledged Solomon as the new king and would probably continue to be Israel's ally and trading partner. Tyre's goodwill was essential for Israel's trade, because the Israelites were not people of the sea, and Tyrians were. Through an alliance with Tyre, Israel would be able to get material from all over the world.

At last, Mara was to be present at a royal banquet. She was seated with the rest of the musicians, watching the servants finish preparing the room. Oil lamps blazed on the cedar walls, and the long table in the middle of the room was already set with trays of figs, grapes, almonds, pomegranates, quinces, and dates. Pitchers of spiced wine were scattered around the room, and Mara had smelled the meat roasting when she entered. Solomon and some of his brothers had been hunting the previous day, so the meat was to be fallow buck and gazelle.

The musicians were clustered on one side of the room, and Mara smiled nervously at Daniel, who played the flute and always teased her about her red cheeks.

He leaned closer to her, "Don't worry, no one even listens to us."

She giggled. "Hadad does."

Daniel nodded in understanding. "You'll be wonderful."

She chatted with him quietly until the preparations were complete. The chatter silenced when the guests started entering the room. Mara recognized most of them. They were David's courtiers and the leading citizens of Jerusalem. Other servants had pointed out most of them to her several times. Solomon had not arrived yet. Though Mara had never been to a banquet before, she had a feeling that Solomon would wait until the last to arrive. Apparently, the envoys from Tyre had not arrived yet either.

The guests were talking idly to each other when three mute taps sounded on the marble floor. Everyone was silent after the first tap, and they all looked expectantly at the double doors.

Thus announced, Solomon walked in with two other men, but Mara saw only the young king.

David was, by now, far too ill to attend a banquet, so Solomon had taken over all of the diplomatic responsibilities. He was dressed in his royal robes, pure white linen and the purple-blue of the Phoenician dye. A thick gold bracelet was pushed high on his arm and he was wearing the thin gold crown. He was, perhaps, as handsome a man as Mara had ever seen. Their eyes met, and Mara forced herself to look away. But not before she saw the blaze of love she had surprised in his eyes.

The envoys from Tyre, Mara learned, were one of King Hiram's sons and another royal official. They were dressed rather gaudily, Mara thought, with jewels displayed prominently. But both of them were rather plain looking, under all the clothes.

Mara played her lyre with the rest of the musicians, but kept an interested eye on the events at the table.

There were several conversations going on, but if she focused enough, she could catch pieces of Solomon's discussion with the Tyrian prince. They were speaking in the language of Tyre, and Mara wondered if the Tyrians could not speak Hebrew or if they just refused to.

Mara heard a voice she thought she recognized and turned her attention to the other side of the table. She recognized Joel there, and was surprised that he would have been invited to such an important banquet. She thought he was just a soldier.

He saw her looking at him, and he winked. She smiled in response, a little embarrassed, and then embarrassed that she had been embarrassed.

Daniel, beside her, nudged her with his elbow. "Stop flirting with the guests," he whispered.

Mara gave an indignant gasp. "I was not flirting. I just smiled."

Daniel chuckled softly. "That was enough."

Mara shook her head and turned her back on Daniel. She had not been flirting with Joel, but maybe it had looked that way. She glanced up at Solomon. He was watching her soberly. What was he thinking? Surely he wasn't thinking that she had been flirting.

She was too scared to smile at Solomon. Someone would surely notice. But she looked at him anxiously and tried to reassure him with her eyes. Apparently, it worked, for he turned his head, smiling to himself—as if he were amused. Laughing at himself again, Mara thought.

The Tyrian prince caught the look that Mara and Solomon had exchanged and he raised his eyebrows. "Who is the golden-haired beauty with the musicians," he asked Solomon.

Solomon glanced over as if he were just noticing.

"She is a slave girl that your father, King Hiram of Tyre, sent my father a few years ago."

"Indeed?" the prince said. "I am surprised we ever let her get away." The prince looked at Solomon suggestively, and Mara, with a contraction of her heart, wondered if the alliance with Tyre was so important that Solomon would give her away.

Solomon looked at Mara idly, as if he had not noticed the prince's look. "She is a moderately skilled lyrist," he said. "Not of the best quality."

Mara would have been offended, but she knew Solomon was saying it to discourage the Tyrian prince. She felt her cheeks redden, and she quickly turned her head away.

She was ashamed she had ever doubted Solomon.

Two weeks later, the envoys from Tyre left. Mara was relieved. Whenever she had seen the young Tyrian prince, he had given her significant looks.

Abigail had asked Mara to keep her company for the afternoon. Abigail had been doing that more and more. Mara wasn't surprised. King David had once loved Abigail, before Bathsheba, and Abigail had been happy to become his wife. Abigail had told her about it.

"I had been married to another man, a crude, violent man called Nabal, but he was very wealthy and my parents thought I would be happy. I was married when I was eleven. David, this was when he was an outlaw from Saul, asked him for food for his men, but he refused. So I brought the food out to David despite my husband's wishes and pleaded with David not to revenge himself on Nabal. When I told Nabal of this, his heart stopped and he died. And so I became David's wife." Abigail told Mara this story while Mara plucked her lyre.

"But why," Mara ventured to ask, "would you marry him when he already had another wife?"

Abigail smiled, a little wryly. "I loved him, and I thought his love for me would make the situation bearable."

"Did it?"

Abigail shook her head, still lovely despite her years. "At first it did, but his attention always did wander."

Mara pitied Abigail, and she resolved again never to let that happen to her.

"Do you think he still loves you?" Mara asked.

Abigail paused a moment. "I'm sure he does, but I am not the only one he loves. People can love more than one person, you know."

Mara disagreed. "I don't believe that."

"You are young. You will see. I never have loved anyone but David, but I have never had the opportunity. I have lived my life in this harem, and now even David doesn't come to see me. Soon he will die, and I won't even have the faint hope."

Mara's eyes teared up. "It must be a dreadful life."

Abigail picked up her hairbrush and started to brush her long, graying brown hair. "It hasn't been so bad. I have had much time to read. I am grateful that I know how. Most women in the harem don't know how, and so they have nothing to amuse themselves but gossip and scandal."

Mara was ashamed at the judgment she'd placed on the women of the harem. Abigail was right—what else did they have? They were David's women, and once David died, they would be passed on to Solomon. But most of the women were far to old to interest Solomon, so they would live out their days in the perfume-scented halls until they were granted respite by death.

She would never become one of them. She was sure of the decision she had made and ashamed that she had begun to have second thoughts.

"Why do kings have to have more than one wife anyway?" Mara asked, a little bitterly. She hoped Abigail hadn't noticed the tone.

Abigail shrugged, as if she had dealt with the same question. "Politics, I guess. Marriages are a good way to make treaties. And power—a king collects women as he would collect treasure. Sometimes, I think it is ridiculous."

"I agree," sighed Mara.

Abigail smiled at Mara. "I am glad you have come to the palace. You are a refreshing change. I hope you do not mind keeping me company."

Mara returned Abigail's smile. "I enjoy it. I am glad we are able to talk."

Mara continued to play, but her thoughts stayed with Abigail, and the harem, and the pleasures of the king.

Chapter 10

David, son of Jesse, king of Israel for forty years, died not long after Mara's conversation with Abigail. He asked for some music in the middle of the night because he was having trouble sleeping, and Abishag came to get Mara. Mara played for him for several hours while Abishag did her best to keep him warm. Nothing soothed him. At last, he said, "Could you have someone summon my son, Solomon?"

Abishag ran to relay the message, and shortly Solomon came running in, his dark hair disheveled and only his tunic on. "Father, what is it? What is wrong?"

"I will die tonight," David stated.

Both Solomon and Abishag made sounds of distress, but David held up a weak hand to silence them. Solomon knelt down beside his father.

"Be strong, Jedidiah, and show that you are a man." Tears started falling down Solomon's face. "Walk in the ways of the Lord and keep his commandments."

"Father, I will," Solomon promised, clutching his father's hand.

"Yahweh promised me, you know, that if your descendants walk faithfully before me with all their heart and soul, you will never fail to have a descendant on the throne of Israel." David's words were forced and labored, and Mara stopped playing so that her soft music would not drown out his words.

"I will do my best, father," Solomon choked out.

"Yahweh will give you the strength you need. Don't try to do it alone, Jedidiah," David said.

Solomon nodded, "I know he will."

"I'm afraid I will leave you with some unpleasant things to be done. I could never bring myself to do them."

"Anything, father. Tell me."

"You remember Shemei, son of Gera, who called down curses on me the day I went to Mahanaim." Solomon said that he did, but Mara didn't know what he was talking about. "I swore to him that I would not kill him, but you cannot consider him innocent. You are wise; bring his gray head down to the grave in blood."

Mara gasped as the words grew louder, and she looked in concern at Solomon's face. For his first act as king, he would have to kill someone. She was sure he had never killed a man before.

"But show kindness to the sons of Barzillai of Gilead. They stood by me when I fled from your brother Absalom."

Solomon nodded. This would be easier to do.

Solomon waited for the rest of his father's charge in trepidation.

Mara leaned forward as David's face twisted. He had to spit the words out, and they left Mara cold inside. "You know what Joab did to me—what he did to the two commanders of Israel's armies, shedding their blood in peacetime as if in battle. You know of the blood that stains his belt and his sandals. Deal with him according to your wisdom, but . . ." David's voice faltered, but he forced himself to continue. "Do not let his gray head go down to the grave in peace." He could say no more.

Solomon's face crumpled at what his father was telling him to do. He had to kill his father's best friend. "I understand, father, what you can not bring yourself to say. It will be done, and it will be on my shoulders."

"Thank you, Jedidiah," David breathed.

Mara started to play again, and she played a song David had written only a month ago. She had just learned it. Solomon looked back at her and smiled in gratitude.

"Jedidiah," David began. "Listen to me. You are king because it is Yahweh's will, and His will cannot be wrong. You do not

80

have to prove your worth to me, your mother, or to anyone else. Certainly not to Yahweh. Do not try. Please."

Solomon jerked his head into a nod, but Mara saw his eyes and knew that the advice was not going to be taken.

Solomon began to sing then, the song that Mara was playing:
"When one rules over men in righteousness,
    when he rules in the fear of God,
    he is like the light of the morning at sunrise
    on a cloudless morning,
    like the brightness after rain
    that brings the grass from the earth."

David sat up a little in his bed, and Mara heard his singing voice for the first time. It was no longer weak and labored, and the beauty of it brought tears to her eyes. He sang with his son:
"Is not my house right with God?
    Has he not made with me an everlasting covenant,
    arranged and secured in every part?
Will he not bring to fruition my salvation
    and grant me my every desire?"

Suddenly, David's voice broke, and he slumped back into his bed. Abishag began to weep, and Mara brushed away her own tears.

Solomon bent to kiss his father's still face. Then he stood up. His eyes met Mara's. "He is gone," he whispered.

Mara put down her lyre and took a few steps until she was directly in front of him. "Yes," she murmured.

"What will I do now?" he asked, his eyes pleading with her for assurance.

She gave him what he needed. "You will rule, and the entire world will know of the glory of your reign. But first . . . you will mourn."

Solomon nodded. "Yes." He walked over to the doors of David's chambers and said to the guards standing there. "You will let it be known that David, king of Israel for forty years, is dead.

He walked with the Lord all the days of his life; may my son say the same about me."

Solomon started to have Mara play for him nearly every day, as he struggled with affairs of state in the throne room, or studied with the wise men of the court, or worked with builders on the plans for the temple he was to build. She saw more of him than she had ever seen before, and she loved him even more.

Solomon had moved another throne into the throne room and placed it to his right for his mother, and she would often come and sit in it. Mara hated when she did; she could not forget the scene she had witnessed between Bathsheba and Solomon.

Shortly after David's death, Mara was off to the side of the throne room strumming softly on her lyre with a few other musicians, watching Solomon talk with Benaiah, whom he had made the Captain of the Armies in place of Joab. Solomon had not yet killed Joab, as he had promised his father—Mara knew he was putting it off as long as possible. Nor had he killed Adonijah. She had heard whispers that Adonijah had not given up so easily, and there were many people who still supported his bid for kingship.

Solomon should do something to secure his throne; people were saying that he was weak.

Bathsheba was announced, and she glided into the throne room, colder than ever. When she had heard of David's death, she had wept for days. Now, she was hard and pale, and Mara shuddered when she saw Bathsheba look at Solomon. David had summoned Solomon to him at his death, and he had not summoned Bathsheba. That was not something Bathsheba would easily forgive.

Not very long ago, Bathsheba had come upon her, very suddenly, in one of the halls of the harem. Solomon's mother, noting her, had forced her against a curtained wall.

Mara remembered gasping at the beauty of the woman at that moment. The flowing dark hair, the pearl-like skin, Solomon's deep, beautiful eyes set in the delicate features of a woman and surrounded by eyelashes as dark and full as feathers. Some strong emotion—Mara had no doubt that it was anger—flushed Bathsheba's usually pale cheeks.

She hated this woman.

"I shouldn't even deign to speak to you, but I will this one time," Bathsheba hissed, her face very close to Mara's own.

Mara forced herself not to bite her lip, and waited in silence for Bathsheba to continue.

"I am telling you now to stay away from my son. He is not for you, not for a tasteless, ambitious, covetous slave girl."

This could not go unanswered. "I only approach your son when I am summoned."

"Don't you think that I don't know what you are trying to do." Bathsheba's eyes were still like stars, reflecting the wavering lamplight of the hallway in a myriad of glints and shadows. "You have already seen that he will not marry you, and I'm sure you are too proud to become one of his concubines. So just leave him alone. The last thing he needs right now is to face the scandal that you are likely to cause."

Mara wanted to laugh at that moment, because the woman knew her own son so little. She didn't laugh, of course. Instead, she said, "I am a musician, a slave in this palace. Solomon is the king, and you are the king's mother. I think you overestimate my power in this place."

That seemed to startle Bathsheba. But she hesitated for only a moment. "You have a certain overblown kind of beauty," she began, sizing Mara up in such a calculated way that Mara wanted to cringe. "There are certainly men around who could admire it. Why don't you find one of them to pursue? Or don't your ambitions allow you to desire anything less than the king?"

There were so many avenues of hate that led to this woman, so many reasons to despise her.

Mara had learned much in the palace, among the perfumed rooms and cedar-paneled halls, and she had learned much in the years before the palace. She knew how to read people, to find their weaknesses, and she knew how to make strong people lose control. And to survive, she had learned to never venture into any of these places. And so she was vaguely surprised when she heard herself saying, very softly, very precisely, "I think, my lady, that you are confusing me with yourself. My ambitions have never extended so far as a throne."

Bathsheba slapped her. It was the reaction that she had expected, in fact, deserved for being so foolish as to say such a thing to this woman.

But Bathsheba was no longer in control of this conversation. Her color was no longer high; she was, instead, deathly white. And Mara could see, with some degree of satisfaction, her hands shaking.

Mara smiled, very stiffly. "Have you ever thought, my lady, that it might be better to speak to your son about these things? He, as you well know, has infinitely more control over things than I do. Maybe you could ask him if your desires are his desires."

"It doesn't matter what his desires are!" Bathsheba said, nothing cool or calculating about her now. "Nothing matters but that he keeps his throne, that he continues his father's kingdom and reign. Nothing matters but that!"

Had Bathsheba been in control, she would never have said something so revealing to anyone, certainly not to Mara. And Mara understood something about the woman now; there was something she no longer had any doubts about. She closed her eyes, to hide the expression. It wouldn't do for her to lose control as well.

"Why?" Bathsheba cried, backing away from Mara. "Why do you insist on conflicting my son? Why don't you turn your attention elsewhere? Why Solomon? Because he is king, because he has a certain fondness for you, because . . ."

"Because I love him." The words were said before Mara had a chance to think about them, and after they were said, she didn't regret them. She saw Bathsheba take another step back. The curtain on the wall behind the woman was a warm green, not, she thought idly, Bathsheba's best color.

"I love him," Mara repeated. Her voice was cool, and she said the words softly. "I have known him for two years, and we have barely ever spoken. But I can see so many things in him to love, so much that is admirable or endearing. Have you ever wondered how blind you must be that you, who are his mother, who held him as an infant, cannot see the same things in him that I have seen so quickly."

She might have hurt Bathsheba, but she couldn't really tell. There was so much anger and pain in the woman's eyes that Mara couldn't really tell how much of it she had caused.

But she knew one thing. Although Bathsheba's idea of love was no doubt very different from Mara's own, whatever emotion Bathsheba named as love was not given to her son, not to Solomon. And for this, more than for any other reason, Mara hated Bathsheba.

"I hate this woman," Mara thought as she looked at her approaching Solomon, now, in the throne room.

Solomon's eyes lit up and he rose as his mother approached. He bowed to her, and she acknowledged the honor with a stiff nod.

"I have one small request to make of you," Bathsheba began.

"You know I will not refuse you anything," responded Solomon, lowering himself back onto the throne.

"Let Abishag the Shunammite be given in marriage to your brother Adonijah."

The words were softly spoken, and with a wave of her hand Bathsheba dismissed them as if they were of little importance. But they were of the greatest importance imaginable, and they hung in the air like a fog.

Mara gasped aloud, but her own intake of breath was drowned by the shocked sounds of the others in the court.

Solomon looked dumbfounded.

Mara had been at court long enough to know what Bathsheba's words meant. Bathsheba herself would surely know. Abishag, although Mara knew she had never given herself to David, was considered a part of David's harem. And the royal harem was a symbol of the king's power.

Mara saw Solomon's hand begin to shake as he sat in silence. She prayed to Yahweh that he would not back down, no matter how much he adored his mother. Adonijah could not have Abishag. If Solomon were weak in this, Adonijah would have a clear claim to the throne of Israel.

She couldn't tell how long the court sat before Solomon responded. Benaiah's plain, rugged face was furious, and she could see him consciously holding himself back from attacking the king's mother. The musicians, herself included, had stopped playing, and all waited for Solomon's response.

It was a response, they all knew, that would determine the line of Israel's future.

Solomon finally rose, and Mara could tell, even before he spoke, what his response would be.

"Why do you request Abishag for Adonijah?" His voice was silky.

Bathsheba opened her mouth to respond, but Solomon silenced her with an uplifted hand.

"You might as well request the kingdom for him—he is my older brother." His voice rose gradually. "Yes, for him and for Abiathar, and for Joab as well."

Again, Bathsheba tried to respond, but Solomon continued. "May God deal with me, be it ever so severely, if Adonijah doesn't pay with his life for this request!"

He was going to do it, finally. He was going to kill Adonijah.

"And now," Solomon continued, "As surely as the Lord lives—he who has established me securely on the throne of my father David and has founded a dynasty for me as he promised—Adonijah shall be put to death today."

Solomon turned to Benaiah, but the captain needed no urging. With a triumphant glance at Bathsheba, he marched from the room.

Shortly, the news came that Solomon's brother had been killed. Mara could see Solomon's face, how he schooled his expression to show no emotion. Inside she ached. How could a man live with the knowledge that he had his own brother killed, even if the killing was just and necessary?

The guards brought Abiathar, the priest who had conspired with Adonijah into the throne room to face Solomon.

The priest was very old by now, and his breath was coming out in gasps.

Mara wondered if Solomon was to put Abiathar to death as well. She glanced at the faces in the court, and she saw that they all thought he would. She thought that he would not.

Solomon did not even rise to his feet. "You deserve to die," he said to the priest. "But I will not put you to death because you carried the ark before my father David, and you shared in all of his hardships. Go back to your fields in Anathoth."

The court let out its collective breath, and Mara could see the surprise and admiration on the faces of the men of the court. A very wise decision. The priest was removed from the priesthood, but he was not killed.

Mara knew from long experience that it was never a good idea to kill a holy man.

"What about Joab?" she thought, knowing the man should die. Knowing that Solomon should have listened to his father and killed him before now. But wishing, somehow, that the thing did not have to be done. Surely Solomon wouldn't have to kill his brother and his father's best friend on the same day.

But Solomon was going to get it all over with at once. She saw Benaiah return and march over to the king's throne. He said something to the king, too quiet for anyone else to hear.

Although no one heard Benaiah's words, Mara learned later that Joab had fled into the tabernacle and refused to come out. Solomon stood up and he responded to Benaiah's report.

"Do as he says. Strike him down and bury him, and so clear me and my father's house of the guilt of the innocent blood that Joab shed."

Mara sighed. Joab gone, too. It had to be. Solomon's throne was too unsteady; he could not afford to be merciful. Mara saw Solomon's lips moving, but she could not hear the words. She only heard Joab's anguished voice as he pleaded with David to change his mind about his successor. "Everything I have ever done has been for you," he had said to the old king.

She felt tears in her eyes, and she wondered if he were worth crying over. But he had saved her, she thought, and he had loved David.

87

She shook her head sharply, and forced herself to listen to the rest of Solomon's speech. "But on David and his descendants, his house and his throne, may there be the Lord's peace forever."

"Amen," she whispered to herself, her small voice drowned out in the cries of assent that came from the men in the court. They would support him now, she saw. He had done what he needed to do. He had proven to his nation that he was strong enough for kingship.

She prayed silently, to whatever god was listening, that Solomon would not have to prove it so terribly again.

Mara glanced over at Bathsheba, who had taken her place in the throne to the king's left. She caught on the woman's face a small smile of satisfaction.

The implications of that smile caused Mara to lose her breath.

"He will come tomorrow," Abishag told Mara that evening.

"And you will leave the palace forever," Mara said. "How I will miss you."

Abishag smiled. "I will miss you too. But I have been waiting for my love for so long, I cannot be sad about leaving."

Mara hugged her friend tightly. "I am happy for you, even if I am sad for me." She took a step back. "Have you talked to Solomon about it?"

Abishag shook her head. "No. I was going to do it the cowardly way, and just run away. Do you think I should tell him?"

"If you don't, I will, after you have gone. He will not come for you, I'm sure."

"I know," Abishag agreed. "He is a good man. He will be a great king if he will just let go of his insecurity."

Mara sighed. "What will I do when you have gone?"

Abishag chuckled and replied. "Maybe you should get married and have a family of your own."

"How would I accomplish that? Who would marry me, a slave?"

Abishag looked as if she were about to say something, but Mara cut her off. "I will not become a part of a harem."

Abishag nodded. "I know. But Yahweh knows what is best for you, and he will work it out for your good."

Mara shrugged. "Maybe. I mean, who would have imagined that I would end up here—safe and secure, if not truly happy—after my village was destroyed, I was sold as a slave, and I escaped from a caravan to get lost in the wilderness."

The two girls were standing on the balcony in the hall of the servants' quarters. The sun was setting, dissolving into shades of crimson and orange.

Mara swallowed hard, trying not to imagine life at the palace without the friendship of Abishag. The days stretched before her like beads, like her own beads of sea-gold, which she still slept with each night, only existing to lead to the next one. "I feel like I have come such a long way for no reason. Surely there is more to life than just surviving."

Abishag gave a little choked noise, and Mara turned to see that her friend was crying. "Mara," Abishag said. "There is more, you just simply refuse to see it."

Mara turned her back on her friend, to hide her face. "I don't understand."

"I, too, was faced with a life lived in the palace, torn from my family, and a life with the man I love only a vague hope. But Yahweh has led me through it and has brought me to the place he wants me to be. He will lead you as well."

Mara shook her head violently. "It is hardly the same. I have no other choice. If I leave, I will face a far worse future than I have here. And here, there is only emptiness."

"There is not. Try to find what Yahweh wants you to do here. He has a purpose for you, if you would allow him to lead you to it." Abishag stretched her hand out to touch Mara's arm.

Mara forced her shoulders not to shake, and she swallowed the ache in her throat. She would not let Abishag leave with this episode last in her mind. She turned around and pushed her lips into a tight smile. "Just ignore my hysterics. I will be fine. And you will be blissfully happy."

Abishag's smile was not convincing. "I would be happier in the knowledge that you were content."

"I will try."

"That is the problem," Abishag responded. "You cannot do it on your own. I know that your life has been so hard that you have only had yourself to rely on, but that is not the case. Yahweh has taken you though everything; you will only be happy when you surrender your life to him, and become content in the knowledge that he is in control."

Mara didn't respond. She didn't really understand. But she saw how earnest Abishag was, and she didn't want to add any more burdens to her friend. For Abishag, she would think about the words. But not now. Not when her only friend was leaving tomorrow morning.

"How will you leave?" Mara asked after a long pause.

"He will wait outside the palace wall. I will just sneak away. I would speak to Solomon, but there is nothing to say."

Mara thought of the young king, still mourning the execution of his brother. "Would you like me to tell him anything for you? I could try to speak to him privately . . . somehow." Mara wondered how she would manage that, but she didn't speak her doubts to Abishag.

"Tell him . . . tell him that I would stay if I thought he needed me. Tell him that Yahweh will work in his life in amazing ways—I can feel it." Abishag smiled at Mara, who was crying again. "Tell him, too, that love does not mean possession."

Mara looked at her friend, startled. "Why does he need to know that?"

Abishag shook her head, "He does."

Mara still didn't understand, but she said, "I will tell him."

"You will see me off tomorrow morning?" Abishag asked.

Mara made an irritated noise. "Of course I will. How can you even ask?"

The next morning Mara got up two hours before sunrise, when the palace was still asleep. She met Abishag in the hallway. Abishag had discarded the simple white linen tunic she wore in the palace for a heavy wool mantle. She wasn't carrying anything.

"You have nothing to bring with you?" Mara whispered.

Abishag shook her head. "I came here with nothing, so nothing I would take would be mine."

The two girls glided silently through the halls of the palace. When the reached the ground floor, Abishag murmured, "The main entrances will be guarded."

Mara shrugged. "If you had told the king, he would have let you go with no problem. Now we have to sneak around."

Abishag chuckled. "True. But this is what comes from doing things the cowardly way. Come, there will be no guard at the kitchen entrance."

They made their way through the kitchen, which was occupied only by a slave girl who could not speak Hebrew. Mara smiled at her reassuringly, and the girl just ignored them.

They exited the palace near the butchery and the other outbuildings used by the kitchen staff. Mara covered her nose as they jogged around a corner of the palace near the stables.

"The guards will notice you when you leave the palace grounds," Mara commented.

Abishag smiled. "They will not stop me. They are expecting me."

Mara snorted. "I still think you have gone to a lot of trouble for no reason. Why will you not face the king?"

Abishag closed her eyes. "I just don't want to put him in a position where he will have to make a difficult choice. He has had too many to make already."

"And you think it would be difficult deciding whether or not to let you go?" Mara wondered.

"He killed his brother when he requested me as a wife. What would his court say if he just gave me away to some shepherd?"

Mara hadn't thought of that.

"He would let me go in the end; I am sure of it. But it would cause him more pain, and I will not do that."

Mara understood, and thanked God that there was such a wonderful person as Abishag in the world, and that she had known her.

"Well, good-bye," Mara said.

Abishag's eyes filled with tears. "Yahweh bless you, always."
The two girls embraced, and Mara willed herself not to cry. She
managed to smile. "Your shepherd is waiting. You won't forget
me?"

Abishag wiped her eyes. "Surely you know by now that love is
as strong as death."

Mara smiled again, and Abishag hurried away. She looked
back once, and Mara was still standing, watching her go.

She was alone again. She was always alone at the end.

When Abishag was out of sight, Mara turned around. She
halted, suddenly.

On the balcony of the second floor, a man stood, watching her.
Their eyes met. "I wonder how he knew," Mara thought. Through
the distance, Mara could not see the expression in Solomon's eyes,
but she knew what it would be.

He would be feeling the same thing she was feeling. Beneath
the sorrow at the loss of Abishag was jealousy. Abishag and her
love would have a life together.

Mara knew that a life with Solomon was completely beyond
hope. She pulled her eyes away from Solomon's and hurried back
into the palace.

PART III

LOVE

"Daughters of Jerusalem, I charge you
by the gazelles and by the does of the field:
Do not arouse or awaken love
until it so desires."

Song of Songs 2:7

Chapter 11

Mara saw Solomon briefly the next day as Solomon was looking into Abishag's mysterious disappearance.

"You were friends with Abishag," Solomon pronounced, in his court voice. "Do you know where she might have gone?"

Mara nodded solemnly.

"Well?" Solomon prompted.

Mara felt a little silly, as if she and Solomon were playing out a game. They both knew exactly what had happened, but for the benefit of the court they had to go through this exercise.

"She has left the palace," Mara explained.

"Where has she gone?"

"I do not know for sure, but she has gone to meet the man she has been promised to for many years. You could probably find her if you really insisted on it."

Solomon frowned. "I do not think it is worth a prolonged search. Did she decide, suddenly, that she did not like life at the palace?"

"She never liked life at the palace. She came only because your father wished her too."

"Hmmm," Solomon mused. "So she is not coming back?"

Mara shook her head.

"And she did not feel she could come to me with her request?"

Mara inhaled the fragrant air sharply; she could see a little hurt in his eyes. "She thought it would be better just to leave. She said that if she thought that you needed her here, she would have stayed."

Solomon leaned forward a little as Mara's voice grew softer. "Did she say anything else?"

"She said that Yahweh has amazing things planned for you." Mara didn't see any harm with the king's counselors hearing that, but she hesitated before she completed Abishag's message.

"And?" Solomon prompted again.

"She said to tell you that love is not possession." Mara said the words so softly that she wondered if Solomon even heard them. She thought by his expression that he had.

"Very well," he said after a moment, waving his hand. "You may leave. I will work on the temple plans now," he announced to the throne room at large.

Mara left him and wondered what he was thinking.

Several months later, Solomon married the daughter of Pharaoh in Egypt. The entire palace was talking about it. Not Solomon's marriage—that was of minuscule importance next to the incredible impact of Solomon's treaty with Egypt. No Egyptian pharaoh had ever deigned to make an alliance with Israel before. This was proof of Israel's growing importance in the world.

With Solomon's marriage came the town of Gezer, which was at the crossroads of two important trade routes. This would open up the route for Solomon to get materials for building the temple.

The alliance was a wonderful thing for everyone involved. Of course, Solomon planned to build the Egyptian princess a separate palace, but until the temple and his own palace was built, he allowed her to reside in Jerusalem.

Mara felt ill every time it was mentioned.

She had to play at all of the feasts that resulted from the marriage, and she felt like the celebration mocked her own feelings. She was not worried that Solomon actually loved this woman; in fact, she would have felt better if he did love her. At least, if Solomon loved his wife, he would have some chance at happiness. But this, this was all wrong.

One evening, shortly after the marriage, Mara was dismissed from the throne room, and was heading back to the servants' quarters. She saw Joel approaching from the opposite direction, and she nodded pleasantly at the man. She had not seen him for several months; she assumed that he had been busy with his duties.

His handsome face was pale and drawn, however, and his eyes were tired. She wanted to ask if he was all right, but she did not dare speak to him before he spoke to her.

"How have you been, Mara?" he asked, pausing in the hall.

Mara smiled, "I am fine, but you do not look like things have been going well for you."

One side of Joel's mouth twitched. "Oh, I have just been a little ill lately. But I am better now. But I am afraid I missed all of the celebration of the king's wedding."

Mara tried to keep from making a face, but she did not succeed very well.

"You are not happy for the king?" Joel asked, raising his eyebrows.

She thought a minute before she spoke. "I think the alliance with Egypt is an excellent thing for Israel."

Joel looked enlightened. "Ahhh. But you do not think it should involve something as personal as marriage."

Mara showed her assent.

"That is the nature of treaties. And the price that comes with being royalty. Perhaps they can achieve happiness through a bad situation."

Mara gave a snort of derision. "I find that doubtful in view of the other wives that will certainly come after this one. I spend much of my time in the harem, you know. There is little happiness found there."

Joel looked sobered. "Yes, I suppose you are right. The crown does not bring happiness, I guess. The lesson for us is not to fall in love with royalty."

He spoke in jest, and Mara tried to respond accordingly, but her laughter was rather choked. Joel seemed to notice her mood, but he did not mention it.

"Poor Solomon. He is my good friend, you know."

"Yes," Mara affirmed. "I had gathered that. He needs friends."

"We all need friends." Joel looked at her intently, and Mara tried to evade his eyes.

She did not understand this man at all.

"Solomon leaves tomorrow to worship at Gibeon. I am glad. He is not always so careful about worship. Yahweh has instructed us not to worship Him at pagan altars. But Solomon says that until the temple is built, the people must worship at the high places. If it continues, the worship will be corrupted."

Mara stiffened her back. "I am sure that Solomon's worship is sincere."

Joel looked taken aback. "Of course it is. Solomon, if anything, is a man of God. But he takes some of Yahweh's commands too lightly. I did not mean any offense; I am just concerned about him."

Mara could see that Joel was sincere, and she wondered if he were speaking the truth. She did not think Solomon was the kind of man to disregard the rules of his God. She hoped he was not.

Something happened to Solomon at Gibeon. The palace was rustling with the event, but no one seemed certain what had happened. Mara did not see Solomon for a week after his return from Gibeon, which was very unusual. He did not call any of his musicians. He spent a whole week closeted with his teachers and the wise men of the court.

Mara was very worried about him.

In the months since Abishag had left, Mara had gone through her duties at the palace in a sort of daze. The few times she had spoken to Solomon had been water in the dryness of her days. She hoped Abishag was happy, but she couldn't help wishing that her friend was still at the palace.

Mara had resigned herself to living out her life this way. Playing music for the king or the women of the harem. Caught up in the maneuverings of the court, but having little influence on anything that occurred. She could leave, she knew. But she had nowhere to go. No man would want to marry her; the world thought she was a slave, would assume she was no longer pure. And the happiness she could have found with Solomon was no longer even a fantasy.

Maybe, she thought, lying awake in the middle of the night, staring at the cracks in the ceiling of the servants' chambers, she would not have very long to live.

She was summoned a week after Solomon's return from Gibeon. The king had a headache, and he wanted to hear some music. She was to report to his chambers. Mara had never heard of Solomon having a headache before, even when he stayed up all night studying with the scribes.

Mara had not been to the royal chambers since David had died. She felt a little nervous.

The guards allowed her to pass through the sculpted doorway, and she ventured a few steps in.

Solomon was lying on the low couch, rubbing his temples with his hands. "Play for me," he said tersely.

Something had changed about Solomon. Mara could see something layered over the Solomon she knew like a cloak, but she could not imagine what could have happened to him.

She started to play, keeping her eyes on the prostrate king. He did not seem to hear the soft music of the lyre, and after a few minutes, she stopped playing. He did not even look up. "You are miserable here," he stated bluntly.

Mara gave a start, amazed by his abruptness. "Of course not . . ." she began, but Solomon interrupted her.

"Don't lie to me. Of course you are miserable. Especially now that Abishag is gone and I am . . ."

He did not complete his sentence, but Mara could fill in the missing word—"married."

"What has happened to you, Solomon," she asked, standing up and moving toward him. "You are so different."

Solomon pulled himself to a sitting position, and Mara could see his headache reflected in his eyes. "Yes, I am changed."

Mara looked at him intently. There were lines around his eyes and between his brows that had not been there two weeks ago, lines that did not belong to a man his age. "I did not see until now how miserable you were," Solomon continued upon the subject Mara had thought they had dropped. "I can see things now, so clearly. I must have been a fool before."

"What are you talking about, Solomon? You were never a fool."

"Maybe not, but it seems that way." Solomon leaned back against the couch. He was composed, as always—certainly not overcome by any strong emotion—but he seemed so exhausted. His dark hair looked startling against the deep blue of the pillows behind him, and his skin looked like alabaster, as if he had not been outdoors for weeks.

"Please tell me what has happened to you," Mara begged, frightened at the change she saw in the young king.

Solomon nodded. "At Gibeon Yahweh appeared to me."

Mara gasped, but she did not interrupt his story.

"He told me to ask for anything I wanted, and he would give it to me. What do you think I asked for?"

Mara thought for a minute, inhaling the musk from the burning jar beside Solomon's couch. What did Solomon want more than anything else? The answer did not come to her immediately.

Her first thought—quickly dismissed—was that he would want her, Mara herself, more than everything else. That was ridiculous, of course: only the fleeting fancy of a vain and too lonely heart. She knew Solomon better than that.

She had always been perceptive, and she had learned, out of necessity, to be observant. And whoever controlled her destiny had given her a lot of time to think over the last few years, without very much to think about besides Solomon. And there had also been an afternoon—ages ago, it seemed—when Solomon had confronted his father and wept before his mother, an afternoon when she had heard things she shouldn't have heard. Mara knew Solomon better, perhaps, than anyone would ever know him.

And so she has able to say, looking up to meet the king of Israel's dark, luminous eyes. "Wisdom, the ability to rule wisely. You asked for the ability to be a great king," she responded, sure that it was the truth.

Solomon nodded, apparently not surprised by Mara's perception. "Yes. I asked for a discerning heart to govern Israel and to distinguish between right and wrong. I knew that without Yahweh's help, I would never be able to rule this people. My answer pleased him. He said that since I did not ask for a long life or wealth or the death of my enemies, he would give me more wisdom than anyone has ever had, or ever will have."

Strange words, coming from a sophisticated, but very young man reclining on a couch, his beautiful, tapered fingers lying relaxed and perfectly still on the pillow beside him. Mara could see the look in Solomon's eyes—almost fanatical—and it scared her.

"Then he said that he would also give me riches and honor, so that during my lifetime there would be no other king like me. And he said if I walk in his ways and obey his commands, he would give me a long life." Solomon raised a hand to massage his temple, an unusual gesture. But Mara was the only other person in the room, and Solomon had never been able to completely maintain his facade of perfect composure in her presence.

Mara smiled at him, wishing she could make him smile in return. "Then what?"

"I woke up," Solomon replied. "I would have thought it was just a dream, something I made up in my mind, but I am different, aren't I?"

Slowly, Mara nodded her agreement.

"Why would Yahweh have done this for me? I am so unworthy." The boy again, the one she had met in the hills near Jerusalem.

Mara knelt down beside his couch. "Who is worthy? Does Yahweh do things for his people because of their worth?"

Solomon gave a bitter little laugh. "You are right. You do not even know Yahweh, and yet you have such understanding."

The recognition of this fact overwhelmed Mara. She had come to understand Yahweh, despite her best attempts, and the knowledge of that fact scared her. "I do know your God," she admitted. "By now, I certainly know him."

Solomon stared at her intently. Then he sighed. "I have now what I have always wanted. The ability to be a great king, to somehow be worthy of the position I hold. But it is such a burden."

"Of course it is," Mara murmured. "But it is also a great gift."

Solomon ignored her last comment. "I can see people's motives now; I can read little clues in their behavior and their speech. And
I find nothing that makes me think well of humanity. It all seems so . . . meaningless."

Mara's heart ached at the bitterness she heard in his voice. The old Solomon had been perceptive about human nature and hurt by the course his life had taken, but he had been willing to see the best in people. This man before her was different. A burden had

101

been added to his load that she could never understand, never even relate to. He had moved away from her, and she knew she would never catch up.

She swallowed the lump that threatened to choke her and stood up. She walked back to her lyre.

"Mara," Solomon said softly, again rubbing his aching head.

"Yes, my lord the king," she whispered.

"My feelings haven't changed," he stated, "at all."

Mara closed her eyes. She was strong—in a way, as carefully guarded as Solomon himself—but there were some things that could still break her.

"Have yours?" Solomon asked, barely a whisper.

"I don't think they will ever change," Mara replied, with equal amounts of tenderness and despair.

Solomon smiled, and she saw some of the heaviness leave his face. "But you cannot continue living the way you have," Solomon said. "I will not see you miserable. Something must be done."

Mara had always had faith in Solomon's wisdom, and now she knew it was beyond her understanding. But she still doubted Solomon's ability to solve the problem of her happiness.

Chapter 12

Mara was brushing oil into Abigail's long, strait hair when a guard knocked politely on the door and, when allowed in, announced that Mara's presence was requested by the king in his throne room. Mara's heart jumped. She had no idea why, but she was afraid. She said she needed to get her lyre first, but the guard told her she would not need it. The king had not summoned her to play, but to talk.

She tried to move through the halls calmly, but she was having difficulty drawing even breaths. Why should she be so nervous? This was hardly an unprecedented request.

But the last time they had spoken, Solomon had promised to do something about her situation. Perhaps that something had been done.

She entered the throne room—David's throne room when he was alive—and blinked a few times. Solomon was seated on the dais, grabbing the arms on the cedar throne as if someone would snatch him out of it. And beside him stood Joel, which seemed strangely inappropriate. But nobody else was in the throne room.

She couldn't remember ever seeing the throne room when it was not bustling with activity. She wondered what Solomon had done with all the men who hung around the king and had jobs that no one had ever been able to explain to Mara. Mara had always secretly assumed that they were just there for decoration.

The tall walls and marble floors of the throne room looked vast without people filling the space. She wondered if the walls would echo when she spoke.

Solomon smiled at her, the resigned smile he always used since he had put on his wisdom, like a garment. Their eyes met, and Mara forced herself to look away from him. She didn't bow to him.

Then Mara glanced over at Joel, to Solomon's left. She nodded politely.

"You must be wondering why I summoned you," Solomon began.

Of course, she was wondering. Mara could not remember the last time she had felt this nervous. But there was no reason Solomon needed to know this. She nodded again. "I'm sure you will enlighten me when you feel it is time."

Mara noticed more lines on his brow that had not been there when she last saw him. He gave a little shrug. "Now is the time. I came to talk about your future."

The words surprised Mara, and she looked over at Joel, whose expression was unreadable. Why was he here to discuss her future? "I see," she said, though she didn't.

"You have lived at the palace for more than four years. How old are you? Fifteen years, sixteen?"

Mara thought for a moment. "I am not sure. I had lived six years when the strangers came." Both men knew what she was referring to, and Mara saw Joel wince at the reference. Solomon's expression, of course, didn't change. "I'm not sure how long I was a slave, maybe five years. That would make me fifteen years."

Solomon nodded. "Most girls marry when they are twelve or thirteen. Have you ever thought about marriage?"

Mara stared at him. "It has never been an option for me. The world believes I am a slave."

Solomon chuckled. "Slaves have been known to marry. What if you could marry?"

Mara had never considered it before. "I guess it would depend on who I would marry."

Joel took a step forward. "If I were to ask for you to become my wife, what would you say?" Mara wondered if that was uncertainty in his eyes. He had always seemed so confident.

"You?" Mara breathed. "But I am a . . ."

"I thought you were a slave at first, so I went to Solomon to ask to pay the price he would have for you. But he tells me you were never his slave, so I asked for his permission to wed you." Mara did not think she had ever seen such tender eyes. His eyes were brown, not as dark as Solomon's. And while Solomon's eyes seemed to reflect all of the light around him, Joel's eyes just seemed to collect the light and form it into some kind of fire that continually warmed them.

"But why would you want to marry me?" she asked, clutching her hands. She immediately released them. She was certainly able to stand in front of these men without revealing her uncertainty.

Joel shrugged a little and glanced at Solomon. "All men need wives, do they not? And how many men have a wife with golden hair, or a wife who would kick them in the shin?" Joel's smile had grown whimsical.

Mara blushed with the shame of the memory. Then she turned to Solomon, and the sight of his closed eyes grabbed her heart like a vice. "You want me to marry him?"

Solomon opened his eyes. "The decision is not mine. How can I not allow you a marriage that would improve your life in every way? I know you are a musician, but you have never been really happy at the palace."

Mara thought about the Pharaoh's daughter, and that was all she needed. She decided. "No, I could not." She took a deep breath, and turned back to Joel. "Very well, I . . ."

"Wait, there is more, Mara," Joel interrupted.

Mara looked confused. "What do you mean?"

"Well, Yahweh has commanded us not to marry foreign wives." Joel looked a little uncomfortable. Mara wondered, for a moment, why that would be. And then she realized that Joel's king, seated in the throne beside him, had himself married a foreign woman.

"Oh, why . . ."

"Foreign women could lead us away from faith in him. It is for our protection," Joel explained.

"And you think I would lead you away?" Mara asked, looking up at him.

Joel watched her silently, intently, but he didn't respond to her question.

"But," Solomon interrupted the silence. "You could become one of us. My father's father's mother was a Moabitess. But she became a Hebrew, and married an Israelite. Ruth was a very strong, devout woman."

Mara hesitated. "What would this involve?"

"If you were a man, you would have to be circumcised. As a woman, it involves a bath of purification, a sacrifice . . ."

Mara waited, certain there was more.

Solomon continued. "And vows made to Yahweh."

Mara had somehow known it would come to this, and her voice was cold as she prompted, "Vows?"

"You would have to bind yourself to the Lord. Serve him, love him, worship him. And you would have to keep his covenant with his people." Solomon paused when he saw the expression on Mara's face, and he rose from his throne. "Why do you look so horrified? You must know that this has been coming for four years, even longer. Before you even came to Israel, Yahweh was drawing you to him. All of the lines of your life have led straight to him."

The room seemed to freeze—Solomon's smile, Joel's kind eyes— and she raised her hands to cover her face. "No," she gasped. "No, I cannot."

Both Solomon and Joel took a step toward her, but it was Solomon who spoke first. "But you said that you knew Yahweh. By now you knew him."

Joel spoke too. "And you said it would be an honor to worship such a God."

Mara kept shaking her head. "No," her voice was louder. "I cannot. You do not understand, I cannot." The last word was a shriek, and she hated herself for losing control.

She whirled around and walked over to the wall. She placed both hands on the wall and leaned to press her forehead against it, trying to take strength from its solidity.

Joel and Solomon exchanged looks behind her back.

"I'm sorry if this brings you pain, Mara," Joel said. "But I think I should know why I am denied happiness."

Mara knew he was right. She turned back around, biting her lip to keep from crying. She took a shaky breath. "It is not because I do not want to believe in your God. In fact, I do believe in him. I have seen his power and his work in the world." She swallowed hard. "But I cannot vow to serve him. He requires all of one's worship. If he is who I believe he is, then no other god can exist on the earth. I cannot admit that he is the only god and still go on living. I cannot."

"Why?" It was Joel who asked the question, because it was clear from his eyes that Solomon already knew.

"Don't you see?" Mara asked, hearing her voice break. Joel shook his head, and Solomon just looked away. She would have to say the words. Squeezing her eyes shut, she did say them, although they forced her to her knees. "If that is true then my father, and Brant, and—oh—Elsa, they all died in darkness."

Mara heard the whispering sound of Joel's clothes as he crouched beside her on the floor. "I see now, Mara. I understand."

She was still holding back tears, but her face had lost all color. "I cannot."

"You would rather dwell in darkness yourself?" Joel asked, so gently.

Mara squeezed her eyes shut and lowered her head to Joel's lap. Somewhere, far away from herself, she felt his hand stroke her hair. She could not betray them now. She started to sob then, as she had not done since the market place in Caphtor—no, not since she had wept with Solomon on the day she finally knew him. She wept now for Brant, whose strong arms had reached to pick her up a moment before his death. And Elsa, who had carried her away from the village and then walked away from her forever, her back straight. She wept for her father, blood matted in his beard, slicing the head off an enemy. Her father, who had raised his arms every morning to greet the sun. She wept for the sun itself, which—the image clear in her mind—was finally being devoured by the sea.

The sun devoured by the sea. She could not rid herself of the image. The words had never made much sense to her but they were the only things still tying her to her home—her real home—and her family. She wondered, briefly, if she were still capable of reasonable thought.

"I don't think I can stand it," she said finally, her voice muffled by Joel's tunic. And, for the first time in her life, she meant it. "How can life be so hard?"

Joel's arms were around her, holding her so tightly she thought she would loose her breath. She wished that she would.

Solomon has watching them both with oddly detached eyes.

Mara could weep no more, and she lay, exhausted, against Joel's chest.

Joel was holding her, but it was to Solomon that Mara turned. "Help me," she whispered.

It was easy to forget, with everything the king was becoming, that Solomon was, indeed, his father's son. But he was, above everything else, and so, when there was nothing else that he could do, he began to sing.

Mara had heard him sing before, and, though his voice was not as pure as his father's, it was strong and true. Mara recognized the song as his father's.

"Oh God, you are my God,
    earnestly I seek you;
my soul thirsts for you,
my body longs for you,
in a dry and weary land
where there is no water."

Mara sat up, and turned her red eyes to Solomon's face.

"I have seen you in the sanctuary
    and beheld your power and your glory.
Because your love is better than life,
    my lips will glorify you.
I will praise you as long as I live,
    and in your name I will lift up my hands."

And Mara gave up then. Gave up trying to order her own life and arrange her own destiny. She admitted what she had known for a long time, and she allowed herself to finally acknowledge Yahweh as the true God, the only God—although doing so would mean her family's damnation.

Yahweh, who had created the world and dwelt among his people, had called her for his own.

Solomon stopped singing, and he smiled, a little sadly, at Joel. Joel's chest rose and fell in his relief.

Mara didn't know how long it was before she rose to her feet. Joel rose as well. "I will marry you, if you still want me."

"I do," Joel confirmed.

Solomon quietly went to seat himself on his throne. Though his face reflected his joy at Mara's decision, his shoulders hunched over a little, one more burden added to his load.

Chapter 13

The circumstances of Mara's betrothal were rather unusual, because she had no family of her own. The ceremony in which she exchanged betrothal vows with Joel should have been witnessed by both families in the house of the bride's family, but instead it took place in Joel's family home. His family were Benjaminites who had moved to Jerusalem because of Eleazar's connection with David. Eleazar had died many years ago, but his wife and two of the daughters lived in Jerusalem. Joel was their only son. Three of the five daughters were already married; one lived in Jerusalem and two in Eleazar's home city of Gibeon.

Joel had taken Mara to meet his mother and sisters the day after the conversation in the throne room. Mara had been comfortable with Joel before they decided to marry. Now Mara felt rather awkward. She could not understand why he would want to marry her. Abishag had told her that all the young girls in Jerusalem hoped that he would make them his bride; his family was wealthy and upstanding. He could certainly have his choice of women. Why would he want to marry her?

Mara had a feeling that he knew how she felt about Solomon. Surely that would discourage a man. Perhaps he thought she was beautiful, but he didn't seem to be a man to be swayed by something so superficial.

She knew he was a friend to Solomon, however. And she also knew that Solomon had been trying to find a way to make her happy. Would Joel have offered to marry her just as a favor to Solomon? Mara couldn't imagine that to be so, but Solomon was the king. Men had done much more than that to earn favor with the king.

Joel did not say much to Mara on the way to his mother's house. He looked at her a great deal, though, and it made her nervous.

"Are you scared of me?" he asked, finally.

Mara looked up, startled. "No, of course I am not." Although that was not altogether the truth.

"You did not used to be," he commented, trying to look into her eyes behind the veil she pulled over her head.

"I am not scared of you. Why should I be? You have been more than kind."

Joel's face showed doubt, but he did not respond.

His mother greeted them at the door to the two-story house. "Welcome," she said, and leaned over to kiss Mara on the cheek. Mara was taken aback by this friendly welcome, and was even more startled when the performance was repeated by Joel's two little sisters.

Deborah and Mary were only a year apart and almost identical. They had big brown eyes, long dark-brown hair, and Joel's friendly grin. Mara greeted them, a little timidly.

Joel seemed very happy to be around his family, and he kissed them all lovingly. Far too many kisses, Mara thought. She was used to maintaining as much personal space as possible.

Mara had noticed how large the house was, compared to the other houses around it, and Joel's mother, Abihail, led them into a large, airy courtyard paved with flagstones. Mara had never been in an Israelite house before, and looked around with curiosity at Joel's family home. Several rooms surrounded the courtyard, but in the courtyard, Mara could see a clay oven and jars, which she assumed were full of cooking necessities. There were also stools clustered around a low table in one corner of the courtyard, presumably for eating meals.

"Shall we sit in the garden?" Abihail asked.

Mara was a little startled, and saw that the courtyard led into an enclosed garden. It was very small, compared to the palace gardens, but it looked cool and fresh.

There were no flowers in the garden, but there were a few palm trees. The trees provided shade for the two benches placed under them. Mara could see the green sprouts of what she assumed were vegetables peeking out of the dirt.

"So Mara," Abihail began, seating herself comfortably on a bench. "You must tell us about yourself."

Mara, who had just seated herself next to Joel, tried not to wince. "It is not a very pleasant story," she murmured.

"You must have had a very exciting life," the younger of the girls said eagerly, ignoring the nudges from her sister. "Joel said you were kidnapped. How I would love to be kidnapped."

Mara stared at her, astonished.

Joel shook his head at his little sister. "Deborah, that is a ridiculous thing to say. You would certainly not wish to be kidnapped."

"Well, it would be exciting. Nothing ever happens to me. The most interesting thing that will ever happen to me is to marry old Jacob, the cloth seller. He is so boring."

"What makes you think you will marry him?" Abihail asked, looking frowningly at her daughter.

"I do hear things," Deborah muttered. "Why can't an Egyptian prince come by, see me from a distance, find me irresistible, and take me to be his bride." Deborah giggled, endearingly. "It would be so much better than marrying old Jacob."

"Jacob is a fine man," Joel said sternly. "And I don't want to hear you speak of any of your elders that way."

Deborah looked properly contrite, but Mara could see the gleam that remained in her eyes.

Joel, apparently, saw it as well. "I don't know where you get these ideas. Egyptian princes are not romantic. If you were kidnapped, you would be treated cruelly. What is more, you would almost certainly not be allowed to worship Yahweh. Is that what you want?"

The gleam left Deborah's eyes, and Mara felt almost sorry for her. Mara had never had any romantic dreams, but she could imagine what it was like to have them destroyed.

"You have distracted us from Mara," Abihail said. "I hope you will forgive Deborah's silliness," she continued, turning to Mara.

Mara smiled at Deborah. "There is nothing to forgive."

This seemed to cheer Deborah up. "Were you really kidnapped by barbarians?"

111

Mara tried to keep smiling. If she were to become a part of this family, she had better get used to it.

Between them, they decided to have Mara's purification ceremony in Gibeon, where the rest of Joel's family lived. The tabernacle that had come with the Israelites through the desert was set up there, and Joel thought that the ceremony should take place at the tabernacle rather than the tent in Jerusalem where, Mara learned, the ark was placed.

Mara could not help but feel a little distant from the history of Israel. It was an amazing history—of famine and slavery, of victory and rebellion, of wandering and homecoming. She was trying hard to make it her own history, and she thought that having her ceremony take place at the tabernacle—a centerpiece of Israel's history—would be a good way to start.

Joel was always very kind in explaining things to her. And he tried to involve her in all of the marriage plans. But Mara realized that she could help very little, because she knew practically nothing. She didn't even know how to cook. This fact gave her several sleepless nights until she felt brave enough to mention it to Abihail.

Abihail smiled in understanding. "I thought maybe that was so. I have already asked Deborah if she would mind living with the two of you until you learn everything you need. She would be delighted, as you can imagine."

Mara was taken aback. "Live with us?" she repeated.

Abihail nodded. "I would send Mary, but Mary, you know, is preparing for her own wedding. I think it would be good for Deborah to be away from here during that time. She dreams too much as it is."

Mara nodded. "Does Joel know about this?"

Abihail chuckled, "He is the one who suggested it."

"Oh." The more Mara thought about it, the more she liked the idea. Having Deborah around would ease some of the pressure of living with a man she hardly knew. With Deborah around, she had learned in the last two weeks, things could not get too intense.

One month after this conversation, Mara sat alone under an olive tree watching the sun sink behind the terraced hills surrounding Gibeon. Today she had ceremonially become a follower of Yahweh. A priest had performed the ritual bath—immersing her in the river—which symbolized Yahweh's purification and made her acceptable to come to him with a sacrifice. And then she had brought a pure, perfect dove—fluttering beneath her hands—to the tabernacle and given it to the priest to offer up to Yahweh. An offering for atonement and an offering for worship.

She had traveled with Joel and his family to Gibeon a few days ago. Gibeon was known for its vineyards, and they had arrived at the peak of harvest time.

"It is harvest time," Joel had commented, looking up at her, as they had approached Gibeon. He was walking beside the donkey she was riding on.

"Yes, I can tell," she had said. "Is there some special significance in that?"

"Gibeon is surrounded by vineyards. The town will be almost deserted now because everyone is living out in the vineyards, harvesting the grapes."

"Is that where we will go?" she had asked him, interested.

Joel had nodded. Mara had learned that Joel's father, Eleazar, had deserted the family business of grape-growing to fight for the young David. Joel, to his family's disappointment, had continued in his father's footsteps, and had refused to move back to Gibeon. But the family vineyards were still well tended by a myriad of cousins and their servants.

Her purification ceremony had been a break in the festivities of harvest time, but Mara could see, even this late in the afternoon, activity among the trellises that supported the vines, and she could still hear fragments of song blown toward her secluded retreat.

Mara had met most of Joel's extended family by now—uncles, cousins, great-aunts, nephews and nieces. They were all very kind, and she was surprised by the warm reception she had received. But right now she didn't want noise or company; she wanted some time to think.

The previous day, one of Joel's nephews—maybe three years old—had come over to her, looking up at her in awe. "Are you a real woman?" he had whispered.

The women around Mara had chuckled at this query, and Mara had smiled in amusement. "Of course I am. What else would I be?"

The boy's grubby face was still transfixed, and his eyes were like saucers. "I thought you must have come from Yahweh. You are all golden." Overcome by his boldness, the boy had run away, hiding his face in his hands.

Mara had laughed with the other women. It was funny, really. But it wasn't.

Because the boy had innocently pointed out what Mara was constantly aware of. She was a follower of Yahweh, and she lived in Israel now. But she wasn't really a part of it. None of it—except maybe her love of Yahweh—was her own. She didn't really belong.

It wasn't even that anyone treated her differently. They were hospitable, friendly, accepting. But she was different, and it wasn't something Mara could ignore.

Mara closed her eyes when she heard someone approaching. She knew who it was.

"Here you are," a warm voice called out. "I had wondered where you disappeared to. I thought maybe my crowd of relations had scared you and you had gone off seeking another adventure."

Mara opened her eyes to see Joel, barefoot, purple-legged from trampling grapes, and grinning.

"Did you really?" she asked, watching as he settled on the warm ground next to her.

Joel studied her seriously. "Not really, I suppose. Although the thought did cross my mind."

Mara adjusted her legs under her. She never knew exactly whether her betrothed was jesting or in earnest. "By adventure, I assume you mean travels," Mara replied. "And none of the traveling I have done in my life has been pleasant."

"I know," Joel said, his mouth turning down. "I suppose that is something. You may not be absolutely happy here, but, from your experience, you know that other places can be much worse."

"What makes you think that I am not happy here?" Mara said, thrown off-guard by Joel's observation. "I hope I have never given you that impression. Surely you know how grateful I am . . ."

Joel held up a hand. "No, no, don't misunderstand. You have been wonderful. I just think I know you well enough to see that

114

something is bothering you. I hope you have been comfortable with my family," he said, looking rather anxious.

Mara nodded. "Yes, they have all been so loving and gracious. I did not realize that people could be so friendly."

Joel chuckled, "Most of them are. A few of them must be caught up in the excitement, because I have not heard a cross word all day."

Mara smiled up at him. "It is such a large family. My family was only four." She had to swallow hard before she continued. "And now it is only one."

Joel turned toward her sharply. "No," he exclaimed fiercely. He grasped her hands in his own. "It is not only you. My family is yours now."

Mara nodded slowly. "Thank you," was all she said.

Her father, and Brant, and Elsa. They were so distant now, and, yet, without any effort at all, she could see them come to life before her. She could not linger on their images however, or she would break down again. She had come to grips with the fact that they were all lost to her, completely, for they had died without the knowledge of Yahweh, but she realized she would never be able to think of it without sorrow. Always an ache.

She knew they were lost, but they were her family. That was where she belonged, in a village by a northern sea, with trees always green, and lakes between the trees.

"You don't believe that," Joel stated softly.

Mara had almost forgotten he was beside her. "Yes, yes, I do. Your family is one that anyone would accept with great joy."

"Then why can't you?"

Mara shook her head violently. She was determined to be honest with the man who would become her husband. "I don't know. I just feel so out of place here. It was different at the palace. I wasn't supposed to fit in. But you are trying to make me a part of your family, a part of this nation. I can't, by the force of my will, make myself feel that I belong."

"It will take time," Joel agreed. "But if you don't open yourself to the possibility, it will never happen."

Mara searched for the words to explain, because she knew that Joel deserved to understand. "I am so different. It is not just what I have lived through. Not just that night when the barbarians came and everything was destroyed. It was everything I had learned before that night. It was the sea and the sun and the snow that had always defined my life. It was my position, a chieftain's daughter. It was everything that allowed me to hold my head up and keep my back straight. I can't get past it, can't get around it. It is who I am." Mara leaned back against the trunk of a tree. "I'm not even making any sense."

Joel smiled. "Yes, you are. But I think there are more similarities than there are differences. You were forced to leave your homeland, and then were forced into slavery. When you were granted freedom from slavery, you wandered aimlessly in the palace until you found Yahweh, and he gave you a home. That is Israel's history as well. You know that. How are you so different than we are?"

Mara thought about his words for a long time. "I never noticed that before," she said at last.

Perhaps he was right. Maybe Yahweh, in his grace, could carve out a home for her among a people who were not her own.

"Thank you," she said.

Joel cocked his head to one side, "For what?"

"For everything. For giving me a family and a home. And taking me away from the palace. For understanding." Mara meant every word.

"Well," Joel responded, smiling slyly. "I didn't do it entirely out of kindness for you. There is a little in it for me."

Mara pulled away from him and continued walking. She understood. Of course, he was marrying her to earn favor with Solomon. But did he have to remind her of it just then? She was beginning . . . to enjoy him.

Chapter 14

Before Mara would have thought it possible, the day before her wedding arrived. She was going to go to Abihail's house to spend the night, but before she left the palace, Solomon called her to his chamber to play for him.

She had not seen him alone for months—not since she had become betrothed. She still loved him—that was certain the moment she entered the room. Despite his unearthly wisdom. Despite Joel's kindness. Despite the distance between them.

But she pushed back her feelings. She was going to be married; she was betrothed, which was just the same as being married. And she had vowed that she would not sully her marriage by thoughts of another man, even a man she loved as much and had loved as long as Solomon.

He smiled at her, but there was no happiness in his eyes. He was lounging on his couch, looking out of his window at the sky. He looked as though he had a headache. "I wanted to hear you play once more before you leave."

Mara nodded, "Yes, I knew that. What should I play?"

Solomon shrugged, so Mara began to play a song that she had been picking at for more than a year, a song that had been running through her head for much longer than that. The melody was intricate, but her fingers plucked the strings confidently. She had become one of the best players of the lyre in the palace.

The music spoke of loss, and pain, and resignation, but it changed, so gradually that one did not notice until it was too late, and the listener was surprised by the love in the last few notes.

Tears were falling down Mara's cheeks when she finished, and she could see the sorrow in Solomon's eyes as well. "You wrote it?" he asked.

Mara nodded mutely.

"Are there words?"

Mara nodded again, but swallowing hard, she was not sure she would be able to get them out. She played for a minute until she felt controlled enough to sing—and then she sang for Solomon.

"I sang to the sun, and he was warm on my face;
   He gilded the water and fought back the dark.
But he died in the sky, and the dark overcame me;
   I stumbled on rocks that my eyes could not see.

I drifted from my home by the water;
     It was night with no light from the heavens,
     In the dark, I lost all those I had loved
     In the pits and the caves and the dens.

I begged for the sun to send light to my eyes,
   But he refused, and I knew that he could not hear me.
So I walked, and I fell, and I ran from the lions
   But they came, even so, and I knew I would die.

Then I saw a light in the darkness.
It was not the sun, but it shone.
I followed the flickering candle,
   And it led me away from the hills.

My world, it was dark, but I followed the candle,
And it led me to a fortress high on a rock.
It led me to a land that was brighter than the heavens.
You led me to a sun that would never go dark."

Mara was amazed that her voice did not crack, and she was glad that she could give this gift to Solomon. The only thing she was able now to give him—her thanks.

Solomon had covered his face with his hands, and she could see him try to keep his shoulders from shaking. He still loved her, she knew. He would not keep her, however. Love, Abishag had told him, did not mean possession.

And the greatest thing he could do for her was to give her a chance for happiness. A chance that he may never have.

She rose from the floor, walked over to the king of Israel, and embraced him. "Thank you," she whispered, not knowing anything else to say. "Thank you."

In a moment, Solomon released her. "I pray that you will not have to face the darkness again."

"I will not," Mara said, very confident of this, if only this. "Thanks to you, I will not."

"I hope you will grow to love Joel," Solomon said, standing up. "I mean that sincerely."

"I know you do," Mara said, thinking of her betrothed.

Solomon hesitated a moment, "But don't forget about me."

Mara remembered saying the same thing to Abishag, when she said good-bye to her. She used Abishag's response. "Abishag said to me when we parted that love is as strong as death."

Solomon nodded. "I will not be able to come to your wedding. You understand?"

Mara nodded. "I never expected you to come."

"But we will see each other again. I will make sure of it." He walked with her to the door to his chamber.

Mara looked up into his face. It had changed so much since she had first seen him in the dryness of the hills. She chuckled, "Just don't go around picking up anymore stray girls in the hills," she told him.

A mischievous glint came into his eyes that she had not seen for a long time. "How dare you speak to me that way," Solomon chided. "You dirty little peasant, I am the son of a king."

Memory—like a wave on the beach of her village, and Mara almost choked on it. "Good-bye, Solomon," she managed to say.

Solomon opened his chamber door. Mara smelled perfume, wafting over her with the air that entered the chamber. She was leaving it now. And she was alone. "Until next time," Solomon told her, with a look she never forgot.

She stayed in Abihail's house that night. Deborah woke her before dawn.

"Mara, wake up. Today you are going to get married. How can you sleep? I haven't slept all night." Deborah's voice was too shrill to sleep through, so Mara opened her eyes.

"I was tired," she grumbled. "One would think that *you* were getting married."

Deborah giggled. "I think there are rules about marrying one's brother. So I will let you marry him. But I get to come live with you for a while. I won't have to hang around watching Mary get things ready for her marriage." Deborah screwed her pretty face up and stuck out her tongue.

Mara was constantly amazed by the differences in the two girls. She had hardly ever heard Mary talk, and the older girl went through her duties with a quiet efficiency that Mara envied. But Deborah was never silent, and though she was quite good at all of the household chores, her work was accomplished in spurts of frantic energy that quickly ebbed away.

Deborah helped her to dress, gushing at each piece of clothing she put on. Her robe was fine linen, dyed in a reddish color, and was intricately embroidered by Abihail's own hand. As a bride, Mara was supposed to wear every piece of jewelry she owned, which, admittedly, was not very much. But she put on her beads of sea-gold, or amber as she called them now. And she wore gold rings, bracelets, and earrings, which were gifts from Joel. Deborah pinned a garland of almond blossoms in her hair, but she did not place the veil over her face yet.

"You are so beautiful," Deborah sighed. "No wonder Joel loves you so much. I hope I will look as beautiful when I am married."

"What did you say?" Mara stammered, looking at Deborah in astonishment.

Deborah's expression was confused. "I only said that I wished I would look as beautiful as you. I know it's unlikely but . . ."

"No, no," Mara interrupted. "Of course you will be beautiful, more beautiful than me. But what did you say about Joel?"

"Oh," Deborah said. "I only said that it's not surprising that he loves you so much. Who wouldn't love you?"

"Joel loves me," Mara repeated.

"Of course," Deborah giggled. "You knew that. You are just teasing me. I suppose I deserve it. I need to get dressed now."

Mara didn't move. She knew that Deborah was mistaken; she just didn't know how Deborah would have gotten such an idea. Certainly, not from the way Joel acted with her. He was always very kind and considerate, but a little distant. She supposed that Joel could have given Deborah that impression to keep the girl from complaining about her brother entering a loveless marriage. But it seemed a strange thing to do.

She decided not to worry about it. She had a lot to go through today. The guests would start to arrive soon. The women would come to this house and the men to Joel's. Then both the men and the women would meet in the place they had determined halfway between the houses. Afterwards, all of guests would proceed to Joel's house, where the feast would take place. The guests were mostly Joel's friends and family. Most of his extended family was coming from Gibeon for the wedding, including his three other sisters and their families. But a few of the people Mara knew from the palace would be there. Hadad, the leader of the musicians, had told her that he would come with his wife. And Ahishar, whom Solomon had recently promoted to a charge of the entire palace and all of its provisions, had told her he would come. Mara and Ahishar had become friends over the years, to the surprise of both of them.

Mara descended the outdoor steps to the lower room, thinking about Ahishar's friendly face.

At the bottom of the steps, a squeal of delight startled her. She looked around for the owner of the voice, and when she saw it her mouth fell open.

"Abishag?" she cried.

Her old friend ran over to her and nearly toppled her with a hug.

"But how are you . . . Why? I don't understand," Mara stuttered, trying to regain her composure and her balance.

Abishag giggled, "Aren't you glad to see me?"

"Of course," Mara said, in a rush. "I have never been so happy. I'm just a little confused. I think I should sit down."

Mara knew that Abishag was of the tribe of Isaachar, and that she and her husband were living in Shunam, where they both were born. But that was so far away.

"How did you know I was going to marry?" she asked, finally.

Abishag showed her dimples. "The king sent a messenger to us with the news. It was quite a thing for simple people like us to get a message from the king."

Mara closed her eyes, as she thought of Solomon's kindness. "So he knew where you were the whole time?"

Abishag shrugged. "I guess he could figure it out."

"I can't believe you came all this way just for my wedding."

"Just for your wedding," Abishag repeated. "But this is a huge thing. I am so happy for you." She paused. "Are you happy?"

Mara nodded. "Yes, finally I think I can be happy."

Abishag hugged her again, and the two chatted until the women started to arrive.

"You had better put your veil on," Abishag said, picking up the thin cloth. "Your face should not be seen on your wedding day."

The women all gathered in the front room, until it was time to process to the meeting point. Mara was placed on a litter and carried, to the accompaniment of the women, through the streets. Joel and the male guests had already arrived at the square in which they were to meet, and Mara struggled to keep from trembling. The litter bearers set her down, and many hands helped her to rise.

Joel was standing in front of her, surrounded by men she recognized as his cousins and his friends. Many of them were carrying swords.

Mara barely heard the songs the guests were singing. There was too much commotion going on at once.

Joel also looked a little harassed, but his face sobered when he saw Mara standing, veiled, in front of him. Very gently, he reached to take her hands as they said the few words that were the extent of the ceremony.

She watched him through her veil, and thanked Yahweh that she would be married to such a good man.

When the words were said, everyone embraced her, and Mara was placed, with Joel, onto his litter. He did not speak to her, but he smiled, and Mara did not feel quite so nervous. The procession made its way noisily through the streets to Joel's house.

Mara had never seen her husband's home, but she did not have time to study it. She was pushed in, the guests eager for her to remove her veil, which could not be accomplished until she had entered the bridegroom's home.

Once inside, the guests quieted. Joel stood in front of her, smiling. He reached down, and lifted the veil, and—to the delight of the gathered guests—he embraced her.

After that, Mara could not remember saying anything sensible. The feasting was loud and long, and she was congratulated by people she had never before seen.

The feasting lasted throughout the afternoon. Once, in the late afternoon, she managed to get away by herself in a corner of the garden. She breathed deeply, trying to free herself from the wine and the rich food. She knew the guests would leave late at night, but many would return each afternoon for several days, taking advantage of Joel's generous table and wine. She didn't know if she would be able to handle it.

"Mara," came a voice from behind her.

She turned around, and reached out a hand to Abishag, who was approaching. "There were too many people and too much noise," Mara explained. "Does everyone wonder where I am?"

"I don't think anyone noticed that you are gone." The sky was growing darker and Abishag smiled. "Joel is such a good man. Yahweh has blessed you as I knew he would."

Mara nodded. "Sometimes, I can't believe my life will change so much. I still think I will be going to the palace tonight. Life is so different away from the palace."

Abishag nodded. "But better, Mara. It is better."

"Yes," Mara agreed.

They sat for a while in silence. "I guess I should get back," Mara said finally, feeling restored.

Mara returned to see that the noise and excitement had risen among the guests. She knew why.

It was time for the last step in the wedding ceremony.

Joel took her hand and led her up the steps, followed by his cousin, Matthew. She knew that Matthew would wait outside the door to apprise the guests when the consummation had taken place.

Joel and Mara entered Joel's bedchamber, and Mara noticed a large bed in the corner, with bronze legs. She looked up at Joel, trying not to tremble.

She had been through so much in her life; she could certainly face her wedding night without trembling.

Joel smiled at her, his eyes crinkling at the corners, and she could not help but return his smile.

"Well," she said.

"Well," he repeated. He was twisting the gold ring on his fingers, and Mara was shocked to realize that he was nervous too. He walked over to her and removed the garland of flowers from her hair.

"In my village," she told him. "Everyone always married at noon, and they would sleep on the grass in the woods." Why had she said that? It was silly. But she didn't feel capable of coherent thought at the moment. Joel's eyes were so brown.

Joel chuckled. "I suppose we could do that, though everyone would wonder where we were going." He reached out and touched her face.

Mara laughed too, and the laughter changed to feelings that were completely unexpected.

He must have seen her change of expression, because his forehead wrinkled. "Please don't be afraid."

"I'm not afraid," she assured him, although she wasn't really sure that she was speaking the truth.

Joel shifted his weight from one leg to the other, and still looked uncertain. "Do you trust me?" he asked, very softly.

Mara looked up at him, determined to be honest. "Trust you?" She thought about it for a long time, and the moments froze in the

silence between them. "I'm not sure that I can really trust anyone."
Not even Solomon, she thought. For she loved Solomon, but she
knew that he was not someone she could surrender herself to.
There was too much instability, too much unreconciled pain in his
soul. But it was not Solomon who was standing before her,
twisting his hands together nervously; it would never be Solomon.
It was Joel . . . and Joel she didn't even really know.

"I will teach you then," Joel said, finally responding to her
statement. His eyes very tender and his hands very strong. "Please
let me."

"I will try," Mara said, no more than a whisper. And it was she
who reached out to embrace him.

Later, Matthew made his way down the stairs to tell the guests
that Joel and Mara were married, indeed.

The next morning, Mara opened her eyes to see Joel, fully
dressed, sitting on a stool next to the bed. He was watching her.

She could hear not hear any noise downstairs. "They will come
back tonight, I suppose," she complained.

"As long as I feed them," Joel responded. His smile faded,
however, and he looked at her intensely.

"What?" she asked, a little uncomfortable with his stare.

"Is everything," he began slowly, "All right?"

He looked so unsure of himself that Mara had to smile.
"Perhaps you are the one who should answer that," she said, sitting
up. She wanted to stretch her arms, but she still felt self-conscious
in front of Joel.

Joel stood up. "I have never been happier," he told her.

Mara could have sworn that he was telling the truth. "Me too,"
she said, and was surprised to realize that she meant it.

Chapter 15

Mara said good-bye to Abishag, again, three days later. The
guests had finally deserted them, and Abishag and her husband
had to leave the next day. The morning of Abishag's departure,
she came to say good-bye to Mara.

It seemed that her life was defined by partings. "I shall miss
you," Mara said. "I wonder if there will ever be a time when I do
not have to part with those I love."

"Not in this life," Abishag responded. "But one day."
Abishag's voice was confident, and it gave Mara comfort.

"But you will be happy?" Abishag asked, looking at Mara
intensely.

"Yes," Mara said. "I am not in love with Joel the way you
are with your husband. But we get along very well, and I will
do my best to make him happy."

Abishag looked a little worried. "I'm sure you will," she said
slowly. "I am glad you will finally have a normal life."

Mara laughed. "Do you think it is possible for me to live a
normal life? Sometimes I wonder."

The two young women embraced, and Mara watched as
Abishag, next to her husband, again walked out of her life.
Abishag's husband was not handsome, but Mara could see the
love between them. She wished that she could have such a life
with a man she loved. But then she shook the thought out of
her mind. Yahweh had blessed her more than she had ever
imagined possible, and she would not wish for things that could
never be.

Mara reveled in the quietness of the house. She finally got to look around the house by herself—well, she wasn't really by herself, for Deborah appeared and did not leave her side. But the experience was pleasant nonetheless.

The house was about the size of Joel's mother's house, which was quite large compared to many homes in Jerusalem. Joel's family was wealthy from the vineyards, and from Eleazar's long service to the king. The tables and stools were of the finest workmanship, and, though the walls were completely bare, the divans and chairs were richly covered.

Joel had told her the Hebrew laws said that for a year after a man was married, he would not be sent to war; but because Joel was a professional soldier, he would still do his duties at the palace. There were not really any wars going on anyway, he had said with a smile. Only a few uprisings here and there. But he went to work at the palace most days, and that left the days for Mara and Deborah to become acclimated.

She had learned quite a bit from Abihail about cooking and cleaning before she was married, but there was still much to learn. She could not seem to cook bread without burning it, and her stew still tasted like something one fed to livestock. She was, however, learning to spin and weave, and she found herself much more adept at that.

She was glad for Deborah's company, for she was not used to being by herself all day. Deborah kept up a steady stream of chatter, and Mara tuned in and out at will.

A few weeks after the wedding, Deborah went to visit her mother and sister, leaving Mara strict instructions on how to complete the loaves of bread for the evening meal. Mara, had, with only a little help, ground the grain into flour, moistened the flour, and kneaded it into dough. She and Deborah had added to it the leavened bit of dough and left it to rise.

After Deborah left, Mara took the dough and formed it into four perfect loaves. She was delighted at her accomplishment. This was the first time she had completed all the steps of the bread-making process without some sort of disaster.

She went over to light the fire in the clay oven, and she brushed the ashes away so she could place the loaves against the hot surface.

When she had done this, she smiled. They should be done by the time Joel returned, and she would show him how skilled she was becoming. They would be delicious—Mara was sure.

Mara's face was damp and red from the heat of the oven, and she pushed away a long strand of golden hair that had escaped her thick braid. She had been working all day, and she couldn't remember when she had been so tired. Life at the palace had never been so exhausting.

She thought she would rest for a moment or two, so she went over and curled up in the shade of the palm trees. Her bread would not take long to finish, and she would just sit and relax until it was done.

Mara closed her eyes, thinking about how proud her husband would be of her four perfect loaves of bread.

When Mara awoke, she noticed how much cooler she had gotten. She smiled sleepily. Then she realized that someone was shaking her gently. She opened her eyes. Still groggy with sleep, she saw Joel leaning over her. His expression was so tender and sweet, that she instinctively reached her arms out to him like a child.

He was quick to accept her invitation, and he lifted her into his embrace.

The embrace woke Mara completely. She realized what had happened.

"Oh, I fell asleep. I am so sorry. I don't know what I was thinking. You must think me a terrible sluggard to sleep in the middle of the day." The words came pouring out in a tumble.

Joel tried to hush her, but she kept apologizing, horrified at the thought of what she had done.

Then Mara smelled something unpleasant. "My bread!" she cried. "Oh no, it will be ruined." She ran over to the oven, but Joel hurried to catch up with her.

"I knew enough of the take it out of the oven," he explained, motioning to the charred remains of her perfect loaves.

Mara was shocked when she burst into tears.

Joel looked a little amazed, but he pulled her into his arms again, trying to comfort her. "It doesn't matter. It is just bread," he murmured over and over.

Mara realized what she was doing, but she couldn't seem to stop it. "They were going to be perfect. I worked so hard," she gulped into his chest. "We were going to have them for dinner. You were going to be proud of me."

This made Joel straighten with a jerk. "Just a minute," he began, lowering his long limbs onto a low stool and pulling Mara onto his lap. He forced her chin up, making her look into his eyes. "Do you think that you have to make bread for me to be proud of you?"

Mara tried to turn away from his warm brown eyes. "I just don't want you to be sorry you married me," she explained weakly, wishing she had been able to control herself better. She wondered when she had gotten so weak.

Joel moved his head, so that his mouth was just a breath from her ear. "Listen to me," he whispered. "It will not take a loaf of bread to make me proud of you. I did not marry you because I thought you would be a great cook, or a great weaver, or anything else. I married you for you. And I will never be sorry I married you."

Mara smiled a little, horribly embarrassed, but happy nonetheless. "We'll see if you still say that after I burn your bread for ten years."

Joel responded to her grin. "Nothing would make me happier than the thought of you spending ten years trying to make me the perfect loaf of bread."

Mara rose from her husband's lap. "But now we have no bread for the meal, and I know you are hungry." She rummaged around in the baskets around the oven. "We have a lot of fruit, though. Deborah and I went to the market today. We can have dates and figs with the stew. I think the stew should be all right."

Her stew of lentils with oil and leeks was a little thick, but it was edible, and Mara sighed her relief.

After a meal that must have been suitable,—for Joel commented on how wonderful it was six times (although the stew was very bland)—and Mara had taken care of the dishes, she went back to the benches near the fountain where Joel usually retired after dinner.

"Will you play for me?" Joel asked when he saw her.

Mara went to get her lyre, happy she could do something well that would please him. She returned, and sat on another bench and began to play.

After a while, Joel asked, "Could I hear one of your own songs. The king mentioned that you had written a song that was very good."

The request was reasonable, and although Mara was not sure she wanted to share something so private, she did not feel like she could refuse. So she played for him the song she had written to Solomon, closing her eyes to hide their expression.

The notes drifted through the overspreading trees on the cool air, and lingered in the branches. Mara was amazed anew at how much the song could affect her.

She would not, she vowed, sing the words for him.

When she finished, she glanced over at her husband.

Joel was staring at her with a slightly shocked, mostly dismayed expression on his face. She could see the hurt in the lines of his face and the way he held his shoulders. After a minute, to Mara's astonishment, he got up and walked away.

Despite the fact that it was he who had requested the song, Mara felt that somehow she had betrayed him. But she didn't know how she could have.

She continued to sit in the cool air, strumming her lyre absently, wishing her husband had not left her alone.

Chapter 16

But I don't want to marry a man I do not even know," Deborah complained. "I want to marry a man I love."

Mara fought a wave of dizziness. She didn't know what was the matter with her this morning. She could hardly believe that Deborah had been with her for six months already. Abihail had arranged a marriage for her youngest daughter, and Deborah was going to leave Mara and Joel. The man chosen for Deborah was not, as Deborah had feared, Jacob the seller of cloth. Instead, he was the son of a wealthy merchant, and, from what Mara had heard, was devout and liked by everyone. But Mara was very sorry to see her go. The two had become very good friends over the weeks they had spent together, and Mara had been happy for the girl's companionship.

"Most girls don't marry men they love. You should thank Yahweh that Caleb is young and devout and quite wealthy." Mara reached into the clay oven and pulled out a perfect loaf of bread. She had finally mastered the art of bread making, and she was a tolerable cook and an excellent weaver. But this morning, the sight of the bread made her nauseous.

She no longer, however, had to tend to the house by herself, for shortly after their marriage, Joel had hired a young, mute girl to help Mara. Rachel, though she could not speak, was able and honest, and Mara was constantly glad for her help. More so, now that Deborah was leaving.

Deborah made a face. "I would rather marry a poor man that I loved, like your friend Abishag."

Mara pulled out another loaf; this one was rather lopsided. "You would soon grow tired of being a poor man's wife. The poor work very hard and are little appreciated. You should thank Yahweh for what he has given you." Mara wondered when she had started to sound so preachy.

But Deborah nodded as if she had said something very wise. "You are right. You are always right. When I marry, I shall have to visit you very often so you can give me advice. You have so much more experience than other women. You have had such an interesting life."

Mara laughed at the thought. "Interesting almost always means full of pain and hardship. I would much rather have lived a boring life."

Deborah did not look convinced. "I don't know how you are happy living as you do after having seen so much of the world. Even if you are married to my brother, it must get boring."

Mara thought about her life. Although her relationship with her husband was still unpredictable, he was always kind and considerate, and they shared many laughs and interesting conversations. During the day, she did housework. And thanks to Rachel, she had plenty of time to visit with the friends she had made and relax, by herself, with her lyre. "It is not boring," Mara told her. "I am very happy. My life before, though it may have been interesting, was empty. Now I have found Yahweh, and he has given my life purpose. And he has given me contentment. He will do the same for you."

Deborah listened to her attentively, but Mara wondered when she had come to the position to be giving advice to another.

Deborah was silent for a few minutes, but Mara could predict the track her thoughts would be following. "But I still want to marry a man I love!" she burst out.

Mara shook her head, and sat down on a stool. She was really not feeling well this morning. "Deborah, listen to me. You don't marry a man because you love him; you love him because you are married to him, because that is what Yahweh has commanded."

She realized that there was a fair amount of hypocrisy in her words. Didn't she, already married, constantly wish she was able to love and be loved by Joel?

She wanted to reason with herself, convince herself that the situations were different, that after what she had lived through the same could not be expected from her, but she knew that it was not the truth.

She should love Joel, if only because he was her husband. It wasn't like he was a difficult man to love. He was so considerate and gentle with her, his conversations were so stimulating and intelligent, his piety and strength so admirable. But it wasn't so easy for her.

Some things were easy. Kindness—both the giving and the taking of it—after having gone without for so long, was easy. So were conversations, about the various things touching their lives, that never approached the intimate places in the soul. Easy, too, were soft embraces at night and words of tenderness, murmured in the safety of darkness. Such things were easy, and Mara thanked Yahweh for them.

What was not easy, and the lack of which made Mara weep when she was alone, was a bonding, a sharing of the self that only came through understanding.

And Mara didn't know her husband, not really, not after six months. She couldn't understand the forces that drove him or the workings of his mind. And she needed that understanding before she could love.

She understood Solomon, understood his twin truths—the love and the pain—and she understood the way they had guided every action he ever took. And because she could understand, and because, in the knowledge, she saw so much of herself, she could love him.

But Joel, strong and confident and devoted, was still a mystery to her.

There was a good deal of guilt embedded in this knowledge, and she asked Yahweh for his help, for his guidance, for him to bring her to an understanding of her husband.

Their dinner that night was unusually quiet. Mara scooped the lentil stew out of her bowl with a piece of bread and bit into it, watching Deborah's face thoughtfully.

The girl was still pouting about her upcoming betrothal. Her full lips were set and her small chin was protruding ominously.

Mara glanced over at Joel; he too was studying Deborah, and she could tell he was concerned from the lines between his eyes.

Deborah looked up from her stew and saw both Mara and Joel staring at her. "Please don't make me marry that man!" she exclaimed, startling both of them.

"Deborah," Joel began, his voice unusually stern. "We have already had this conversation, several times."

Mara leaned back from the table as Rachel laid a tray of dried fruit down. Deborah took a fig from the tray and chewed it as she spoke. "Why can't I have any say in the matter? I am the one who has to live with him for the rest of my life."

"You don't have any say because children never have a say in issues such as this. Your mother has said that you will marry Caleb, and you will obey her."

Had Deborah been more mature or more perceptive, she would have known to go no farther with this conversation. Joel's face had a set look that Mara would have known how to interpret. But Deborah was still a child in all the ways that mattered, and she would never have Mara's understanding of nuances. So she whined, "It was hardly Mama's decision."

"Excuse me?" Joel's words were perfectly polite.

"Well," Deborah said rashly, arranging her curly hair with her hands. "I know quite well that it was you who arranged the marriage. Mama would just go along with whatever you said. Sometimes, I wish you would stay out of my life."

Something changed in Joel's face, but it was not really a change of expression. He rose to his feet. "You will leave this table immediately."

Deborah was young and rather vain, but she was certainly not a fool. She jumped off her stool and ran out of the room as quickly as Mara had ever seen her move. She could hear the girl weeping through the walls.

Mara had not moved from her stool, and she turned back to look at her husband. He sunk back onto his seat and covered his face with his hands.

She had to say something. "Deborah will come around," she said softly. "She just takes a little longer than others."

Mara moved her stool closer to Joel's. He raised his head from his hands, and Mara gasped. She had never seen such hurt on Joel's face before. The incident, which to her had seemed so minor, was evidently of the greatest importance to her husband. And because her nature would not allow her to let any man she cared for remain in pain, she reached out to take one of his hands.

The gesture seemed to mean something to Joel, for he turned to look at her.

"She is so young," Mara continued. "And she has so many romantic notions about life. She will learn, and it will hurt her some. But she has a good heart. Don't blame her too much for this." She had to add that last, for Deborah was, after all, her friend.

"Blame her," Joel repeated, still holding her hand. "Blame *her*?"

And in that moment, before any more words were spoken, Mara learned something about her husband—something more than surface information, something that went deep down into who the man was.

Of course he wouldn't blame Deborah for her outburst at the dinner table. He would blame himself.

Deborah was his family. And it was family on which every strong emotion in this man centered. The bonding and the love were unbreakable, the foundations of his life. But it was more than this, for with the love came responsibility. He was the head of his family, and all the guilt his family deserved he took upon himself.

"I don't blame her," Joel told her, confirming the understanding she had just come to. "I blame myself."

And Mara knew too that the only real insecurity that Joel ever faced, that he could not really overcome, was centered around his family and his duty to them. But her husband was in pain, and although she could now understand it, she did not want it to continue. "But you can not blame yourself for Deborah's actions. Why would you blame yourself?"

"Why?" Joel was clutching her hand. It hurt. "Because it is the responsibility of the parents to train the children in the way they should go. Our father died months after Deborah was born. I had to be a father to her. So if she will treat family and her elders the way she did just now, I have no one to blame but myself."

Mara wanted to cry. She forced herself not to. "I understand what you are saying. And, yes, parents are responsible for teaching their children, but, ultimately, Deborah must take the responsibility on herself."

Joel didn't even seem to hear what she had said. But he was staring at her, his face damp with perspiration. "I must have failed. I could not be the father she needed."

Mara had a picture then, of her husband as a father. She knew what kind of father he would make. The very best. And then—and this thought stabbed—she thought about Solomon, and the kind of father he was already becoming. The thought was too painful to face, and so she had to push it from her mind. She said to Joel, "No father could ever have taught Deborah the way you did. She is young, but she is kind-hearted, generous, loving, devout. You have not failed."

Joel looked away from his wife, to the shadows that were dancing on the walls from the branches outside the small window and the wavering light of the lamps. "I must have failed. I must have." Then, suddenly, he turned back to look at her. "But how could a boy, not more than fifteen years old, be a father to his sister?"

Mara did cry then, and she moved into his lap, wrapping her arms around his neck. She could feel Joel respond to the closeness of her body, feel his arms, hard, around her. And holding him, Mara wept for the pain that he was feeling. She prayed to Yahweh, pleading with him to ease the pain or take it away.

And as she held him, while she wept for him, she had to breathe a prayer of thanksgiving, for Yahweh had answered her prayer, at least in part. He had allowed her to understand something about her husband. Something from which sharing could grow.

And, finally, she prayed again for a child, which Yahweh had not yet granted her. She prayed it now, especially now, for she knew, as surely as she knew her own name and her father's eyes, that if Yahweh granted her a child in this world, she wanted Joel to be its father.

The next day was Deborah's betrothal ceremony. Mara stood next to Joel in Abihail's house and watched with excitement as the young couple exchanged vows and the parents gave their children to each other.

Caleb was not as handsome as Joel, but he looked very friendly and good-natured. Mara thought that Deborah would be happy with him.

Mara could not see Deborah's face, but her voice was clear and confident, and Mara was proud of her friend.

After the ceremony, when Deborah came to embrace her, Mara was surprised by the joy on the girl's face. Deborah whispered in her ear. "I'm in love. I took one look at him and fell in love."

Mara hoped that Deborah was speaking about her newly betrothed. "Caleb?" she murmured.

"Of course," Deborah responded. "Oh, I am so happy."

Mara was a little startled, but she could see that Deborah meant it. She was glad that Joel's sister would be able to have her wish and marry a man she loved. She was glad, but maybe a little jealous.

She thought of Solomon, which she had not done for quite a while. His harem was growing every day, she had heard, and his words of wisdom were repeated by everyone. He was lost to her, forever.

Then she looked at her husband. Joel had been unusually quiet ever since dinner yesterday, his smile more forced, his eyes not as open. She wondered if he regretted showing weakness in front of her. But he had never been that kind of man—not like Solomon. She hated feeling so uncertain around him, and she wished that she was better at reading him.

He was a very strong man, and a very devout Jew. There was nothing about him that she did not like, except the way he made her feel. She wished that she could love him.

That night, the evening meal seemed very quiet without Deborah's chatter. Joel broke the bread in silence, and used it to scoop out the soup Rachel had made into Mara's dish, and then into his own.

"Caleb seems to be a good man," she ventured, watching carefully for his response.

He smiled easily. "He is a good man. And he admires Deborah greatly."

That seemed to be all that could be said about that subject, so silence fell again.

Mara thought and thought for something to say.

"The king is starting construction on the temple, isn't that right?" Mara asked, taking up the most popular discussion in Israel at the moment.

Joel nodded. "Soon. Much of the wood has arrived from the forests of Lebanon, and the builders will begin any time. It will be a long process, though, before it is completed."

"I imagine it gives the king something to accomplish. Something he can do to give his reign some purpose."

Joel agreed with her. "He needs it."

Mara's face grew soft at the thought of the young king, who had already grown tired of the pleasures of kingship.

He had consolidated the kingdom by dividing the kingdom into twelve administrative districts, which weakened the tribal allegiances. He had made alliances, not only with Pharaoh, but also with Hiram of Tyre, and it was from this alliance that Solomon got the materials with which to build the temple. He had encouraged trade with other nations, and the Hebrew merchants were gaining more and more wealth for the country.

Joel had explained all this to Mara, some with admiration and some with disapproval.

It was a different world from the world of David's kingship. David had been a warrior and a poet, passionate and intense about everything. In his reign, there had been little subtlety or guile. He had forged the kingdom with his sword and had held
it by the force of his strength and the power of a name blessed by Yahweh. Solomon was different; Israel under Solomon was different. For Solomon's goal was not to make a kingdom, but to make the kingdom great.

A different world. A world that would reflect Solomon's gifts rather than his father's.

Joel frowned at the look on Mara's face, so Mara smiled at him. She had learned that if she smiled at her husband, he would have to smile in return and his sour mood would vanish.

It worked again this time. "Poor Solomon. He married again, did you hear, to the daughter of the governor of Megiddo."

They both shook their heads in regret. "If he does not quit soon, he will have more wives than his father did," Mara commented. She wasn't sure why she had said that. Although she was distant from Solomon now, she still understood him. She knew that he would not stop marrying until he had more wives than his father did. She also knew that he would never admit it. Marriages were for diplomatic reasons, or to solidify trade routes, or to promote alliances. All true, and all relevant. But she knew it was more than that. Harems were power— women like gold, spices, or cattle. And Solomon was determined to display his power in the most obvious and lavish of ways.

"Poor Solomon," Joel repeated. "Life is not as he would have hoped."

Mara could not help but agree with this statement, and it worried her.

Chapter 17

A few weeks later, Mara entered her bedroom shortly after breakfast. Joel had already left for the palace, and she was about to begin her morning chores.

Her eyes caught her beads of amber, her sea-gold, resting next to the piece of polished silver that served as her mirror. She walked over to pick them up.

Such a small thing, not even very valuable in the Israel Solomon was creating. But they had been forced to carry more of a burden of significance than such a small trinket should carry. They were the only thing she had left of her homeland, of her father, who had given them to her.

And then, for no good reason—or perhaps with every reason in the world—she thought about Cala, one of David's concubines in the harem. She had loved amber. She had also, over a period of months, been ill every morning. And Mara had watched as Cala's belly, normally as flat as a board, had grown rounded and large.

Mara took a deep breath to fight the nausea she felt. She looked down at her own belly. It was still flat.

She had to lie down, and so she moved over to her bed. She had never lain down in the middle of the morning before. But she felt so ill. Perhaps it was allowed.

When Rachel came to find her, Mara was still lying on the bed, clutching her beads of amber in one of her hands and her stomach in the other.

She should tell Joel. It had been three more weeks and she was fairly certain by now. But, for some reason, she was afraid. What if she was wrong? What if she was just ill, and had gained a little weight? Her monthly cycle had never been perfectly regular, so it would not be completely unusual if . . . It seemed cruel to tell Joel if he was only going to be disappointed.

And there was something beyond that, something Mara couldn't define, that was keeping her from telling him.

Mara was resting in the courtyard after lunch. She hadn't eaten anything. She was sure that Rachel knew, but even if Rachel could speak, Mara knew that she wouldn't.

It was time to tell Joel, she thought, looking at the broad leaves of the palm trees blow in the light wind.

He was her husband and the child's father. This was what he had been longing for, although he certainly had never told her as much. Joel deserved to be told.

But Joel would not be back until evening, and she had the whole afternoon in front of her. Mara decided, because she was feeling better and because she was becoming the kind of person who did things like this, to go and visit Joel's mother, Abihail.

Abihail embraced her when she was let into the sitting room. "Mara, I haven't seen you in a few weeks. I have missed you."

Mara returned the hug. This was a woman she could confide in. "I have been rather ill lately."

Abihail nodded, "So Joel told me." She paused, really looking at Mara for the first time. "No, you haven't been ill. Yahweh be praised for his blessings." And she embraced Mara again.

"How did you know?" Mara asked, smoothing her long hair and feeling her cheeks flush. "I wasn't even sure myself."

Abihail smiled, brimming over with the excitement of the news. "Oh, you will come to recognize these things. How long?" she asked cryptically.

Of course, Mara understood her. "Two months."

Abihail pressed her hands together. "Does Joel know?"

Mara hesitated. "I haven't told him yet."

"But does he know?"

The hesitation was longer now. "I don't think so. He thinks I have just been ill."

Abihail shook her head. "Joel is a very perceptive man, but even the best of men are often blind about the most obvious things. When are you going to tell him?"

"Tonight," Mara responded, sure now that it was the truth. "I'm going to tell him tonight."

Joel brought a guest home that night, one of the commanders of the army. A pleasant man and one she knew, but she hated the sight of him that night. She could hardly tell Joel that she was with child if the man was with them.

They chatted for a long time after dinner, and Mara helped Rachel do the evening chores. It was much cooler out, and she could feel herself shaking.

Rachel touched her on the shoulder, a wordless gesture of concern.

"I'm fine," Mara responded. "Not really cold, just impatient. I need to talk to my husband alone."

Rachel nodded her head, in complete understanding.

Eventually the man left, and Mara went to bid him farewell.

She took a deep breath when the door was closed. Joel looked at her expectantly.

She opened her mouth, but no words came out. She didn't know why she was having such a hard time telling him. It was good news. Wonderful news, in fact.

"What is bothering you this evening?" Joel asked, seating himself on a finely crafted stool.

Mara sat down as well. It was a good thing, since her legs were not effectively supporting her. "What do you mean?" she responded, instead of answering the question.

"I mean that you looked several times as if you wanted to push Joseph forcefully from the room, and you haven't looked me in the eye all evening. What is the matter?"

"I just needed to talk to you, and I couldn't talk while Joseph was here."

145

"So talk to me now." Joel was smiling a little, and his eyes, as always, were kind. After a moment of silence, he drew his brows together. "Nothing is wrong, is it? I mean, you are all right?"

Mara nodded. She took a deep breath, and she spoke, her own words surprised her. "It is just I visited Abihail, and she doesn't look nearly old enough to be a grandmother." She had no idea why she was approaching the issue in such a haphazard manner.

It took Joel only a second. "A child?" he whispered.

Mara nodded again, looking at him through her lashes. "A child." She gave a little smile.

And she learned something else about Joel to admire then, something she hadn't known before. She could see the blaze of joy ignite in his eyes with her words, but she could also see him smother that joy with concern, concern for her. "And you, you are all right?"

"Yes, I feel rather ill, but I gather that is normal."

Joel reached out to touch her cheek. "I didn't really mean physically. I meant, are you all right with this? Are you happy?"

Mara smiled then, her full, bright smile, and something warmed in her as Joel returned it. "I am. I want a child more than anything." It was the truth, although she hadn't really known it until that second, looking into her husband's face.

Joel allowed himself to indulge his joy then. He pulled her into his arms, and twirled her around. Then, startled, he put her down. "I'm sorry," he gasped sheepishly. "Did I hurt you?"

"Of course not," she reassured him, laughing with pleasure at his joy and her own.

She had been a fool to be wary of telling him. She couldn't remember now why she had been so afraid.

The next month was the happiest month Mara had ever known. Joel, who had always been kind and gentle with her, treated her as if she were made of crystal. Her friends were joyful and supportive. She wasn't quite as ill as she had been. And she had begun to plan for the child.

It was such a pleasure to be able to give Joel this child—maybe even a son—after he had given her so much. He had taken to, at the strangest and most unexpected moments, leaning over and kissing her belly. Kissing their child, he said.

She could understand his feelings. He was born to be a father.

It was mid-afternoon and the house was quiet. It was so quiet since Deborah had left them. Rachel was busy working in the courtyard, and Mara had been ordered, with firm hand gestures, to rest in the cool of the trees.

She wasn't about to argue with Rachel, especially since she was feeling strangely weak today.

Mara rose and walked over to Rachel. "Do you know where my lyre is?" she asked, glancing around at the stone oven, the pottery filled with oil and grain, and the stools scattered about. It was unlikely to be around here.

Rachel nodded and pointed up to a window in the wall behind her, the window to the bedchamber.

"Thank you," Mara said and hurried up to the bedchamber. Her lyre was lying on the floor next to the dressing table. She bent to pick it up, and suddenly cried out. She had had these strange sharp pains occasionally last night and the previous day. But they had not been as bad as this.

Mara forced herself to take a few deep breaths. The pain subsided, and she slowly walked back down to the courtyard. She would not complain about them. She would certainly be strong enough to bear whatever pains came with pregnancy.

Rachel glanced up at her as she approached, and her face filled with concern. Mara was about to wave it away, when the piercing pain returned. Mara managed not to double over, and she just grasped her stomach tightly.

Rachel studied her, then smiled and pointed again at the bedchamber window. There was no doubt about what she was telling Mara.

Mara agreed. She needed to lie down.

She made it back to her bed before the pain returned again. This time, she was lying down, and she pulled her knees up to her chest, trying to smother the pain.

Surely pregnancy was not supposed to hurt this much. How did women manage to have so many children if they had to go through this for several months before each one?

Mara forced herself to think about her breath going in and out of her body. All she needed, she assured herself, was a little rest.

She never remembered Cala, from David's harem, hurting this much.

Maybe she was just not strong enough to take it. But she had always been strong; at least, she had always thought that she was.

The pain wouldn't go away. Mara breathed heavily, praying, and willing her body to obey. It didn't. The pain continued, and it continued to get worse.

She was used to pain, physical pain even. So many times in her life she had hurt, so many things had been done to her: blows, and cuts, and lashes. But it had been so long since she had ever really been in pain. And she could never remember anything hurting the way this hurt.

Something was wrong.

She should summon Rachel for help, but she knew she couldn't rise from the bed, and she didn't think she would be able to call out loud enough for Rachel to hear her.

Why wasn't Joel here? Why wasn't he helping her?

"Yahweh," she whispered. "Make it go away."

It didn't go away. She lay on the bed, thinking about pain, about the ways life could hurt you, about the ways life had hurt *her*.

Elsa knew how to bear it, could take a dagger wound in the shoulder without crying or flinching. But Elsa had always been stronger than she was, and Elsa had been gone now for years.

Mara wondered where her father's sister was now. Was she alive at all?

She had to think about something other than the pain, so she thought about Solomon. But Solomon, in her mind, was intricately tied to pain of another variety, so that was hardly a help.

Joel. . . . But then Joel had caused this pain, had planted this seed inside of her.

What else was there to think about? Everything in her life led her back to pain, to this specific pain, low in her belly.

The room was so bright, the light hitting her like a blow. She could see the familiar furnishings of the room, the bare walls, the clean floor, but they did not look familiar. In the bright light, they seemed foreign, hostile, even her beads of sea-gold on the table.

She didn't know how long she had been lying there on the bed. She must have pulled a blanket up over her. She was hot, but if she took off the blanket she would be exposed to the hostile light and the room.

Rachel came in to check on her. She took one look at Mara and covered her mouth with her hand.

Looking at her, Mara became conscious of something else. There was something sticky on her hand. She pulled her arm out from under the covers and looked down at it.

She knew what it was; she had seen it often enough.

Blood.

Rachel saw it too, and darted for the door. At the door, she turned around, looking back at Mara, silent tears starting to run down her cheeks.

There was no one else in the house this afternoon. She would have to leave Mara by herself. "Go," Mara told her weakly. "Go, get help."

Rachel nodded and obeyed, leaving Mara alone.

Blood. There was blood on her hand, and on the blankets and her clothes. She was bleeding. She shouldn't be bleeding.

But the pain was still there, dulling the knowledge of the blood.

It was funny, she thought, as her hurt closed in around her, how dark a bright room could look.

Chapter 18

It was the pain that woke her again. She was in the same position, in the same room, but it was dark outside, and the room was lit by a few smoky lamps. She lay very still. There were voices murmuring on the other side of the room. She couldn't hear what they were saying.

Then she heard another voice, one she knew, and this one she could understand. "Mara!" The voice came from the hallway. "Where is Mara?"

The voice was closer now, and she heard the harsh silencing noises from the other two people in the room.

She could hear Joel's breathing, even from across the room. They would have had to go to find him. He may have been drilling, outside of the city. Then it would have taken him a while to get back. From the sound of his rough breathing, it had not taken him as long as it should have.

They were whispering now, and she couldn't hear them. She wondered if she should let them know that she was awake. She decided not to. That would mean she would have had to hear things she did not want to hear. So she stayed perfectly still and listened.

She couldn't understand anything until she heard Joel's voice rise as he asked, "Is she going to be all right?" There was an edge to his voice that Mara couldn't quite identify.

"She has lost so much blood," she heard, and then more words too soft for her to hear.

"What?" after a moment, Joel again. "What else is the matter? What else is there?"

A woman's voice, one she couldn't identify. "She hasn't cried at all."

And with those words, the room grew dark once more.

When next she woke, it was bright again. Same room. Same position. She opened her eyes, and looked at the wall. The sharp pain was gone now. All that was left was a dull ache, and the soreness. She wondered if Joel had left her, gone somewhere else to rest or to eat. Surely he wouldn't have done that. He wouldn't have left her.

She had to find out, so she forced herself to turn over, even though she knew it would hurt.

He was there. Sitting on the floor against the wall, his hands clasped over his knees, his eyes never leaving the bed. There were lines between his eyes and next to his mouth and near his temples. Mara was glad she was too far away to see the expression in his eyes.

She just looked at him and opened her mouth. She couldn't seem to form any words.

He got up and moved over to the bed. "Would you like some water?" he asked softly.

She nodded, and watched him pour water from a pitcher into a cup. She tried to reach out to take the cup, but she couldn't seem to manage that either. Without speaking, he leaned over and held up her head with his hand. Then he placed the cup to her lips. The water was cool and mild, and her mouth was parched, but she got no comfort from the sensation.

There was a stool beside the bed, and Joel seated himself. Hesitantly, her husband reached over to touch her cheek. "My dearest, my Mara," he murmured. "I thought I had lost you."

It meant something to her, even then, in that room, even after the pain and the blood. But if she thought about it too much, she would not be able to bear it, so she pushed the words away from her conscious thoughts.

"The child?" she whispered. She didn't know why she had even asked that, because she already knew the answer. She had lost too much blood.

Joel shook his head. She saw the sorrow in his eyes. She knew what he needed, and that he needed it from her, but she couldn't give it to him. Not now. So instead, she turned over again, turned her back to him.

It was too bright in the room again, and she tried to block the light with her blanket.

She didn't want to be here. She didn't want to face the sorrow in her husband's eyes, the dull ache in her stomach, the blood.

Why had she ever left the palace? She had been safe there. And if she had always carried emptiness like a chasm inside of her, and if she had never felt the joy of belonging or of shared laughter, at least there had been no blood.

There was blood outside of the palace, everywhere.

At that moment, she was able to feel rage. Rage at Solomon, for letting her leave the palace, not keeping her within the sheltering safety of its walls. And rage at Joel for bringing her to this room and for the weight of his body at night. And rage, finally and especially, at Yahweh, for giving her this home and this family, as if it had been a blessing, and then taking it all away from her.

She was not a person who angered often or easily, but, for just that moment, she felt the anger like a heat inside of her chest, like an invader inside her body.

And then the rage was gone, as quickly as it had come, and the only anger she had left was for herself, for allowing herself to trust, for leaving herself vulnerable, for losing control of her life.

No one had brought her to this moment but herself. She knew—oh, how deeply she knew—what happened when she let herself love, but she had done it anyway, and she could blame nobody for it but herself.

And still, despite the myriad of overwhelming and conflicting emotions—because the legacy she carried from a fiery, bloody night in midsummer was self-knowledge—she knew that in all the turnings of her life she had never sunk to the depths she was drowning in at the moment.

"Mara." The voice came through the fog of her emotions, as if from a great distance.

"Mara, please look at me."

Joel would not know, could not know, what it would take for her to do that. To pull herself out of the fogs and move back into the world she had to live in. But he was her husband, and it was his child that had been lost as well, so she forced herself to turn back over and look him in the eyes.

"Mara," Joel said again. His eyes were so brown. Why, she wondered, was she constantly dwelling on that fact. "I am the last person to be talking to you about strength. I know how strong I am, and how far that strength will take me. And I also know that if I had lost you, as well as the child"—here his voice cracked—"Both of you, I don't know how I would have gone on. And you, you lost your entire family, before your eyes, and yet you were strong enough to, not just go on, but to keep your calm intelligence, your peaceful reserve, your laughter. I would not pretend to know more about strength than you."

Again, his words were a balm. But there was only so much that a balm could do for an open, bleeding wound.

Joel continued, reaching to take her hand. She let him, because she hadn't the strength to pull away. "But I do know one thing about strength. I know, as sure as I know my own father's name, that it takes more strength to face your emotions than to hide from them."

And that nearly broke Mara. "Strength?" she cried. "I don't care about strength. I don't want to be strong. Is strength supposed to be some kind of reward for a life full of pain? I don't want to be strong. I want to hide." She was revealing too much, sharing too much of her soul when he had offered only a little of his own. But there was no way to take the words back now.

She saw Joel vulnerable then, his shoulders hunched and his head bowed. "Do you know where to hide? Where you can be safe from them? If you do, please tell me, and I will join you there."

And then she did weep. For there was no where to hide. Nothing to prevent the sorrow and the blood. Not even the palace—especially not the palace.

While she wept, Joel continued to hold her hand. She saw him, once, move, as if to take her in his arms, but he stopped himself. And as she wept her husband was blessedly, mercifully silent.

He didn't speak at all; he just squeezed her hands until it hurt.

And then, because Yahweh's grace has nothing to do with humanity's strength or weakness but is poured out on his people regardless, she slept.

It was amazing how different a morning could feel. When Mara opened her eyes again, it was morning. She could tell, for the sunlight was coming in the windows at a low angle. She must have slept the remainder of the previous day and all through the night.

Joel would no longer be in the room. Certainly, by now, he had gone to rest or eat or refresh himself. But Mara turned over just to be sure.

He was still there. On the floor, against the wall. But this time he was asleep.

With his eyes closed and the lines of his face smoothed out in slumber, he looked younger, innocent.

Mara managed to smile. *My dearest*, he had called her. *I know that if I had lost you and the child, both of you, I don't know how I would have gone on.*

He must have meant the words. He wouldn't have lied to her, not at such a time.

And in the silence of the morning, with only Joel's steady breathing to break the stillness, Mara learned the last thing she needed to know about her husband. She was his family, and she knew—by now she certainly knew—what family meant to this man.

He loved her. Perhaps not passionately, or romantically, or in the way she may wish to be loved, but he loved her as his family. It was something. It was enough.

For she loved him.

She wasn't sure how, or when, or even why, but she did, with everything she had in her to give—which, she admitted, at this moment wasn't very much.

Solomon she had loved, and perhaps loved still, but her love for Joel was different, more complex, more mature.

Yahweh had answered this prayer. Had showed her how to love her husband. And she was grateful, could be grateful, even now, even in this room.

Joel opened his eyes, and shook his head to rouse himself. "How are you?" he asked softly.

"You are still here," she said, not answering his question, watching his tall, broad form cross the room. He looked desperately in need of a washing.

Joel put his hand, again, on her cheek. "Where else would I be?"

She was his family. It was enough. She would make it enough.

Somehow, you keep getting up in the morning. Keep washing, keep eating, keep winding thread for the loom. Mara knew this by now, and she knew that the pain would get vaguer and vaguer until it was just another of the aches that let her know she was alive.

After a few months she found herself smiling to herself as she worked on the cloth she was weaving. The previous night, she and Joel had stayed up late laughing about the escapade of one of the palace gardener's sons. Pouring perfume—dense Arabian perfume—over Benaiah's head from on top of the wall as the commander of Israel's armies stood at the palace gate. The poor man could not wash the scent away, and he would smell like an Eastern princess for days.

The relationship between Mara and Joel had grown closer in the previous weeks, something, Mara knew, a shared sorrow could do. And everyday she found herself loving new things about him. Missing him while he was away. Cherishing every tender word he said to her.

Of course she didn't tell him how she felt. There were limits to the extent she would let herself be vulnerable.

As if an extension of her thoughts, she saw her husband at the door to the room. It was much too early for Joel to be home.

She rose to greet him.

"I have found you a maid servant," he said, after apologizing for interrupting her work.

"What?" Mara asked. "I don't need a maid servant."

Joel shrugged. "Perhaps not, but a friend of mine is in debt, and he needs to sell his daughter as a maid servant. I told him I would buy her."

"A slave," Mara exclaimed. "No! I will not have a slave living in this house. Certainly not a little girl."

Joel understood her outrage, and he explained. "It is not what you think. It will just be for seven years. Then she will be set free. It is not a cruel system. It allows people to survive."

"I don't care," Mara insisted. "I will not stand for it. I cannot have a slave working for me. I will not. What kind of father sells his own daughter?" The image of her own father, a tall silhouette against the red of a burning hut. She pushed it out of her mind.

"He has no choice. He has no sons, only five daughters, and they will starve to death otherwise."

Mara hesitated. Perhaps this was the truth, but still . . . "No, I don't think I would be able to handle it." It was a different system—she understood that much. But the idea was repellent to her. She knew, too intimately and too terribly, about slavery.

"At least, if she lived with us, we would treat her kindly. Some families would not. She would be a part of our household."

Mara thought about it. She knew that Joel did not have to put up with her objections. He was the husband, the head of the household, and he could buy the girl if he wanted.

But he wanted her approval, she could see that, and he was concerned about her feelings.

She nodded reluctantly.

It seemed ironic, somehow, that she would have a slave to work for her.

Joel brought Ephrath home with him that evening.

Mara had thought she was prepared for the little girl's coming, but she found she was not.

Mara saw a girl who looked about ten years old, and she had dark, fine hair and a thin, plain face. Her eyes showed that, in her life, she had endured much, and they reflected resignation at what was to come. But she held her shoulders stiffly with a pride that was really a defense.

Mara saw herself, so many years ago. She closed her eyes, and she could actually see herself.

When the Huntar finally reach the south, Mara can smell the sea. Soon, she knows, the Huntar will trade her to somebody else. They come to a port with many ships. It smells of salt and dead fish—familiar smells to her, but something she has not smelled in a long time.

But the sun is hot and huge in the sky, and the sky is so pale it is barely blue. The water of the ocean is blue, slapping on the sides of the ships. Mara walks next to Elsa with the other captives behind the wagons carrying the furs and amber.

There is too much noise, sailors shouting at each other, and men bartering for goods. If she closes her eyes, the chaotic colors and blinding light disappear, but the sound still whirls around her, dizzying her, sickening her. And then the sounds completely disappear.

"Mara! Mara!" comes a sharp voice, as two strong hands grasp her shoulders.

Mara opens her eyes to see Elsa's concerned face close to her own. "Are you all right?"

Mara nods. It is too hot, and she is very hungry. But she is used to it by now.

The brown-eyed Huntar chief meets a heavy-set man with flashing eyes. The man looks into the wagon, inspecting the amber and furs. He then walks past all of the captives. He stares at Mara, with a calculating, dispassionate look. "Beautiful," he mutters, but it is hardly a compliment.

Later, they are taken onto the man's ship. Danel is his name. Mara doesn't know how much he paid for them, and she doesn't care. She is a slave now. But she is only eight years old. She doesn't really know what that means.

Mara snapped back to the present. She looked down at the girl again.

If the despair in the girl's eyes was from partings that had come on her suddenly, rather than the hardness of one who had faced them all her life, Mara loved her more for it.

She knelt down on the ground and opened her arms to Ephrath.

Ephrath looked at her uncertainly, but Mara smiled at her encouragingly. The little girl ran into Mara's arms.

Mara held her tightly, whispering, "It is all right. You are safe. I will take care of you." All the words that she had longed for someone to say to her.

Mara continued to hold the girl, but she looked around at her beautifully furnished home and up at her kind, handsome husband, whom she loved.

And she realized, for the first time, how far Yahweh had brought her.

Chapter 19

Construction on the temple moved very slowly, and six months later only the foundations were built. Solomon's harem continued to increase, mostly with wives, but he also increased his number of concubines. The number surpassed the size of his father's harem, but Solomon did not stop. Most of the marriages were for political reasons, and Mara was sure that many of the wives had never seen Solomon in person. Mara pitied them, and she pitied Solomon.

She was also worried by the fact that she was not with child again.

She prayed about it daily. She longed for a child—yearned to make something of herself in the world, to love and shelter the child as she had never been in her own childhood. But it was more than that. She needed to give Joel children. Family was everything to him, and he needed children of his own. He would never complain; she knew that he wouldn't. However, it was one thing for a man to be understanding about burnt bread, but Joel would certainly be disappointed in her if she was not able to bear him children.

Surely, Yahweh would not repay Joel's kindness in marrying her by refusing to give him a son.

Mara picked at a knot in the thread on her loom, and prayed again for a child.

Joel came home in the evening, and Mara went to greet him. "Good evening," she said with a smile. "How was your day?"

Joel told her, as usual, that everything was fine.

"Any news on Solomon's temple?" she asked.

Joel's face changed only a little, but after living with this man for more than a year, Mara could tell that the question annoyed him. "Do you have to ask that?"

Mara was confused by Joel's terseness. "But I always ask that."

"That," Joel began, growing visibly more irritated, "Is exactly my point."

Mara was hurt, and her face showed it. "Why are you so upset?"

Joel looked at his beautiful wife sternly. "A man does not like to come home every evening to be greeted with questions about another man."

While Mara stood, trying to figure out why Joel was upset, her husband stomped away. Why would he be so upset about her asking about the temple? Everyone was talking about the temple. She wasn't even really asking about Solomon, and, though she sometimes did, she did not see why that should make her husband angry.

It wasn't as if he had anything to be jealous about. She never even saw the king; she could hardly be unfaithful to Joel. She loved Joel—she didn't even want Solomon. But, of course, he wouldn't know that.

She couldn't stand for Joel to be angry with her, so she went to find him.

"Joel," she said nervously, when she saw him among the palm trees in the courtyard. "I am sorry if I made you angry. What can I do to make it better?"

Joel looked up at her, and his eyes were very tired. "I don't think you can," he said.

Mara could tell that he was hurt, not angry; he was hurt by her. This she could not bear. "Joel," she pleaded, kneeling down beside him. "Please tell me what I have done. What has hurt you?"

Joel opened his mouth to explain, when a sound came from across the courtyard. Phinehas, their porter, had cleared his throat discreetly.

They both stood up.

"I am sorry, my lord," Phinehas said softly. "But you have a guest."

Joel's brows went up. "A guest? But we were not expecting anyone."

"Even so," Phinehas said. "There is a man here."

160

Joel looked at Mara in curiosity, and Mara shrugged her own surprise. "Very well," Joel said. "Show him into the sitting room."

Joel and Mara went to greet their unexpected guest and waited while Phinehas led in a solitary, cloaked man.

The couple watched in amazement as the man gracefully removed the cloak and smiled at them. There were more lines around the mouth than when Mara had seen him last and there was a slightly bitter expression in the glittering eyes, but the smile lit up his whole face and there was no mistaking the young man.

"Solomon," Mara exclaimed, starting to move toward him, but stopping herself just in time.

"My lord the king," Joel said, politely, visibly shook by the king's presence in their house. "We are your servants. What can we do for you?"

Solomon laughed, and Mara was glad to hear no bitterness in it. "Do not be so stuffy. I am the king, after all, and if I want to visit some old friends, I can certainly do so."

Joel smiled, and Mara tried to hide her excitement.

"Will you share a meal with us, then," Joel offered. "We were not expecting anyone, but I am sure there will be enough." He looked at Mara questioningly.

Mara nodded, "There is plenty. Do stay and eat with us," she urged.

The king grinned. "I was hoping you would offer, actually. I have gotten some new cooks in the palace, and all the food they cook is terribly rich. I have constant indigestion."

They laughed as they walked back to the dining room. Mara hurried to the stove, where Rachel was boiling some beef stew.

After they had washed their hands meticulously, Joel and Solomon seated themselves. Mara told Rachel that she would serve the food, and she laid trays of food onto the table. She had been saving some excellent dried fruit for a special occasion, and this seemed to be it. She laid out, as well, some spiced wine.

When she had placed all the food on the table, Mara joined the men at the table.

Mara looked over at Joel, to see what his expression was like. Her husband was smiling broadly, pleased as she was at both Solomon's presence and his affectionate sincerity.

Mara watched as Joel started to serve the meal. She was glad Rachel had made the stew tonight, because her own never tasted quite as good.

The discussion focused mostly on the temple, and Mara could see Solomon's enthusiasm for the project. It was an enthusiasm, she knew, that he had inherited with the crown from his father. Solomon explained the shape and furnishing of the temple, descriptions they had heard several times before but never tired of hearing. Then he explained his trade with Hiram of Tyre, whom he had gone to visit, and he raved about Tyrian craftsmanship.

When the subject came to matters of state, some of the excitement left Solomon's eyes. He talked about some of the cases he had tried, including one he had tried just today about two harlots who claimed the same child.

"Cut the child in half!" Joel exclaimed, shocked.

Solomon nodded, winking at Mara. "Indeed. What other way was there?"

Mara chuckled. "You didn't really?"

"No," he sighed, feigning disappointment. "Before I could carry out such a wise decision, one of the women exclaimed that she would rather the other woman have it than see it killed. So I had to assume she was the real mother."

Joel and Mara applauded this wisdom.

At the end of the meal, Solomon sat back with a contented smile. "I have enjoyed this," he told them. "Living in the palace gives one such a warped view of life. I can see through everyone, and all their petty ambitions and motives are laid bare. People have lost their interest for me. But not the two of you. You are refreshingly . . . real."

Joel smiled at his friend in concern. "We are not unique. You have just forgotten how to see people. Too much wisdom is not the easiest of gifts."

"You are right, of course," Solomon agreed. "But I can't seem to remember that."

They gave thanks for the meal, and Solomon stood up. "I should be getting back. I don't think anyone knows I am gone."

They said farewell, and Solomon turned to Mara, "Walk me out?" he asked.

Mara nodded, glancing back at Joel, and walked with Solomon to the door.

"Are you happy?" he asked her.

She nodded. "Yes. I must thank you again for everything you have done for me."

"No, no," Solomon argued. "I have done very little. And I would have done even less had I allowed myself to be selfish."

Little lines appeared between Mara's eyes. "I wish you were happy as well."

"What makes you think I am not?" Solomon asked, straightening his back with the pride that had always characterized him.

"I know you, remember." Mara sighed softly. "At least you have the temple."

"Yes," Solomon agreed, his face brightening. "The temple gives me something."

"And when it is completed?"

Solomon closed his eyes against the thought. "I will find something else. I am king. I will find a way to give my reign purpose. I will, if nothing else, be a great king to Israel."

Mara understood him. She still loved this man, though distantly now, and not in a way that threatened to consume her. Things were too different, and he was not, after all, Joel.

Solomon recognized the difference. "I had to see for myself if my sacrifice was worth it," he said finally, in explanation.

"And was it?"

Solomon looked into her eyes. "Yes," he affirmed. "I have to say that it was." He lifted his hand to caress her cheek. "Good-bye, little Mara," he breathed.

There was something to his voice and the shape of his mouth that made tears form in Mara's eyes. It was not just a casual farewell; it seemed so final.

"Solomon," she said, her voice breaking. She was very much afraid. "What is it?"

Solomon gave a little shrug. "Sometimes," he began, as if he were not answering her question. "When your reality is not what you want it to be, you cling to a fantasy—no matter how unrealistic—and you invest in that fantasy so much of your feeling and so many of your dreams. And when you realize that the fantasy is merely a piece of air," Solomon's eyes were distant, and his voice as mellow and rhythmic as a song. "It hurts."

Mara reached out to grasp his hand. "I'm sorry." It was the only thing that she could say. For she knew exactly what he was talking about. He could read people, all people; he could certainly read her. He would know that she loved Joel.

She had loved Solomon more than anyone in the world, and now she didn't. It was better this way, for everyone, but it was still—in a very real sense—a betrayal. "I'm so sorry," she repeated.

"No," Solomon replied, squeezing her hand. "I shouldn't have said anything." He smiled then, his old smile.

"I thought you had left," came a hard voice from behind them.

Mara twirled around, and she winced at her husband's angry face. Surely he would not have so little trust for her, for Solomon, that he thought they were . . .

Mara didn't finish the thought.

"I was just leaving," Solomon said easily. "I hope to see you soon."

Receiving no response except a smile from Mara, he pulled on his cloak and slipped out of the house. Mara would have thought it was a retreat, but she realized that if he had stayed the situation could only have gotten worse.

Joel continued to stare at Mara, and Mara forced herself not to squirm under his eyes.

"Why are you so angry," she asked finally.

Joel gritted his teeth. "I had hoped that I would not have to remind you that you are married to me."

"Of course you don't have to remind me," Mara cried. "I would think you would have enough faith in me to keep you from reminding me."

Joel raised his chin. "And what was it, then, that I came upon here a minute ago?"

"I was saying good-bye to Solomon. Surely, you could see that. We have shared much." Mara's voice grew softer with the last phrase. She had never wanted to hurt Solomon.

"Yes." Joel's voice was bitter. "I am aware of that. More than you have shared with me."

"I share my life with you," Mara exclaimed, growing angrier. "What more do you want? Must you have, as well, all that I share with Solomon?" By loving him, she had given more to Joel than she had ever given to anyone. How could he be questioning her loyalty?

Joel took an angry step toward her, but stopped himself. "I have waited," he began, his voice carefully leveled, "for more than a year. I thought if I were patient, you would forget about Solomon, learn to love me. But I am tired of waiting, tired of being good and kind and patient." His voice lost its levelness at the end, and his voice rose to a shout.

Mara stared at him, open-mouthed. "Learn to love you?" she repeated. "What are you talking about? Why would you expect love if you give none in return?" She was furious with herself when her voice broke. "What kind of a man are you?" She knew that this was not fair, for he did love her, after his fashion. But it was not the kind of love that she wanted.

It was Joel's turn for astonishment. "Give no love," he muttered. "Why on earth do you think I married you?"

Mara had thought about the question so many times throughout the months that the answer came easily. "As a favor to Solomon. Because you pitied me. Because you needed a wife, though why you would choose someone as inept as me is still a mystery. Because you wanted a family."

Joel almost choked on his outrage. "You surely do not think anything so ridiculous. Of course, I love you. How could you not know something so obvious to everyone else?"

This made Mara even angrier. "How was I supposed to know it? You never said so." Her voice grew softer as she thought about the implications of her husband's words. "You never said so."

Joel was still angry. "I thought it was obvious, and I didn't want to pressure you . . . to scare you. But I am tired of waiting, and I need to know now if you think you can ever love me. Or is my hope entirely in vain?"

Mara had to sit down. He loved her. He had always loved her. Not just as his family. How could she have been so utterly stupid? She had always prided herself on her perception.

She looked at the man in front of her, slightly blurry through her tears. The man she loved. Who loved her in return.

She realized that she had been wrong, about so many things.

Mara stood up with a gasp, and smiled at her husband blindingly. "Joel," she began, timidly.

Then, to her horror, Joel was on the ground in front of her. "Mara," he started.

"No," she said, panicking. "Do not kneel to me. Get up, Joel."

Joel shook his head, but could not resist a wry smile. "You had better appreciate it while it lasts, for I do not think I will be able to manage it again."

Mara gave him a watery smile, but her smile faded as he spoke.

"Mara, I love you. I have loved you for years, maybe since I first saw you, when you ran into me chasing that ridiculous bird. I love you more than my life. I will love you until I die. I love you more than anything in this universe, except Yahweh alone. Do you understand now?"

Mara would have felt like a fool, had she not been so happy. She pulled at Joel's arms, urging him to rise. "I am so sorry," she whispered. "I love you, too. For so long, I have loved you. I was just too scared to tell you."

Joel looked as if Yahweh had suddenly granted his greatest desire. She thought, with a thrill, maybe Yahweh had. "But why?" he asked. "Why would you be afraid to tell me anything?"

"I won't be again," Mara murmured. "Ever."

He bent down to kiss her, and Mara realized that Yahweh had given her the one thing she had thought she lacked—a life with a man she loved.

PART IV

VANITY OF VANITIES

"What has been will be again,
what has been done will be done again;
there is nothing new under the sun.
Is there anything of which one can say,
'Look! This is something new'?
It was here already, long ago;
it was here before our time."

Ecclesiastes 1:9-10

Chapter 20

Mara rose when she heard Sarah crying, and she left her lyre under the trees of the courtyard. She thanked Yahweh, as she walked back into the house, that he had finally given her a daughter. She loved her four boys fiercely, but she had hoped that her fifth child would be a girl.

Ephrath had already consoled the infant, but she handed her over to her mother. Ephrath was sixteen years old now, and in only a few months, her time of service would be over. But Ephrath had already made clear to Mara that she did not wish to be released. She would have her ear pierced, she said, and become her bondservant for the rest of her life.

Mara had tried to talk Ephrath out of it, but the young woman was adamant. "My life is to be spent serving you. What could be more worthy?"

Mara had been touched, and she admired the humility in the girl and her spirit of servant hood. It was a spirit that Mara had been working on for years. They were all to be servants of Yahweh, and it was hard, sometimes, for Mara to adapt her own will to that of Yahweh's.

She kissed Sarah gently, and smiled lovingly at Ephrath. "She still will not sleep?"

Ephrath shook her head. "She seems determined to see everything that happens."

Joel had taken the two older boys, Jedidiah, who was six years old, and Samuel, who was five, with him to visit the temple. The building had been up for two years, and the craftsmen were nearly completed with the interior. Samuel had declared proudly that he wanted to be a goldsmith when he grew up after Joel had taken them to see the work on the temple the first time. Joel said that their son would station himself wherever the master goldsmith was working and not move until Joel dragged him away. Mara smiled at the thought.

Jedidiah, however, had proved to have a great talent with words. Joel had taught Mara to read before the children were born, and Mara had been diligent in teaching them. Joel had chanced to mention Jedidiah's talent to Solomon, and Solomon suggested they send the boy to the school for scribes he had instituted in the palace when Jedidiah was old enough.

The two younger boys, Benjamin and Eleazar, were playing in the courtyard, pretending they were soldiers like their father.

The afternoon was drawing to a close, and soon Joel would return with Jedidiah and Samuel. Rachel, who was still in their service, was working on the evening meal, and Mara went to help.

Mara heard the boys as soon as they came in. "Mother, mother," they cried, running to greet her. "It is finished. The temple is finished."

Mara looked at her dark-haired boys. She remembered when she had first given birth to Jedidiah. The boy had the dark hair and eyes and strong features of his father. Mara had sighed, "Where am I in him?" she had asked her husband, wistfully.

"You are in his spirit," Joel had replied.

The three other boys, it was clear from the day they were born, would also look just like their father. So Mara had been shocked when her daughter had arrived with blue eyes. Sarah's hair was dark, but her eyes were undeniably blue.

"It is completed?" she asked her sons.

"Yes, and the master goldsmith said he would miss me, and that if I wanted I could come be his apprentice." Samuel looked as if he would burst with the news.

Mara looked up at Joel, who had come to join them. "But I thought he was a Tyrian. He is not thinking about taking Samuel back to Tyre with him?"

"Certainly not," Joel said with a chuckle, tousling the boy's hair. "He is staying in Jerusalem to work on the king's palace. He will be here for many years."

"When will the temple be dedicated?" Mara wanted to know.

"At the feast of the Tabernacle," Joel answered, "Still several months away."

Mara nodded, thinking with a twinge, about Solomon. She was sure that the construction of the temple had occupied most of his time for the last seven years. Something significant to pour his gifts and resources into. It was finished now, and she couldn't help but wonder how he was feeling.

When the feast of the Tabernacle finally arrived, all the people of Israel who could come crowded into Jerusalem. On the day that the priests and Levites were to move the ark from Gibeon, a huge crowd gathered near the temple, on the enormous site that would later be Solomon's palace.

Solomon had extended Jerusalem considerably to the north. And his palace was, from what Mara had learned from Joel, to be even greater in size than the temple.

A platform had been built especially for the dedication, but all of the room in the temple grounds was filled with the heads of the tribes of Israel, the chiefs of the Israelite families, the palace officials and other very important men in the kingdom. The rest of the onlookers were forced onto the palace foundation, but most of them could still see the platform.

The three younger children had been dismayed at being left at home with Ephrath, but Joel had been insistent, and only the two older boys stood with Joel and Mara among the masses of people.

The crowd, amazingly, silenced when the procession came into sight. The ark was brought into the temple with solemnity, and sheep and cattle were sacrificed one after another. For a time, the stench of blood and the squealing of dying animals were all that Mara was conscious of. She felt a little dizzy and reached out to Joel for support.

He looked down at her, concerned. He knew what blood did to her.

But once the animals started to burn and the odor of roasting meat filled the air surrounding the temple, Mara was able to focus again.

She was grateful because she would have hated to miss what happened next. When everyone had withdrawn from the temple, a cloud filled the building.

A cloud. Everyone knew what it meant. A cloud, just as there had been a cloud in the tabernacle as they had journeyed through the desert. Yahweh's presence among them. Mara was conscious that the extent to which the sight moved her testified to how much she had made this people's history her own.

After a long silence, Solomon walked up to the platform. Mara could barely see him—a straight figure, elegantly dressed—but fortunately the crowd remained quiet enough for her to hear his voice.

The king blessed the people who had gathered to see this great day. "Praise be to the Lord, the God of Israel, who with his own hand has fulfilled what he promised to my father David."

A woman behind her pushed into Mara, and Mara almost lost her balance as Solomon continued. She felt Joel's hands steady her, and she moved closer to him, listening as Solomon spoke. "The Lord has kept the promise he made: I have succeeded David my father and now I sit on the throne of Israel, just as the Lord promised, and I have built the temple for the Name of the Lord, the God of Israel. I have provided a place there for the ark, in which is the covenant of the Lord that he made with our fathers when he brought them out of Egypt."

The crowd cheered them, in recognition of Solomon's accomplishment, and his father's vision, but mostly out of praise to the God that had done so much for them.

Mara didn't cheer. She had only spoken to Solomon one time since he had come to eat with her and Joel, before any of the children were born. And that had been at a banquet, a formal setting—certainly not an opportunity for sharing or honesty.

Seeing him at that banquet had hurt her, in a way she could barely articulate. He had changed so much over the years, perhaps not in the ways that mattered, but in all the ways that Mara could see. He was bored with the conversation, with the laughter, and with the excitement around him. He had spoken harshly to the serving girls, something he had never done in his youth. And there had been something cold in his eyes when he looked at her.

"It has been a long time, Mara," he had said, pausing in front of her as he circulated around the room.

"Yes," she had answered, "A very long time indeed."

"Congratulations of the birth of your children. May Yahweh bless them." There had been two children at the time, and Mara had thanked him for the notice.

And that had been all. It was not that she had expected anything serious or intimate, but he had not even smiled at her.

She supposed, thinking back to that moment, while the hoards of people cheered around her, she could understand why he had acted the way he did. Coldness was a protection when fires threatened to consume you. She understood that concept very well.

And in Solomon's position, he could not afford to have anything consume him.

When the crowds finally silenced, Solomon raised his arms to pray. His prayer was full of love and awe, and the sense of his own smallness before Yahweh. "But will God really dwell on earth? The heavens, even the highest heaven, cannot contain you. How much less this temple I have built!" A sincere prayer, Mara could tell. And from his heart. With nothing of the forced coldness she had witness in him the evening four years ago.

He asked for forgiveness for his nation and the mercy that they knew characterized the God of Israel, making him different from every other god Mara had ever encountered.

When Solomon finished the prayer, he stood up and said, "May the Lord our God be with us as he was with our fathers; may he never leave us nor forsake us. May we turn our hearts to him, to walk in all his ways and to keep his commands, decrees and regulations he gave our fathers."

Solomon, on the platform, had kissed her in a curtain alcove, many years ago. It was hard to imagine that now. Hard even to find the uncertain boy in the king who stood before the nation. He was sophisticated and confident and infinitely wise. But he was sincere in his love for Yahweh and in his humility, and he continued to speak. "And may these words of mine, which I have prayed before the Lord, be near to the Lord our God day and night, that he may uphold the cause of his servant and the cause of his people Israel according to each day's need, so that all the peoples of the earth may know that the Lord is God and that there is no other."

Mara joined the people in saying "Amen."

She repeated to herself, "All the peoples of the earth may know that the Lord is God and that there is no other." And the words brought back an old ache, as she thought of her father, and Brant, and Elsa, who had never known him.

She prayed then, for the people of her island, if any of them remained, after the bloody summer night when the stars shone so brightly they ached. And she prayed, despite the sick feeling in her stomach, for the people on the mainland, who had betrayed her island to their destruction. And she prayed, as well, for the tribe that had kidnapped her and Elsa, and for Danel, the Tyrian trader who had bought her. She prayed for them all, and was surprised to realize that she really wanted for them all to know Yahweh and find the peace that she had found.

She could forgive them all—finally—after all the years she had hated them. There was little hate left in her, some sort of miracle that had happened while she was distracted by the joys and hassles of her family.

Nothing, she thought, really, left to hate.

An image came to her then, of Bathsheba's lovely, still-hated face. She tried to shake it away—she couldn't.

Bathsheba she could still hate, when she looked at the king standing on the dais. Bathsheba she would always hate.

Mara opened her eyes and saw Joel looking at her strangely. "Everything all right?" he asked, holding a hand of each of their sons.

Mara nodded, struggling to smile up at the man she loved. "Yes, everything is fine." But she couldn't get the picture of Bathsheba out of her mind.

Israel celebrated for two weeks. On the second day, Joel and Mara were astonished to be summoned to the presence of the king.

Mara had been thinking about Solomon more and more, worrying about him. There was a good deal of sorrow involved in her thinking, and a good deal of guilt. So when she and Joel received the message, she felt something clutch inside her throat.

They went to the palace immediately, and were not led, as they had been expecting, into the throne room, but into a private sitting room. Solomon was lounging on a low chaise. He rose gracefully when they entered.

"My dear friends," he greeted them. "It has been too long since I have seen you." His words were to both of them, but his eyes were on Mara.

He embraced Joel, and then he embraced Mara. His touch brought back memories, tenderness even, but nothing of desire. Mara noted that fact, and she saw that Solomon did as well.

"You were at the dedication of the temple?" he asked.

"Of course," Joel responded, shaking his head. "We are loyal Israelites. We would hardly miss it."

"The temple is everything it should be, isn't it?" The words seemed strangely uncertain, coming from the powerful, urbane man in front of them.

Joel chuckled. "Nothing man could create on earth could be worthy of Yahweh's greatness, but it is everything that human hands could make it."

Solomon's handsome face—still more handsome than any man Mara had ever seen—was relaxed, but there was an emptiness to his incandescent eyes that worried her.

"Your father would be so proud," Mara said, wishing, even as the words came out, that she hadn't said them.

"My father would be jealous. He always wanted to build the temple himself. But, because of the blood on his hands, it was left for me. Ironic, isn't it?"

"What is?" Joel asked. Mara already knew what he meant.

"That it is the greatest thing I will do in my entire reign, and I have my father to thank for it." Bitterness, even more than Mara had remembered.

"You have Yahweh to thank for it," Joel corrected, turning around Solomon's words.

Solomon nodded. "You are right," he agreed, his face transforming. "You are right, as you always are, Joel." He turned to Mara then. "I will build my palace now. The architects say that it will take even longer to complete than the temple did."

"Why?" Mara asked him.

He understood what her question really was, and, because the wisdom that could search into the hearts of others could certainly search out his own, he was honest. "I have to do something."

Mara turned to look at her husband, and she saw sadness in his eyes, which mirrored her own. She wondered if there was anything she could say to Solomon that would make any sort of difference.

As it turned out, she wasn't given the chance. Embracing them again, Solomon led them to the door. "Do not worry about me," he chided them, his old, sincere smile illuminating his face. "Don't forget, I am the wisest man alive today . . . and"—his smile faded—"perhaps the greatest fool."

Shortly after the festival, Joel came home one night with some news. He waited until the children were in bed to tell it. "Solomon has married again."

This was not unusual news, but Joel knew that it was something Mara would want to hear.

Mara shook her head and didn't even ask who it was, "How many is it now?" she asked wearily.

"If you can believe it, I have lost track." Joel sat down on a stool next to their bed, while Mara washed herself behind her screen.

"It is too many," Mara muttered. "What god does this one worship?"

"She is Sidonian; she would probably worship Melquart."

"Why doesn't Solomon stop his wives from worshipping false gods?" Mara asked, though it was not a new question. "It sets such a bad example. Even after the great festival to Yahweh, even after the sincerity of his prayer and the glory of the temple, he still does not put a stop to it."

"The last time I saw him," Joel began, "Right after he called us to see him, I got enough courage to say something about it."

Mara came out from behind the screen. "And?" she prompted.

Joel shrugged. "He looked genuinely surprised and said it would be cruel to take them away from their homes and not allow them to worship their own gods, even if they are false. He said that he hopes they will come to worship Yahweh as he does."

176

Mara sat down on the bed and sighed. "I suppose he thinks that is the generous thing to do. But it is so foolish. How can he be so foolish?"

"He has not been as blessed as I have," Joel said, coming to take Mara in his arms.

Mara pulled away from him. "No," she said gravely. "He has not."

Joel raised Mara to her feet. "I will not allow you to do that," he said sternly. "You cannot blame yourself for Solomon's mistakes."

Mara was newly surprised by her husband's perceptiveness. "But he loved me. He wanted to marry me. I think he still loves me." The thought was somehow saddening.

"He does," Joel affirmed. "But that does not make his actions your fault. He chooses his own way."

"But I could have helped him. He would have been happy with me, and maybe, somehow, I could have stopped him from his foolishness."

"I think you take too much upon yourself. How do you know he would have been happy with you," he said, almost cruelly. "He would still have had his other wives. He would not have married only you."

"But I would have tried to keep him happy. Maybe I could have. If he was happy, he would not try so hard to find things to satisfy him. Can you really tell me that he would be the same man he is now if he had been able to marry the woman he loved?" Mara's voice reached out to Joel, unconsciously hoping for some reassurance.

He had little to give. He opened his mouth to speak, but stopped. He shook his head. "No, honestly I cannot tell you that. But how do you know that you could have done something? Everything might have worked out the same way, and you both would have been miserable. Not to mention myself." His smile was wry.

Mara seated herself again on the bed, and she buried her face in her hands. "But I still feel guilty. I am so happy. I love someone else. And Solomon is . . ."

"Responsible for his own actions. He has to face Yahweh with his sins, just as you do for yours. But refusing to marry Solomon is not one of your sins." Joel sat down next to her, turning her toward him. "Do you regret marrying me?" he asked.

His lips were smiling, but there was a little uncertainty in his eyes.

Mara reached out to touch his beard. "How can you even ask such a thing? Marrying you was one of the wisest things I did in my life. And I didn't even know it at the time."

"Mara," Joel murmured. "Listen to me. Had you married Solomon, there would be three people miserable. Because Solomon's actions, despite your vanity," he smiled to relieve the sting of his remark, "are not solely out of a love he was denied. There have been too many things that have made the man what he is, and only one of them is his love for you. There is no doubt of Solomon's love of Yahweh, but he has many things to work through before he finds peace. I pray one day he will."

Mara nodded, accepting Joel's assessment of the situation, because she knew, in her heart, that it was the truth. "I pray for him, too. May Yahweh bring him, one day, to stand in the light of His glory in peace."

Chapter 21

Each year that passed marked further progress on Solomon's palace. On the seventh year of its construction, people commented on how it had taken only seven years to build the temple. How much longer would Solomon work on his own palace?

They were still asking that seven years later when it was completed.

Solomon's fame had grown, as had his wealth and his wisdom. Emissaries came from every country around, bringing gifts and seeking knowledge of the king wiser than any other man.

Caravans arrived, just after the palace was completed, from the land of Sheba, far to the south. Nobody knew exactly how far away the land of Sheba was. The issue was taken up at the city gates, and never finally settled. But the general view was that the caravan had been traveling for more than two years.

The most popular place to be, in the days when the caravan arrived, was right outside the city wall, watching the procession make its way into Jerusalem. Each hour brought new wonders to see. Long rows of camels carrying gold and spices and gems, wagons filled with silk and ivory, and the litter of the queen herself, who had traveled for months to find out for herself who this king was who had made such a name for himself.

Mara, watching the procession with her children, could not help but feel a little awed. It was Solomon who had done this for Israel; Yahweh had used Solomon single-handedly to form Israel into the great power it was.

The queen of Sheba's coming was celebrated with a huge banquet, to which Joel, who had moved up in the ranks of the army until he was second only to Benaiah, and his wife were invited.

"But I want to go too," Sarah complained. She was fifteen years old now—certainly old enough to marry. She was beautiful, with her mother's features and blue eyes, and her father's curly brown hair and wide grin. Many men had come in pursuit of her hand in marriage. But she was their only daughter, and Joel was being very picky about who would marry her.

Mara, who was in no hurry to lose her daughter, was glad of her husband's procrastination.

"I'm sorry, dear, but you cannot go." She hated denying her daughter anything, but some things had to be accepted.

"But Jedidiah and Samuel are going," Sarah complained, working at a knot in her weaving.

"You know Jedidiah is a scribe, and he always goes to the king's banquets. And Samuel is invited because he did so much work on the king's palace." Mara's voice was patient, but she secretly pitied the girl. It would be terrible to be left behind. "Benjamin and Eleazar are not going either," Mara reminded Sarah.

"Benjamin is so excited about his marriage that he doesn't care about anything."

Mara smiled at the thought of her son, who had recently married a lovely girl. Soon she would have grandchildren. Who would have thought?

"Mother," Sarah began.

Mara interrupted her. "No more, Sarah. The decision is not up to me anyway. You were not invited."

Sarah silenced under this indisputable fact.

"Tamar is coming over to visit you," Mara continued. "You always enjoy that. She is not invited either." Deborah and Caleb's daughter was two years younger than Sarah, and the two girls had always been best friends.

"Yes," said Sarah, cheered by the thought.

Ephrath came in then, and told Mara that she best start bathing in preparation for the banquet.

This sent Sarah into another fit of depression.

Solomon's palace was at least four times larger than his father's had been, and it towered over the skyline of the city. Mara had not been in the palace, however, until she and Joel arrived for the feast.

The feast was to last for several days, but she knew they would not stay that long. Joel took her hand as they were led through the cedar halls and marble covered floors into the banquet area. The room was enormous, and it needed to be because hundreds of people were invited to the feast.

A table was set on the dais for the king, Mara assumed, and his guest of honor, the queen of Sheba. Behind the table was Solomon's throne.

Very little in Mara's life had made her sadder than the sight of Solomon's throne. It was extraordinary. Gold and ivory, with steps leading up to it. On both sides of each step was a sculptured lion, and beside the armrests were two more lions. Fourteen lions, as lifelike as statues can be, staring down at the assembled people from the empty throne. The throne, a symbol of Solomon's power, wealth, and greatness, made Mara want to cry.

Mara looked over at Joel. Her husband's face was lined now, and his hair was graying, but his smile still covered her heart and his touch made her tremble.

He raised his eyebrows. "Quite a place, isn't it?"

Mara rolled her eyes. "I should certainly hope so after fourteen years of construction."

"That's quite a throne."

Mara shook her head, and she couldn't respond to her husband's comment.

The conversation stopped as three mute taps proclaimed the king's entrance into the room. It was a strange way for the king of Israel, who had built himself this splendid palace, to announce himself. It seemed so understated and quiet. One would expect blaring trumpets and ringing voices, but Solomon had always used the three taps of a staff on the marble floor. It was not as though, Mara thought with a sigh, he needed a great noise for people to notice his arrival. Solomon was hardly a man that people could ignore.

He entered now with the queen of Sheba on his arm, but, as always, Mara did not see his companion.

He had aged like they all had, but gracefully, and the silver streak in his hair only made him more debonair. He raised an elegant hand, greeting his guests, and waited until the queen of Sheba had seated herself before he sunk into his throne.

He still grasped the sides of his throne as if someone would snatch him out of it.

Mara turned to her husband in the noise of the banquet hall, and she saw Joel looking at her sadly.

"You would think he would be proud of his palace," she commented.

Joel glanced back at the king. "What makes you think that he is not?"

Mara gave her husband an exasperated look. "Surely you can see his face, even from here. He is so tired. After he completed the temple, he was radiant. It was something he had accomplished that he could be proud of, but this . . ." She waved her hand around to take in the banquet, the room, the entire palace. "He should know by now, in all his wisdom, that this is not the way to achieve happiness."

Joel agreed, but he said nothing.

Mara studied the queen of Sheba, when she finally turned her attention to the honored guest.

The woman was very dark and handsome; she looked about Mara's own age. She was dressed rather strangely, in fabric that shimmered when she moved. Her arms were almost completely covered with bracelets, and she had several gold chains around her neck.

"What do you think?" Joel whispered, seeing her observation of the queen.

Mara tilted her head. "I do not know. She is too unreadable."

Joel seemed to agree. "She has come for several reasons. I do not know what the primary reason is. Probably she seeks to establish trade with Israel."

"Now that seems rather practical for you, my love. I would prefer to think she came out of genuine curiosity and desire to see a king as splendid as Solomon."

Joel chuckled at his wife's sally. "Very well. Solomon's fame has traveled so far it would not be impossible. I only wish his obedience to Yahweh increased with his wisdom and his power and his fame."

Mara's face saddened, and Joel seemed to regret his abrupt change of conversation. To remedy the fact, he leaned toward Mara. "Isn't it amazing," he said.

"What?"

"That you are still the most beautiful woman in the room, even at your exalted age, even with the adorable lines next to your eyes, even with the gray hairs that I caught you looking at yesterday." Joel's eyes crinkled up, and Mara, forgetting where she was, reached to touch her husband's face.

One would not think—in a room that large, with so many varied and important people present, with the queen of a large, rich nation sitting beside him—that Solomon would have noticed a gesture that small from a slave girl he had once known.

But he did.

Mara looked up and saw him gazing at the two of them. But one thing Solomon had learned over the years was to guard his face, and his expression, even his eyes, were vacant.

Chapter 22

Little Solomon did surprised Mara anymore, and she was certainly not surprised when an attendant stopped her and her husband on their way out of the palace, explaining, with downcast eyes, that the king requested their presence.

Mara met Joel's eyes, and they followed the scarlet-liveried attendant through the rich hallways to one of the king's sitting rooms.

Solomon rose from his chair gracefully, and he smiled at her coolly. "Thank you for coming," he said.

"As if we would refuse," Joel responded, slightly amused.

Solomon shrugged slightly. "Yes, I suppose that is true." He walked over to the other side of the room, and it was only then that Mara noticed they were not alone in the room. The queen of Sheba was lounging in the corner of the room, her golden gown falling in folds around her dark body.

"I asked King Solomon if I could meet you." She was speaking to Mara. "I saw you from the dais and was curious."

"I am honored by your curiosity, but I'm afraid there is little about me to interest you," Mara responded. Surprised, and a little awkward about the situation. It had been a long time since she had been anything other than a wife and mother. She was no longer a foreigner to the people in Jerusalem.

Sheba didn't rise from her position. She just stared at Mara, smiling enigmatically.

Mara looked over at Solomon. His eyebrows were raised slightly. "It seems she was curious about your origins. It is your hair, again, you know."

"And did you tell her?" Mara asked.

"Of course not," Solomon replied. "I would not be so bold." Mara had rarely heard this tone of voice from Solomon. It was cool and suave, slightly condescending. She had known he had this side to his personality, but he had never shown it to her before.

Mara glanced over at her husband. His lips were pressed tightly together. She knew that he was offended with Solomon for using his wife so blatantly as an object of curiosity. But what could he do? Solomon was the king, after all. And there had been no direct offense.

Mara turned back to the eastern queen. A little recklessly, she seated herself without permission on a low stool near the queen's reclining bench. "I am from a country far to the north," she began.

Sheba leaned forward slightly. "From the lands where the druids are?"

Mara gave a little start. The queen knew more than she would have expected. "No, the tribes that have druids as holy men were to the south of us. We were even farther north. We did not live in tribes. In my homeland, all the villages were united under one rule, and they worked together for trade and war. Our village, like the other villages on our island just off the mainland, would not unite with the others. So we were destroyed."

Sheba nodded slowly. "And so you were taken as a slave?"

"Yes, by a tribe to the south of us, although different tribes than the ones with druids. That tribe traded me to a Phoenician trader, who sent me as a gift to the king's father, David. That is why I came to Israel, and a few years later Joel married me."

"I see. You must tell me about the lands you traveled through." Mara raised a corner of her mouth. "There is little to tell."

"Now we know that is not true," Solomon interrupted, "for you have told me quite a bit about it."

Mara looked at Solomon accusingly. Why was he allowing her to be used in this way? Why should she have to bring up all of these old memories, just when she was starting to put them to rest?

She looked over at Joel. His face was getting more and more menacing.

"Why have you come to Israel?" Mara asked suddenly, to the queen. Inappropriate, of course, but at the moment she hardly cared.

Sheba chuckled. "News of Solomon's wisdom had reached me in my country, and I had to make the journey to see if the stories were true."

This was a lie. Mara knew it as much as Solomon must know it. But she played along. "And have you found them to be true?"

Sheba shook her head. "No, I haven't." Mara heard Solomon suck in his breath. A small thing, but it gave more away than Solomon was in the habit of giving. The queen continued. "The stories haven't done justice to the wisdom I have found in Solomon. And, you should know, I am a collector of wise men. It is a thing I know about."

Solomon gave a little bow of acknowledgment to the compliment, and laughed softly. "Perhaps you came to find wisdom, but it is I who have been graced with your companionship."

Sheba rose from her reclining bench. "Will you come with me to my chambers?" she asked Mara. "There is something I would like to show you."

Mara looked a little startled and glanced back at Joel. She couldn't read his expression, so she turned to Solomon. "Do go," he encouraged. "I will chat with your husband until you return."

Mara nodded, hesitantly. The queen led her down a few halls and they entered a huge suite of rooms, decorated in gold and scarlet silk.

"What is it that you want to show me?" Mara asked when they arrived.

"Oh nothing," the queen said. "I just wanted to talk to you privately. The men were getting in the way of our conversation."

"Really?" Mara responded. "I hadn't noticed."

Sheba sat down and motioned for Mara to do so as well. "Tell me about your relationship with the king."

"What?" Mara exclaimed. "There is nothing to tell. He is the king." This was not the conversation she wanted to be having.

"Nonsense," Sheba said with a wave of her ringed hand. "I saw the look he gave you in the throne room. He is in love with you, isn't he?"

This was getting to be a very dangerous discussion. Mara wondered how she should handle it. "Maybe once," she said at last. "When I lived in the palace. Maybe he thought he was in love with me." She knew the words did not do justice to Solomon's feelings for her; she knew his love for her went deeper than most of the strains of his life. But she could hardly say that to this foreign queen.

Sheba rose and walked over to a small side table. She took a gilded box and held it out to Mara. "Have one," she offered. "It is a candy from my country. You will never taste anything like it in your life."

Eager to do something with her hands, Mara took one of the pale, sticky candies. She tasted it, and couldn't help but voice her delight. Sweet, rich, melting. Indeed, never had she tasted anything quite as delectable. "Delicious. Thank you."

"So," Sheba prompted. "Solomon might have been in love with you once. Years ago. But he still looks as though he might kill himself when he watches you with your husband."

"Don't be ridiculous. He looked nothing like that," Mara said scornfully. This woman was really too perceptive to be comfortable with.

Sheba nodded. "Yes, that is true. The king guards his expressions. But one can read him just the same. For when nothing affects him emotionally, he doesn't have to hide himself. It is only when he is hurt that he has to be careful. And I have never seen his expression so guarded as it was when he was watching you and your husband. He was very, very hurt."

Mara turned away from the woman's dark eyes. She knew Solomon was hurt. It was something she had learned to live with. But it didn't seem fair to have it stated so blatantly, so clearly. "He is hurt from many things. There is no reason to assume that it is me."

"I agree with that," the queen granted. "But there is something about you that makes his hurt worse."

Mara could not keep on discussing this issue. Yahweh had healed her in so many ways, made her happier than she had ever dreamed she could be. But there were still some things, even after all these years, that she couldn't stand to think of. One of them was the love that Solomon felt, still felt, for her.

"So why did you really come to Israel?" she asked abruptly. "And don't tell me any stories about being curious about Solomon's wisdom."

Sheba chuckled, not at all startled by the turn of the conversation. "Actually, that is partly the truth. I did hear many things about the wisdom of the king of Israel. I was interested in seeing for myself if it is true."

"But what is the real reason?" Mara prompted.

"Does there have to be just one reason? I will admit, I also heard about the riches and the wealth of the king of Israel. I heard about the ships he sends out all over the world, about the tribute countries send him, about the wealth he amasses. He is the kind of partner I could use in trade. It is not so easy to get furs and diamonds where I am from in the East."

Mara nodded. This sounded more realistic.

"And I also heard about this god that the king serves, about the temple he built for this god, and the things that this god has done. And I am interested in learning more about him."

Mara smiled. "And that may be the best reason of them all to make the journey."

The queen smiled back at Mara, and for just a moment, there was a kind of bonding between the two women—between the queen of an exotic eastern country and the wife of a soldier, a former slave girl.

"And what have you learned about Yahweh?" Mara asked, when the moment had passed.

Sheba took one of the candies she had offered to Mara. She thought for several minutes before she spoke. "I can see what your Yahweh has done for this country. Not so long ago, it was only a collection of tribes, barely surviving in the face of attacks from the surrounding countries. And now, it is one of the most powerful presences in this part of the world. Solomon is certainly one of the most rich and powerful kings in the world today. If your god has done all that, he must be powerful indeed."

"He is," Mara affirmed.

"And I have witnessed Solomon's wisdom first-hand. I ask him impossible questions, and he answers them effortlessly. He says that his wisdom is a gift from Yahweh, a gift that he asked for specifically. If your god can give him this wisdom, your god must be wiser than any of the gods we worship."

Mara was silent, watching the play of emotions on the face of the woman beside her.

"For his power and his wisdom, I will worship Yahweh. He will be added to the other gods in our temples."

Mara shook her head. "But Yahweh does not deserve to be placed along other gods. For Yahweh is the only god. If you worship Yahweh, you cannot worship any other gods."

"That is what the king was trying to tell me. But it doesn't seem reasonable for a foreign god to replace all the gods that we have worshipped for centuries. Surely you can't expect that."

Mara rose from her seat. "It is not what I expect. It is what Yahweh deserves. For he is the only true god."

Sheba rose as well. "I don't understand," she said, pushing off the subject with a shrug.

Mara could see that she didn't.

The two women returned to the sitting room where Joel and Solomon were waiting. Solomon's face was distant and masked, and Joel looked worried.

"We were talking about the glories of your reign," Sheba said to Solomon as the men rose. "How single-handedly, you made Israel what it is today." Her voice was throaty, and her gaze admiring. Mara wondered what exactly her intentions for Solomon were.

Solomon chuckled. "Well, not single-handedly. It was my father who defeated all our enemies. Otherwise, I would have to be worrying about who would attack us next. Instead, I can put all my energy into making Israel greater than it is."

"And it is Yahweh," Joel put in, "Who has given us everything we have."

Solomon nodded slowly. "Yes, he has." The king turned to look at Mara. His dark eyes were so blank, that she wondered if he were even seeing her. "So, how will it feel to return now to your little house in the city after spending an evening in the palace talking to kings and queens?"

Cruel words, and Mara raised her chin indignantly. "I will be as happy as I have always been with the family Yahweh has blessed me with."

She wished, after she spoke the words, that she had not said them. For just a second, she saw pain raw in Solomon's eyes. She had intended to wound Solomon with the words, and she was ashamed. Much of Solomon's pain was of his own doing, but he didn't need her to add anything to it.

"A blessing indeed," Solomon said softly. "Perhaps even comparable to a palace, and a throne, and a treasure-house filled with riches."

"Perhaps," Sheba said skeptically. "But what kind of comfort is family, if you have nothing?'

"And what kind of comfort is gold if you are alone?" Solomon was no longer guarded, and he had to turn his back to them.

Mara wanted to cry—even more so, after she looked at Joel's face, which was filled with compassion.

The queen looked delighted at having seen Solomon in weakness. "A very interesting night, indeed," she commented, to no one in particular.

"We must go, your majesty," Joel said, raising his voice. "You have honored us by requesting our company."

Solomon turned back to face them, and smiled graciously—a smile that did not reach his eyes. "The honor, as always, is mine."

Joel and Mara bowed to the king, and then to the queen of Sheba, and they left the palace.

"What did you and Solomon talk about?" Mara asked, as they left the palace grounds.

Joel laughed, a little bitterly. He was not a bitter man. "What did we talk about? Let's see. We talked about the stallions he had just acquired, and the chariots he has commissioned to be built, and the new architect from Tyre who will arrive at the palace next week."

Mara understood the frustration in his voice. "Should we even try to get through to him? Should we keep trying, after all these years."

Joel shrugged. "We can keep praying. And wait for the opportunities that Yahweh opens up for us. Solomon is in Yahweh's hands, and Yahweh loves him. Leave it up to him." Joel paused for a moment. "And what did you discuss with the queen of Sheba?"

"My relationship with Solomon, her reasons for coming to Israel, and the worship of Yahweh," Mara responded. It was her turn to pause. "Do you suppose she is in love with Solomon?"

Joel looked a little surprised. "It is possible, I suppose. He is a very magnetic man."

"Yes, and wise, and powerful, and attractive, and charming. I would be surprised if she were not in love with him. But if she is, it is not the kind of love I understand. Rather, it is about the give and take of power." Mara shrugged helplessly.

Joel grinned a little. "So, are you going to be happy going back to your little house after spending an evening in the palace talking to kings and queens?"

Mara reached up to touch his beard. "I thank Yahweh every other second for making me as happy as I am." And for the first time that evening, she knew that what she said was the absolute truth.

Chapter 23

There was a time, Mara thought glumly, when she could have handled this evening's difficulties without a thought, without even a momentary hesitation. Hiding her feelings and schooling her expressions had been her life, and leaving herself vulnerable by showing how she felt would have been incomprehensible. But that was years ago, and the life she was living had softened her, left her out of practice.

For, in the life she led now, there was no reason for her to try to keep anything she was feeling to herself. She knew Joel would never hurt her, and even had she tried to hide something from him, he knew her well enough after so much time that it would have been a futile effort. She could still, successfully, smile politely at an acquaintance's irritating ramblings or compliment a friend's new piece of furniture that may not be exactly her own taste, but that was the extent of her masking.

Which is why she was finding it so hard not to show her dislike of the young man sitting across from her.

She had tried not to smile at the man's surprise when Joel had introduced him to her. She was aware that she was no longer young and her waist was not as slim as it had been in her youth, but she knew that she was still an attractive woman. Her hair was silvering in places, but the gold still was striking among the darker people of Israel. The young man's reaction to being introduced to her reinforced this knowledge. She couldn't help but be pleased, and she saw the satisfaction on Joel's face as well. The pride, she knew, was to their shame, but there was something about this young man that provoked in her a strong desire to keep him in his place.

She couldn't quite figure out why she felt this way about him. He was tall and well formed, with neat features and fine dark hair that seemed permanently set in sleek waves. He smiled readily and often, and he had overcome his awkwardness at their introduction with admirable speed.

But she couldn't bring herself to like Jeroboam, son of Nebat, the Ephraimite.

He and Joel were talking enthusiastically about the building project Jeroboam was working on. Jeroboam had been among the men conscripted by Solomon from the tribe Ephraim to work on the wall around Jerusalem. Joel had told Mara that the young man did his work so well that Solomon had put him in charge of all the forced labor for both the tribes of Ephraim and Manasseh. It was quite an accomplishment for a man of Jeroboam's age.

If Solomon had recognized such qualities in the man, and if Joel was ready to affirm these qualities by inviting him over to their home, there was no reason for Mara to distrust Jeroboam.

It was something about his eyes, Mara thought as she watched him scoop a mouthful of lentil soup out of the clay bowl. He kept meticulous eye contact with Joel the whole time, his eyes never wavering down to his food or around the dimly lit room. Only occasionally would he look over at Mara—enough to let her know she was part of the conversation, but not enough to let Joel think that Jeroboam's attention was on his wife.

But despite the correctness of his gaze, there was something about Jeroboam's green eyes that Mara didn't like. They displayed a wide range of emotions—amusement, sympathy, excitement—but the emotions didn't seem to spring spontaneously from somewhere inside Jeroboam's soul. It was all so calculated. Every word, every glance, every gesture thought through and intended for a specific purpose. What that purpose could be, Mara didn't know. She didn't even know if her feelings were accurate or fair.

But she had to struggle to keep a smile on her face as she listened politely to the men's discussion.

Apparently, her struggle was unsuccessful, for Joel fixed her with an intense stare. She knew what he was telling her. "Be polite. The man is our guest."

Jeroboam pushed his bowl back from the edge of the table and leaned back a little. "The meal was excellent," he said to Mara.

Mara smiled and thanked him for the compliment. He had already praised the food earlier in the meal, after he took his first bite. But two compliments were not too much for one meal—in fact, it was just the right number. This man made no mistakes.

"Shall we move out to the courtyard?" Joel asked. "It is a beautiful night."

Jeroboam assented, and all three of them rose.

"You have a daughter still living at home?" Jeroboam asked, a casual question, with no urgency in the words.

Mara couldn't stop the quick, sharp breath that escaped her. Absolutely not! She was not fooled by the calculated disinterest in his voice. This man was not the man she would give her daughter to, not a man who could even be considered.

"Yes, but Sarah is visiting a friend this evening," Joel responded, with his deep, sincere smile.

"No, no, no!" Mara said silently, to herself. The men left the dining room, and Mara remained to remove the dishes.

But momentarily, Joel returned, alone.

"No!" Mara said aloud.

Joel's thick eyebrows shot up.

Mara read the question in his look. "He is not for Sarah!"

Joel, again, was silent. Mara thought, perhaps, she should have approached the subject differently. This was not the way she normally spoke to her husband.

She tried to soften her words. "You are not considering him in such a way," she asked, "Are you?"

Joel shook his head soberly. "I am not. I do not even know if Jeroboam has such a thing in mind."

"He does," Mara murmured, under her breath.

Joel ignored her comment and continued. "I do not know him well enough, but there seems to be something artificial about his worship of Yahweh. And such a thing I cannot allow in a potential husband for my daughter. But I do need to know why you are treating Jeroboam so coldly."

Mara looked away from Joel's eyes. Something about him, still, that could pierce into her heart, could expose her entire self. "I don't know. I just don't like him."

"That is not like you, Mara," Joel said gently. But, yet, not so gently.

"Don't you see something in him that you instinctively distrust?"

Joel's brown hair was graying now, and it had never stayed in such perfect waves as Jeroboam's did. "No, I truly don't. What I do see in him is the need for love, the need for someone to show him Yahweh's love in a very tangible manner. But we cannot leave our guest alone any longer." And with that, Joel turned and walked briskly to the courtyard.

195

Mara was ashamed. As she picked up the empty bowls and the nearly empty trays of dried fruit, she asked Yahweh to change her heart. She prayed that she would be able to show Jeroboam the love that he needed.

Shortly, she joined the men under the palm trees in the courtyard. It was a beautiful night. The moon was nearly full, hanging in the sky so low that it seemed to be perched on the silhouette of Solomon's palace in the distance. And the rainy season had just ended, so the dust that stayed in the air during the summer had not yet risen, and the wind from the east was not very strong yet.

Still, the two men were talking about Solomon's building projects. Jeroboam was an ambitious man, and he was full of ideas for the future. Everything he had said about the king was respectful and admiring, which is why Mara was so stunned when Jeroboam declared, "But King Solomon is making a mistake by forcing his people into slavery."

Mara could feel, rather than see, her husband freeze up. "To my knowledge, the king has made none of his people slaves."

"Well, of course he doesn't call it slavery, but forcing the men from the villages around Israel to work for him, to build all of his construction projects, makes them nothing better than slaves. And that, combined with the heavy taxes, is not the best way to keep the nation's allegiance."

Mara had to clinch her fists to control her anger. She could not sit here, in her own home, and hear Solomon spoken of in such a way by a man no older than her sons.

"I think we are hardly in the position to judge the wisdom of the king's actions," Joel said firmly. It was a rebuke, although a polite rebuke. Often, between themselves, Mara and Joel would discuss Solomon's unwise actions, but never in public, and never to anyone who would not understand that it was only love that was guiding their words.

"Oh," Jeroboam claimed, raising a hand in a perfectly timed gesture, "I did not mean to sound like I was judging him. Who am I to do such a thing? But I am in command of the forced labor for two of the tribes, and I am in a good position to see what they feel about the arrangement."

There was probably some truth to that remark, but Mara was not about to let that overshadow the impertinence the man was showing. She closed her eyes and prayed, again, for understanding.

"My son, Eleazar, you know," Joel began, fighting the same fight as Mara. "Is a stonemason, and is also constantly exposed to the labor force. He says that although there is some discontent in the present state of affairs, everyone knows what King Solomon is and has done for this nation. He has turned Israel into one of the strongest nations in this part of the world. After doing this for our nation, only a very few would break loyalty with the king."

"Perhaps," Jeroboam assented. "Perhaps." Mara could tell that he was not convinced.

They sat in silence for a few minutes—long minutes to Mara, who was thinking about Solomon's handsome, frozen face and hunched shoulders—then Jeroboam said, unexpectedly, to Joel, "You must be a wonderful father."

Mara couldn't see his face very well in the shadow, but his voice seemed sincere and a little wistful.

"I hope I was," Joel responded. "I do know that Yahweh blessed me with my four sons and my daughter—more than I would have ever thought to ask for."

Even in the shadows, Mara could see the look in Joel's eyes as he gazed at her.

Jeroboam could see it too. "I never really knew my father." Mara wished that she could see his eyes, so she could tell whether this, too, was a calculated gesture. But his voice seemed so hurt.

"Nor did I," Joel responded.

Silence again, this time for longer than before. Mara stared at Jeroboam through the darkness. She could see how his face revealed a struggle going on somewhere inside of him. She could see that, and, despite his disparaging comments about Solomon, she could pity him.

"How," Jeroboam said finally. "How do you know how to be a father to sons when you have never had a father of your own?"

This was a deeply personal question, and it revealed something about Jeroboam that Mara needed to know. Something that would explain the reason he felt the way he did about Solomon, about all men who would have some authority over him.

Joel didn't answer right away. "That is not something anyone can answer for another person. But I will tell you what I did. Yahweh is my father, the father of all of Israel. So I used him as an example for my own life. Not," he added, with his rueful grin, "That I came anywhere close his standard. But he is something that I can hold my own life up to."

Jeroboam nodded, and Mara wondered—hoped—that he was nodding out of understanding and not out of courtesy.

Then the young man turned suddenly to Mara. "Did you know your father?"

Mara smiled, very slightly. "For six years I did." The night seemed to grow darker, but Mara didn't turn to see if a cloud had covered the moon. Her eyes didn't leave Jeroboam's perfectly proportioned features.

"He died?" Jeroboam's question was very soft and hesitant, as if he was not sure whether it was appropriate.

It probably was not, but Mara did not care. "Yes," she responded, feeling that Yahweh was guiding this discussion, but not sure what the outcome should be.

"I watched my father die, of a fever, in our home. I was four years old and I saw him die." The words were spoken to Mara, and they could have been intended to provoke sympathy, but Mara didn't really think they were. There was something too raw and forced about them.

Mara had seen her father die to, an arrow in his bare back. But she didn't share that fact. For some reason, she knew her own grief would not be able to relieve Jeroboam's. Instead, she reached out and squeezed the young man's arm.

She should have felt awkward about making such a gesture, but she was a grandmother now, and Jeroboam could have been one of her own sons.

They sat in silence, until Jeroboam rose to leave.

It was amazing, Mara thought, the way Yahweh could answer a prayer so quickly and in such a dramatic and moving way.

A week later, Mara covered her graying golden hair with a veil as she left through the narrow alley of her house that led to the street. She had been thinking a lot about Jeroboam: both his pain and the comments he made about Solomon.

She knew that many of the things Solomon did—particularly his indulgence in letting his foreign wives bring their religious practices into the country—would not be pleasing to Yahweh. She also knew that Yahweh would not remove his love from Solomon, and she agreed with her husband that the nation would stay loyal to Solomon for the sake of David and for the great thing Solomon had made out of their nation. But to hear someone speak so bluntly about Solomon in public was unnerving. It was not something that would have been done fifteen years ago.

She started uphill toward the building site that Eleazar was presently working on. Eleazar was their one son who was not yet married. He was still young, and Mara was not worried. But she would often go to the building site with figs, olives and bread, for if she did not, she was not sure that he would eat at all during the day. It was nice, really, to still be able to mother her sons, even though they were all grown.

For the last few months, Eleazar had been working on finishing the gap in the wall around Jerusalem. It was a long walk to reach the site, but Mara still enjoyed the movement and the fresh air. She was not, she thought, as old as her children liked to think she was.

When she reached the construction area, she paused for a moment. From her position, it looked like complete chaos. There were hundreds of workers surrounding the wall, piles of stone, brick and wood, various tools and building instruments. Amazing, Mara thought, that anything could get done in such a mess.

When she got close enough, she paused, wondering where Eleazar was today. He had chided her several times for walking too close to a heavy stone being lifted or coming too near to an open pit. She thought there was probably some logic to his admonishment, so she tried to avoid as much of the actual work area as possible.

While she stood there, a man approached her. "Are you looking for Eleazar?" Bildad asked, with a friendly smile.

He had been a friend of her sons from childhood. "Yes, do you know where he is today?

Bildad wiped some of the perspiration off his forehead with the back of his hand. "I saw him over where they are laying the new foundation. Come, I will help you find him."

Mara accepted his offer and walked with him through the maze of men and materials.

It wasn't very long until they spotted Eleazar. He was supervising the workers who were building a wooden construction that, apparently, would have some purpose in the building of the wall. Mara couldn't even begin to imagine how the strange-looking contraption would actually be used.

Seeing her son, bareheaded, in a simple tunic, intent on the progress of the construction, Mara had the strange feeling that she was seeing Joel at this age. Mara chuckled to herself. What a silly thing to think. She had not even known Joel when he was Eleazar's age, which in itself was hard to comprehend. All of her sons looked like Joel, with his brown hair and eyes, and his broad smile.

She saw Joel's smile on Eleazar's face when he glanced over and saw her watching him. Momentarily, he came over to join her, and Mara thanked Bildad for his help.

"Mother," Eleazar greeted her. "Were you worried that I was not getting enough to eat?"

This was close enough to the truth for Mara to ignore it. "You seem to be making a lot of progress," she commented, gesturing at the narrowing gap in the wall.

"Yes, we should have it finished before the next winter." The two of them walked farther away from the work, and Mara handed Eleazar the figs and olives she had brought him. They sat while he ate, and Mara watched his active face wistfully.

"Are you feeling sentimental today?" Eleazar asked, noticing her expression.

Mara laughed. "More and more, lately," she affirmed. "The house is so quiet without you boys filling the rooms."

Eleazar looked as if he would speak, but before the words could form, a figure passing them called out, "Don't be slacking on the job, Eleazar!" The friendly face belied the words, and the bellowing laugh made Mara smile. The man was carrying a large bundle of straw, and he didn't stop to chat with them.

"That is Aziza. He is in a good mood because today is the last day of his service. He will be returning to his family in the north. It has been a long time for him."

Mara nodded. "It must be very hard for the workers to be separated from their homes for so long." With Jeroboam's words fresh in her mind, she studied the faces of the men around her closely. They were not just intent or focused; many were unhappy or angry.

Eleazar did not respond to his mother's comment, and his face looked sober. Jeroboam was right about one thing: the forced labor was not the way to earn Solomon a great deal of gratitude.

Mara continued to watch Aziza carry his bundle of straw. He wove in and out of the workers, dodging under ladders and curving around piles of stone. She didn't even know the man, but she could tell by his walk how happy he was.

She turned back to look at Eleazar, wondering what he had been planning to say before Aziza had interrupted them. But apparently, she was destined never to know, for she heard a loud outburst from the construction site.

"Mother, don't look," Eleazar ordered.

Of course, she looked. From their distance, they could see the crowds start to surround a large stone, with something, perhaps a man, crushed beneath.

"Stay here, mother, you don't need to see this." With that, Eleazar hurried over to join the growing crowd.

At another time, Mara would have smiled. Her children, who only knew her as their mother, could not possibly know how many times she had seen death, how closely she had experienced violence and brutality. And so she saw no reason to shield herself from whatever she might witness under the wall.

She followed Eleazar, but more slowly.

By the time she reached the place, so many people were surrounding the man that she couldn't see who it was. But it was only a moment before somebody told her. Aziza, who was to return home the next day.

Mara felt sorrow clutch at her heart, although she hadn't known the man.

She turned when she heard a sharp voice and felt the crowds start to part, letting someone through. Jeroboam, his back perfectly straight, made his way to the center of the crowd. On his neat features was not the expression she would have expected. He did not look concerned or grieving. Rather he looked angry.

Standing on the site of one of Solomon's building projects, in the presence of a conscripted laborer who had very likely died under a falling stone, it did not take a lot of perception for Mara to understand with whom it was Jeroboam was angry.

It turned out Aziza didn't die. His leg was almost completely crushed by the stone, but amazingly, it didn't kill him. He would never walk again, of course, and he was very young.

Mara was still thinking about him two days later, as she rested a moment before preparing the evening meal. She thought about Aziza. and Jeroboam's anger. And then, because it was the natural flow of her thoughts, she thought about Solomon. She wondered if he realized how many lives his decisions affected, how his random commands could make or destroy families.

And then she was ashamed of herself, because she knew Solomon very well. Of course, he would know how his decisions would affect his people. It was one of the many truths his life and position had forced him to live with.

She tried to shake herself out of these thoughts. If she thought about Solomon too much, she might start to weep. His life was not something that could make her smile the way it used to.

She was grateful when Phinehas entered the room to announce Deborah. Mara rose to embrace her friend, a grandmother now as well.

It was evident by Deborah's face that she had not come over for a friendly chat. Her face was very concerned. "What is it?" Mara asked quickly, steeling herself for whatever news she might be hit with.

"I don't quite know," Deborah began, taking a seat on an embroidered stool. "Oh, don't look so worried. Nobody is dead or dying."

Mara released the breath she had been holding. "Then what is it?"

"Well, I have heard strange news, and I don't know how it works together, or even how much of it is true. I was hoping that Joel had come home and he could tell us."

"No," Mara responded. "Joel is doing evening duty at the palace; he won't be home for an hour or two. What have you heard?"

Deborah's curly hair was pulled back in a thick braid. She pulled on it as she explained. "Well, something happened with Jeroboam, son of Nebat—you've met him, haven't you—and Ahijah outside of Jerusalem."

"Ahijah the prophet?" Mara prompted.

Deborah nodded. "I haven't found out what exactly happened, but whatever it was made Jeroboam think he should be king."

Mara gasped. "After Solomon?"

"No," Deborah shook her head. "Now."

Mara stood up. "Jeroboam is revolting against Solomon?" she exclaimed.

"That's what I don't know. I mean, it's not like he is laying siege to the palace or anything. I'm sure they are talking about it down at the city gates, but I guess it is too late for us to go down there."

Mara glanced out the small, high window. It was almost dark. "Yes, it is. Joel will know, surely, when he returns."

"I imagine Caleb will know too. He has been at his stand all day. I had better hurry home so I can have the meal ready before he returns."

"Thank you for stopping by," Mara said, as she walked with Deborah to the door.

"We will pray to Yahweh that whatever this is will not hurt the king or end in bloodshed." Deborah hugged Mara again, and left the house.

Mara returned to the main room and sat down on the stool Deborah had vacated. Maybe Joel would come home early.

She rose again immediately. She had better start preparing the meal.

As she put the soup together in the courtyard, Mara kept looking at the sun, setting behind the roof of the house. It must be time for Joel to be home soon. Surely, he would know that she would be anxious to hear about whatever happened.

The soup was prepared, and Mara had laid out the bread and olives. Joel still did not arrive.

What could be keeping him? Was he wasting time after his shift in the palace?

This, Mara knew, was completely unfair. Joel always came home as quickly as he could. He wasn't even later than usual. It just seemed like it because she was so concerned.

Sarah had come into the courtyard and was rearranging the olives in the tray. She was chatting, but Mara was barely listening. Mara had stirred the soup far more than it needed to be stirred when she finally heard a door close inside the house. She ran under the columns into the house and nearly collided with her husband.

"I'm glad to see you too," he jested, leaning over to kiss her.

She cut the kiss short. "Tell me what has happened."

Joel raised his eyebrows, the way he always did when he questioned her behavior. His eyes, she noticed, looked a little tired. "May I eat?"

Mara smiled weakly. "I am sorry. Of course. Everything is ready."

Rachel had already set the table, so it was only a few minutes before Joel had washed , and Mara, Sarah and Joel seated themselves at the table.

After Joel took his first bite, Mara looked at him expectantly.

"I take it you have heard something about what has happened?" Joel asked.

"Not enough to understand," Mara replied, watching her husband carefully. If something was very wrong, Joel would still be at the palace with Solomon. The thought comforted Mara, a little.

"This is the story we have heard, the story Jeroboam has made known," Joel began, putting down his piece of bread. "He was on his way to visit his mother when he encountered Ahijah the prophet in the desert. Ahijah grabbed Jeroboam's new cloak and tore it into twelve pieces. He gave ten of these pieces to Jeroboam and told him that Yahweh was going to tear the kingdom away from Solomon and give ten of the tribes to Jeroboam."

"No," Mara exclaimed. "It is not true. Jeroboam is lying."

Joel shrugged. "Ahijah supports his story."

"But Ahijah has never liked Solomon," Mara insisted.

Joel shook his head. He was very tired, she could see. Even his shoulders were hunched. "Ahijah has often chided Solomon, for good reason."

Mara had to admit that this was true. But Yahweh could not take the kingdom away from Solomon. He had promised the kingdom to Solomon as long as he lived, and to his son after him.

"There is more," Joel told her.

Mara waited for the rest.

"Ahijah said that Yahweh was not taking the entire kingdom away from Solomon, but only for the sake of David, his father." Joel's eyes held Mara's for a long time.

Mara looked away, although she knew it was too late to hide her expression. She knew what Solomon's reaction would have been to these words, how closely they would mirror Solomon's own fears and pain.

"Could this really be Yahweh's plan?" she whispered finally, looking back at her husband. Deborah was the only one who was eating. Joel's bowl and Mara's sat, uneaten, on the table.

"I don't know. How can we know? Solomon is Yahweh's anointed; our loyalty must remain with him and his line. But Ahijah's word is not something I can simply discount."

"Do you think he could do this? Take the kingdom away from Solomon. How could he raise enough support? Would the tribes follow him?"

Joel paused a moment. "Ephraim and Manasseh certainly would. Perhaps some of the others. Solomon's taxes have been growing and growing. People are very discontent."

"Benjamin wouldn't, though," Mara said, more of a question than a statement.

"Not while I am alive," Joel said calmly, his eyebrows lowering. Although they lived in Jerusalem rather than with the rest of the tribe, Joel was still one of the most influential men in the tribe of Benjamin.

"Yahweh made a covenant with David," Mara mused, her head starting to ache. She reached up to rub her temples. "He will not break it. Yahweh does not break his covenants."

"No, he doesn't," Joel agreed. "But sometimes our ideas about his promises are not the same as his ideas."

This, too, was true. Mara could not understand it all; she could not reason through it. So she willed herself to trust Yahweh and wait to see what would happen.

"How is Solomon?" Mara asked, hesitantly.

Joel shook his head and didn't respond.

"Did he ask for your counsel?" she tried again.

Her husband nodded. "I advised him to act as though this were not a big thing, just an overly ambitious man seeking a crown. And to remove Jeroboam from any place of influence, maybe exile him."

"Will he take your advice?" Mara asked. A futile question. She already knew the answer.

Joel shook his head, affirming what she already knew. Of course, Solomon would not act rationally in this situation. Solomon was as insecure about his throne now as he had been when, barely a man, he had fought with his brother for it. Solomon would kill Jeroboam.

Solomon tried. The next day, Mara learned that he had ordered his soldiers to find, arrest, and execute Jeroboam. The young man, however, was no fool; he learned of this order and escaped from Jerusalem. The word was going around the city that he planned to go to Egypt, perhaps to enlist Pharaoh's help.

More of Ahijah's prophecy was repeated around the city before the gossip started to die down. Yahweh had promised Jeroboam that if he walked in his ways and followed his commands, then he would build a dynasty for Jeroboam as great as that of David himself. The words were debated at the city gate, discussed over dinner tables, whispered in the palace hallways.

They were not, however, brought up in Solomon's presence. Nor were they discussed in the house of Mara and Joel. Nothing could be settled with such discussions, and Mara knew that the more she talked about it, the more she would worry.

Whenever she thought about Jeroboam, she couldn't help but feel a little betrayed. She had disliked him from the beginning, but somehow, he had persuaded her to sympathize with him, understand him. Perhaps the entire discussion in their courtyard about fathers and deaths had been calculated, as she had originally feared. It would have been better, she thought, if she had continued to distrust him. It would have been easier.

Because any thought of Jeroboam or Solomon now brought her pain, she tried not to think about the situation. And she held on, desperately, to the things that she knew.

She knew that Yahweh would not break his covenants: with David, with Solomon, or even with Jeroboam.

She knew that Solomon was still the king of Israel, and he had built Yahweh's temple, had single-handedly raised Israel from a struggling collection of tribes to a consolidated, powerful nation, and was still as wise as any mortal man could ever be.

She knew now the last of Ahijah's words of prophecy: "I will humble David's descendants because of this, but not forever." Even if it were true, it was not forever.

And she knew, above all, that Yahweh loved his people, and that whatever was planned for them under the rising and setting of the sun, it would be for their ultimate good.

Chapter 24

One evening, months after Jeroboam had fled to Egypt, when all of the gossip and debate had ceased, when Jeroboam's name was no longer even spoken in Jerusalem, Joel and Mara were resting in their sitting room. Sarah was visiting Tamar for the evening, so they were alone. Phinehas, still their porter, entered the room and told them that they had a guest.

Joel and Mara looked at each other in surprise. They were not expecting anyone. "Show him in," Joel said, rising to meet whoever had appeared.

A solitary, cloaked figure entered the room, and Mara knew who it was before he removed the cloak.

"Solomon," she exclaimed. "How good of you to visit us."

Joel gave the king his own greeting, and Solomon seated himself with a smile on one of the divans.

"How have the two of you been?" he asked pleasantly, smiling at them in an open manner, as if he were not the king of Israel, as if this were not the first time he had visited them in their home since that distant evening a year after their marriage.

They told him they were well, and they chatted about various idle things until Mara asked, "How long will the queen stay in Jerusalem?" The caravans from Sheba were still encamped outside the city gates.

"For many months. It is too long a journey to come and turn around right away." Solomon looked very tired. "How did you like my new palace?" he asked. He was mostly asking Mara, who had been inside it only once at the banquet several months previously. Joel was there constantly.

"It is beautiful," Mara said truthfully. "I cannot believe how grand it is."

Joel nodded his agreement. "But, as I have said more than once, it is a bit extravagant, don't you think?"

Solomon looked mildly irritated, but after a moment, he relaxed. "Of course it is extravagant. It took fourteen years to build. Somehow, I had hoped that it would give me more satisfaction than it does."

Mara saw that this was the truth. His eyes, as she had noticed at the banquet the last time she saw him, were rather empty, and he seemed to have a headache.

"You will not find your satisfaction in anything you can build," Joel said carefully.

Solomon nodded. "I know that. Of course, I know that. I am the wisest man alive." He sighed deeply. "What a burden."

"It doesn't have to be," Mara insisted, leaning forward in her eagerness. "You just have to learn to use it correctly. You let it burden you."

Solomon shook his handsome, graying head. "I think it is too late. I have made a mess of things."

Neither Joel nor Mara could argue with that statement, and that fact seemed to make Solomon even more unhappy.

"Did you hear that I had high places built for Chemosh, the god of Moab, and Molech of the Ammonites. My wives wanted a place to worship. But now some of the Israelites worship there, and I have led them to it." Solomon hunched his shoulders. "What a great king I have become."

"Well then change," Mara urged, reaching to touch his arm. He pulled from her as if she would burn him. But she continued, "You do not have to continue the way you have been going."

"It's too late," Solomon repeated.

Joel gave Mara a look, and she leaned back into her chair. There was nothing they could say. They worked to change the subject, and soon Solomon was telling them about his latest activities.

Eventually, the subject came to battle. "Benaiah returned this afternoon," he said to Joel. "Did you hear?"

Joel shook his head. "Surely they have not subdued Rezon's men that quickly." Joel had been complaining to Mara for the last few months about the way Solomon had him stay in Jerusalem instead of going north to fight. Rezon, who had caused trouble for the kingdom since the time of David, had been attacking Israelite cities from his station in Damascus. Solomon's explanations about Joel needing to stay here to keep order among the troops that remained did not ring true with him. But Joel had not said anything to Solomon. Solomon had been acting unpredictably ever since Jeroboam's attempt at revolt.

"No," Solomon explained. "He was wounded. Not fatally, don't worry, but his leg seems to be permanently damaged."

Joel's face fell at the news. Benaiah was a good friend.

Solomon looked at Joel intensely, and Mara—for no reason she could understand—sucked in her breath. Solomon said slowly, "Benaiah thinks what is needed is an aggressive attack, rather than just defensive fighting, to stop this rebel for good. So I have worked with him on a plan that will force Rezon out of Damascus."

"Good," Joel said with a nod, his eyes reflecting the way he was judging, measuring, reasoning out the military matter at hand. "Surely one man and his group of bandits should not cause so much trouble for the nation of Israel."

Joel paused, his eyes on Solomon. Mara knew he would be expecting to lead the attack. He was, after all, second only to Benaiah in the army.

She still held her breath, wondering why she was suddenly so nervous. The light from the oil lamps was flickering, casting strange shadows on the walls. Solomon's silhouette looked momentarily vast and monstrous on the wall behind him. Mara looked away from it quickly.

"I am sending Igal to lead the attack," Solomon stated casually, but he kept his eye on Joel's reaction.

"But, my lord, why not send me?" Joel asked, visibly surprised at the words.

Solomon shifted in his chair slightly—a revealing gesture. "Igal has much experience in this sort of battle. He will lead well."

"I see," Joel replied, attempting not to look hurt at the king's decision. To be passed over as commander was a direct affront, but he was not a man who would question the king's decision.

Mara saw the hurt in her husband's eyes, and she moved to put an arm around him. His tunic, she noted irrelevantly, was course under her hand. She gave Solomon a questioning look. Something was happening here. Something significant. Something not right.

"Please do not think this has anything to do with your own abilities," Solomon urged, his expression sincere but not meeting Joel's eyes.

"Of course not. You have the right to your own decisions," Joel said, forcing the disappointment from his face. "I am, after all, getting older."

Mara made a little sound of protest, and it was that sound more than Joel's words, which seemed to propel Solomon to his feet. "Don't be ridiculous. You are not old. You are the best warrior I have, next to Benaiah. But I cannot send you."

Joel nodded, though it was plain he did not understand, and he got to his feet as well.

Solomon kept talking. "It will be a difficult campaign, anyway. Very risky. Benaiah estimates that maybe half of the force may die. You should be thankful you remain here."

The words were ill judged. Mara couldn't believe they had actually come from Solomon's mouth. Solomon, who judged every word before he spoke.

"Thankful!" Joel exclaimed, forgetting for a moment that he was speaking to the king. "Thankful to sit safely while my fellow soldiers go to their deaths? I don't think so."

Because she knew Solomon so well, and because, in a very real way, his history was part of her own, Mara suddenly understood what Solomon refused to say, what had brought him to their home this evening, and what was hanging like a curse in the air.

She lost her breath and started to shiver uncontrollably. "Solomon," she said, her voice shaking. The tone of her voice made both men turn to her in concern. She swallowed hard and forced herself to take in air. This was too important—it meant everything. "Solomon," she repeated. "It would not be the same thing. How can you even think such a thing? It could never, ever, be the same thing."

Solomon turned his head away from her, his shoulder-length hair hiding his eyes.

Joel looked at the two of them in confusion, but he was a quick man and, after a moment, he understood as well. "No," he said—a soldier's voice, cutting through the nuanced confusion. "You can not keep me here just to save my life. You will not be, like your father, sending me to my death on purpose."

Mara pushed the agonizing thought of her husband's possible death out of her mind. However real and horrifying the idea was, that was not what this was about. This was about the richly dressed, burdened man standing before her, whose presence filled the room like incense.

She knew about guilt. And she knew Solomon's soul. She could not let Solomon take onto himself his father's guilt, as well as his own.

"You are not your father," she said, trying to steady her voice, praying that Yahweh would give her the words to say. Solomon would still not meet her eyes. "Solomon, listen to me, you are not your father. Joel is not Uriah, and I am not Bathsheba. It is not the same thing. History does not repeat itself in that way. It is not the same thing." Her voice seemed to echo in the otherwise silent house.

"Isn't it?" Solomon asked, a little desperately, finally looking up at her. Mara had to turn away from what she saw in his eyes. "Isn't this what my whole life has been leading up to? I despised my father for his sins, and then I commit them all, one after another, in a glorious fashion my father would never have imagined. This would just be the pinnacle of my career, a bitterly ironic salute to the utter folly of my life." Mara thought for a moment he would weep, but this was Solomon, after all, and she had only seen him lose control once in his life.

"No!" Joel said again, taking the king forcefully by the arm. Mara saw that the touch had startled Solomon. "I will not let you keep me here out of some imagined guilt of yours. If you had thought I was unable to lead the attack, I would accept it. But this . . . this I will not accept."

"Do you want to go to your death?" Solomon asked, his voice more biting than pained. Mara heard laughing voices on the street outside their house. Normal people, enjoying the evening. It was hard, at this moment, for her to believe such things existed.

The voices silenced as Joel answered the question. "My death is in the hand of Yahweh, as my life has been. But I will do my duty as a soldier, for you and for Israel and for Yahweh. You must let me."

211

Joel's voice was firm, and Solomon, in his wisdom, saw that he would not change his mind. So the king turned to Mara, only his eyes uncontrolled. "Do you want your husband to die fighting a battle he did not have to fight?"

Mara brushed impatiently at her own eyes. Of course, she did not want him to die. And, selfishly, she did not want him to leave her side. "No, but he is a soldier, and it is his duty to go. Would you force him to be a coward?" She met Joel's eyes briefly, then turned back to Solomon. "And I cannot allow you to go on thinking that his death would be on your conscience. If he does die. He may not, you know." Of course, he would not die, she told herself.

"You will die," Solomon said to Joel, his face damp with perspiration and his eyes shooting out the light they reflected. "I know that you will die."

"Then allow me to face death with some dignity," Joel insisted. Next to Solomon, he looked older, plainer. But Mara knew and loved every line in his face. "It is not something you can control."

Mara knew the king of Israel better than any one else in the world. She certainly knew what he was hiding when he started to chuckle just then, as bitter a sound as she had ever heard. And she understood why the hiding was necessary.

"Very well," Solomon said lightly, again the picture of languid urbanity. "If you insist, I will not stop you."

He turned away, and, with a graceful movement of his shoulders, shrugged another burden onto the load that was already far too heavy for one man to carry alone.

Joel left a week later, to fight the band of Rezon, the outlaw. He had been away before, fighting, sometimes for a month at a time. And Mara was used to the waiting. It was what she had learned was in store for the wife of a soldier. But there had been no real wars during Solomon's reign. Solomon was a king of peace. And Mara had never, truly, feared for her husband's life.

But she did fear now. Solomon's words kept repeating in her ears, like the sound of drums going into battle.

She was kept busy with preparations for Sarah's betrothal. Before he had left, Joel had accepted the proposal of a young merchant. He was a godly man and had a very large estate.

Mara prayed that her daughter would find the love she had found.

Joel was gone for more than two months. One day, in the middle of the afternoon, Mara sat down suddenly.

"What is wrong?" Ephrath asked anxiously.

Mara looked up at the woman who had become her best friend. "I have this dreadful feeling. My husband is not going to return alive."

Ephrath made a cry of distress. "How can you know that? Yahweh will keep him safe."

"But I think it is Yahweh's will for him to leave me." Mara buried her face in her hands, giving in to weakness for the moment. "How will I make it without him?"

Ephrath reached an arm around her mistress. "Look at you," she said, trying to sound light. "Mourning for something that has not even happened."

"You are right," Mara agreed. "I must not mourn. But I must prepare myself."

Mara started to pray, asking the Lord to give her the strength to face whatever he had planned for her, as he had always done in the past, even before she knew to ask him.

A few days later a messenger came from the palace. The young man looked distraught. "You husband is wounded. They have brought him to the barracks. You must come at once, before . . ." The messenger did not finish, but Mara understood.

How she made it to the palace grounds she never remembered. She couldn't see the streets, the buildings, the people surrounding her. She couldn't smell the pungent air, or hear the laughter and chatter around her, from people whose lives were not about to change forever. All she saw, hurrying with the messenger toward the military barracks on the palace grounds, were her husband's face and Solomon's face. Only those two things in all the world.

She reached the barracks and was led urgently into a dim room. She ran to her husband, who was lying on a cot in a corner next to a window. Mara could tell, as soon as she saw him, that he had only made it this far out of his will to see her. The wound, in his chest, had been bound neatly, but Mara saw in his eyes that there was nothing left for anyone to do.

She was going to lose him.

The world came back into focus. Mara knelt beside the cot and reached for her husband's hands. "My love," she said. "My love, I am here."

Joel opened his eyes, and managed to smile. "They fought a little better than we had expected," he said, wryly, but far too weakly.

"That is all right," Mara reassured him, voicing a hope she didn't feel. "You will be fine, soon." Her voice broke on the last word.

"No, I will not," Joel argued, trying to smile. "But, my dearest, I am not sorry. I did my duty, and I have served Yahweh all of my life. And you, love, have made me more happy than any man deserves."

Mara could not stop her tears, and she bent to press kisses onto his dear face and his shaking lips. How many women, she thought, are blessed with the gift of a final farewell? How many men die on the battlefield, their wives never able to say good-bye?

Before she could say anything else, a man burst into the room, and she looked up to see Solomon, his face nearly distorted. He was wearing his royal robes, and Mara guessed that he must have been holding court in his throne room when he heard the news.

"Is that Solomon?" Joel asked, gasping a little. His eyes did not seem to be able to focus. Mara nodded. "Let me speak to him."

Mara gestured to the king, and he walked over to bend over Joel's cot. "I am so sorry," he said. "I knew this would happen, and I did not stop it." There was no masking in the face now, no guile or protection. Only pain, as raw as a wound, as raw as the wound in Joel's chest.

Joel raised a weak hand. "No, it was not your fault. I will not have you blaming yourself. It was my time. I knew it, and I think Mara knew it." Mara nodded through her tears. "But I will not die knowing you add this to your list of guilt." It was like him, to worry about someone else now, at a time that should be completely his own.

Solomon had found some measure of control by now, and his expression, again, was carefully schooled. He bent to kiss Joel on the cheek. "My friend," he said simply. He took a few steps away from the cot, looking over at Mara.

Mara met his eyes for a moment, but she could not take the time to read the expression in them. She knelt again beside Joel and kissed him.. "Oh, my love. You have given me my life and my family. How can I ever thank you enough?"

To her amazement, Joel laughed, not the full, hearty laugh that had always characterized the man, but a laugh nonetheless. "You have never understood that I was reaching for my own happiness, when I reached for you. You have nothing to thank me for. I have been so blessed."

Mara started to cry in earnest then.

It was only a few moments before Joel died.

Mara looked up, then, at Solomon, who had been standing a short distance away, watching them. There were tears, Mara thought, in his eyes, but he would not let them fall.

"He is dead," she whispered. Her life had been full of partings. She was used to it. She had come to expect it.

Solomon nodded.

Of one accord, the king and the former slave girl knelt down on the floor beside the dead man and prayed. They thanked Yahweh for his life and for his death and for the sweetness of his spirit. And for the chance they had been given to know him.

When Mara stood up, she started to cry once more. She had not even told Joel that she was with child again.

After Joel had been buried, with the pomp and tears that had befitted a man as loved and respected as he had been, the king summoned Mara unexpectedly into his presence.

She was led into one of the rooms next to the throne room, and Solomon looked at her with shadowed eyes. "What can I say to apologize?" he asked. He was standing very still in the center of the room, his hand resting on a richly appointed chair.

Mara shook her head. She thought there were no more tears in her to shed. "Didn't you hear what Joel said to you? It wasn't your fault. You are not your father. You did not send him on purpose to die."

"Didn't I?" Solomon inquired bitterly; idly, he brushed a random piece of lint off the top of the chair. There were rings on his fingers, which glinted in the light when he lowered his hands to his sides.

215

Mara took a step toward him. "Of course, you did not. If I thought you had I would kill you where you stood." The words surprised her, reminded her of her own father.

"Perhaps I would deserve it," Solomon said, showing the level of his control by keeping his hands perfectly relaxed at his side. "How do you know I did not unconsciously want him to die in battle? Have I not resented him for years? Have I not been jealous of his happiness?"

Mara walked purposefully over to the king and took his face between her hands. She hadn't touched him in years; she could smell his skin when she breathed. "That is not the same thing. You acted in spite of your feelings when you allowed us to marry, and I don't believe you have ever regretted your decision." She was closer to him now than she had been in so long, but nothing was the same . . . could ever be the same.

"No," Solomon agreed, pulling away from her. "I haven't. But I have so often wished I had not had to make the decision. I wanted to have you; you will never know how much I did. And now, because of an order I gave, your husband was sent to his death. How can you say my actions are better than my father's were?"

They had reached the point where Mara had nothing more she could say. "But I will never become your wife," she concluded finally. "Joel's death gains you nothing."

Solomon was forced into a chair by the strength of his emotions. He knew she was right; he was so wise, after all. But he could not feel that she was. "I am lost, Mara," he said, his voice like a child's—no control now. "I am hopelessly, helplessly lost." He reached his hand out to her, his eyes luminous in the torch-lit room.

She ran to take his hand. Maybe there was, after all, something she could do for him. "You showed me the light, so many years ago. Do you remember?"

He cradled her hand and said nothing.

"Let me help you," she begged. She was praying—oh, how she was praying.

The king of Israel, known throughout the world for his wisdom and his wit and his glory, looked up at Mara. "Help me," he pleaded, his voice no more than a breath.

She had asked him the same thing, in the throne room of David's palace, with Joel, young and strong, standing beside them. Solomon was David's son, more than anything else. And she knew the thing that might reach him. She began to sing:

> "Blessed is he
>> whose transgressions are forgiven,
>> whose sins are covered.
> Blessed is the man
>> whose sin the Lord does not count against him
>> and in whose spirit is no deceit.
>
> When I kept silent
>> my bones wasted away
>> through my groaning all day long.
> For day and night
>> your hand was heavy upon me;
> my strength was sapped
>> as in the heat of summer.
> Then I acknowledged my sin to you
>> and did not cover up my iniquity.
> I said, "I will confess
>> my transgressions to the Lord"—
> and you forgave me of my sin.
>
> Therefore let everyone who is godly pray to you
>> while you may be found;
> Surely when the mighty waters rise,
>> they will not reach him.
> You are my hiding place;
>> you will protect me from trouble
>> and surround me with song of deliverance."

It was a song of David, Solomon's father. David had been a man who had known about the power of forgiveness.

Mara stopped singing. Her voice had broken once or twice, but she saw that Solomon was on the floor, weeping.

Mara had the strangest feeling that she had lived through this moment before.

She thought about when he had last broken down in this way, and she remembered. It was a hot summer day, too many years ago, and Solomon was on the floor in front of his mother.

The thought that made Mara the saddest was the fact that Solomon was still weeping over the same thing.

She had said to Solomon, before Joel had gone off to die, that history didn't repeat itself. But she had been wrong. She and Solomon had never really gotten past this moment; in everything that had happened since, they had never really left that room.

"You are wise," she began, the right words finally coming to her—a gift from Yahweh. "Wiser than I can even imagine. You know what it is you need to do."

Solomon's hands were covering his face, hiding his eyes . . . his mother's eyes.

"Forgive your father," Mara continued softly. "Surely you, as much a sinner as he, do not have more reason to hold his sin against him than the perfect, holy God. Yahweh has forgiven him. You can too."

Solomon looked up. "I have become everything I despised in my father. And I have none of his goodness. I know that."

"Then forgive him for being a sinner, for being a man. And allow Yahweh to forgive you as well. He will," Mara whispered. "I promise you."

Their lives had come full circle, and they were still in David's palace. Mara prayed that one of them would lead them forward, away from the past that couldn't seem to die.

Then she saw, again, the image of Bathsheba's face—her beautiful, cold, most-hated face.

And Mara, with an ache, realized that she was the one who had to do it.

She swallowed hard. "I said, back then . . ."

Solomon looked up, and she could see that he was in the same place.

"I said," she began again. "That I hated your mother, for what she had done to you. And what I meant was that I hated Yahweh for letting her do it. I have never forgiven her," she admitted. "I have always hated her. And I have always been angry at Yahweh because of her."

Solomon stared at her in vague astonishment. Perhaps, even in his wisdom, he had never known this about her.

Mara continued, thinking of Solomon, thinking of Bathsheba. "But I am forgiving her now. I can think of her without anger. Without hate. I can pity her. And I can love her because of you."

The words were difficult for Mara to say, even to Solomon. But suddenly she knew that she meant them and her heart was finally free.

Solomon swallowed hard, and Mara could see again the struggle going on inside him between the love and the pain, the twin truths of his life. "I never hated my mother, although I suppose some of the fault for the sin was certainly hers. But my father, I did hate him . . . on some of the worst days."

Mara could see them moving forward, away from the past. The room around them was blurred, indistinct, a haze of colors and shapes. It could have been any room, in any palace, in any city in the world.

"Perhaps I was always afraid to admit it, because he was such a good man, such a godly man. I admired him with half of my heart, and hated him with the other." He wiped his brow with the back of his hand and met her eyes. She hadn't seen the expression in his face since before King David had died, and she could feel something healing around her heart. "But you are right. I need to forgive him. He was a sinner, but not such a sinner as me." He smiled at her, a very small smile, but a smile nonetheless. "I will forgive him," he stated. Then he added, "I will try."

Mara realized that this was the best she could hope for. "Yahweh will help you, as he always has."

Solomon smiled at her as he rose to his feet, much of the bitterness departed from his eyes, but all of the sorrow still apparent. "You have always helped me, as well."

She walked toward the door then, so he could talk with Yahweh on his own. Her work was over. There was only so much someone could do for another, even if the bonding went as far back as theirs did.

So she left Solomon to face the life he had made for himself and the sun that was already setting above them, and she prayed, as

219

she and Joel had been praying for years, that Solomon could at last find his peace.

Epilogue

THE SUNSET

"Now all has been heard;
here is the conclusion of the matter:
Fear God and keep his commandments,
for this is the whole duty of man.
For God will bring every deed into judgment,
including every hidden thing,
whether it is good or evil."

Ecclesiastes 12:13-14

Joel pulled his mother to her feet, grinning broadly. Her youngest son looked more like his father than any of the others, Mara thought with a sad sigh—her husband's last gift to her.

He was fourteen years old now, and taller than she was. He was apprenticed to a goldsmith, like his older brother Samuel, and he had just come home to visit her.

She had been feeling old lately. She had been living, now, for more than fifty years, and she was growing tired. She had been losing her breath a lot lately, and it would have worried her if she had given it much thought.

But Mara had fifteen grandchildren, and they kept her busy. And her young son, who had never known his father, was a constant comfort.

"Jedidiah says the king is ailing," Joel told her, knowing his mother was always interested in news from the palace. "He does not think Solomon has much time left."

The thought made Mara's heart ache. She had hoped, after Joel's death, that Solomon would mend his ways and live in peace with Yahweh. But though she really believed he had reached a crossroads in his life during their meeting after Joel's death, he was still to weak too change entirely. He could not turn from his old ways so easily, and he continued to allow his wives to worship their false gods. Sometimes, the city would whisper, he even joined them in their worship. The wealth that Solomon's court required strained even Solomon's great coffers, and the taxes kept increasing with each year.

No one would rebel against Solomon, who had, after all, ruled the kingdom in peace for forty years and built the great temple to Yahweh. The king whose wisdom was still talked about in all of the countries around them—no one since Jeroboam.

But Rehoboam, Solomon's oldest son and the one he was equipping to succeed him, was weak; and there were many men in the nation who were not.

Mara sighed. She had been thinking a lot about the past lately, about her father and Brant and Elsa. And about the years she had spent being passed from one tyrant to another. She thought about the empty years at the palace, broken only by her friendship with Abishag and the brief glimpses of the king, whom she loved. And the first year with Joel, which she had wasted because of her stupidity. She thought about her first child, who had died before being born.

All her children were grown now, even Joel, who was working as a man.

The porter—no longer Phinehas; he had died several years ago—came into the courtyard and said, "There is a messenger here from the palace."

Mara looked up, knowing what the message would be. After living as long as she had, there were things that one knew.

A young man entered, looking a little nervous. "The king has sent for you, madam."

Mara nodded calmly. "What is your name?" she asked.

"David," he responded.

"You have a great namesake," she said. "Well, David, lead the way."

David led her to the palace and through it to the king's bedchamber. There were many advisors and guards standing around, but the king dismissed them all. David took his place in the room next to the door, and Mara hurried to the king's side. It had been fourteen years since she had hurried to the side of Joel, in the barracks, for exactly the same reason.

"Well," Solomon said with a half smile, looking up at her from his pillow. "It appears that the illustrious reign of King Solomon of Israel is coming to an end."

Mara smiled at him, responding to the look in his eyes. "You do not seem sad." It was the truth. There was a peace on his face that she had never seen before.

And in the smallest part of her mind that still held girlish fancies, she was hurt that the he had come to that peace without her help.

"I am only sad at the mess I have left for my son. He will not have an easy time, and he is not as wise as he should be." Solomon's face was lined, and his hair was nearly all gray. His eyes were still bright, and they were focused on Mara, who was bending over him.

"He, too, will have to live in the shadow of a great father, and somehow overcome it." Mara placed her hand on his as she spoke. She thought of her own father. So much of her life had been defined by fathers and their children.

Solomon shook his head slowly. "Please Yahweh, he will do it better than I did. Do you think, that ever in this world, there was a man who wasted his life as completely as I have?"

Mara could not answer with any encouragement. "No," she answered. She saw Solomon's face resign itself to the fact and she continued, "But no man ever had so much potential; no man ever had so much he could waste."

Solomon gave a breathy laugh. "I have always loved Yahweh. Even when I," he winced at the thought, "Offered incense at the altars of false gods. I never stopped loving him."

"I know," Mara reassured him. "I know." He was telling her, only her, the deepest truths of his life. She wanted to tell him that he didn't have to, that she already knew.

Solomon continued, and Mara could see his lined hands clenched in front of him. It was significant. "I tried so hard to live and reign better than my father. And instead, I have become such a man my father would weep over. I thought that if I kept building things, and making alliances, and claiming women, that I could somehow find something to make my life meaningful, something that was new. But I failed to find the meaning in life in Yahweh, and that was my whole problem."

Mara closed her eyes. "You do not have to confess to me," she said.

"I'm not. I have already confessed to Yahweh all my sins, all the lists of sins that I have committed. At least as many as I can remember. He has forgiven me. I just want to explain to you."

Mara shook her head. "I know it all already. I know you so well. Even in the height of your sin, I could understand, and pray that you would seek forgiveness."

"It has taken me too long. And now—hah" he laughed. "I am able to die and my son will inherit the consequences of my sin."

Solomon turned his head. "You, David, named for my great father, step forward."

The young man came forward, visibly shocked.

"When someone decides to try to take the crown from my son, who will you serve?" Solomon asked the young man.

David was offended. "I have served you, my lord, for my whole life, and I will serve your son after you. But may the Lord grant that you live forever."

Mara smiled at the young man, and Solomon nodded. "Thank you," he said.

The king laid his head against his pillow. "I am dying now. But I wanted to see you before I died. I did not want to die with you hating me."

"Oh, Solomon," she said, her eyes filling with tears. "I have never hated you. Surely you know that I have loved you since I met you."

Solomon smiled at her. "That, at times, was my only comfort. And, at times, the reason for my despair. For I knew I was never worthy of your love. But I have loved you, always loved you."

"I know," Mara told him. "I know that."

"Could you," Solomon began, hesitating. "Could you kiss me once more before I die?"

Mara let her tears fall, and bent over the king, kissing him gently on the lips.

With her tears resting on Solomon's face, a mischievous gleam came into his eyes, a gleam she had not seen in years. "You dare to kiss me," he asked, with feigned affront, taking him back, taking them both back. "You dirty little peasant. I am the son of a king."

Memory, like a surging tide on the shore, and Mara choked on it. So long ago, she thought. A lifetime ago.

And because their lives were always circling back to the beginning, she knew what she had to say. "And I am the daughter of a king," she whispered. Her voice broke on the last word, but she forced herself to continue. "But I"—here she was able to smile—"am not covered with mud."

Solomon returned her smile, one final moment of bonding, but then he seemed to weaken. "I will see you again, though," he said, with confidence.

"It will be very soon," Mara said softly.

The thought seem to upset Solomon more than anything else. "Do not say that. You have many years."

Mara shook her head. "You do not really think that I could live long on this earth when you are gone, when both of you are gone." Her voice cracked.

She had loved two men in her life, and she was losing, now, the second one.

"My Mara," Solomon said, his voice now a breath and his hands now relaxed on the pillow beside him. "I repent of much in my life. But the one thing I look on with no regret are those few days I ran away from the palace to wander in the hills, and came back with you."

She turned away for a moment to hide her tears from him, and she saw the sun ride low in the sky through the open door to the balcony.

Then she saw the branches of the trees rustle and leaves blow across the courtyard. The wind, which carried away the leaves and the dust and the clouds, would carry away the spirit of a good man. Her father had taught her that years ago, and so she knew, before she turned around, that the king was dead.

She turned back and lifted a hand to shut his eyes. "Good-bye," she whispered.

Another parting, in a life full of them. But the last one. Mara was sure that this would be the last one.

Mara looked up at David, who had been weeping as well. He hastily wiped away his tears, but he did not look ashamed. He had loved the king, she realized, and she loved him for it. She smiled on him kindly. "You may tell the people that Solomon, son of David, king of Israel for forty years, is dead. May the Lord look on him in mercy and finally grant him peace."

Several weeks later, in the chaos that followed the death of the king, David heard it mentioned in passing—just idle gossip to pass away the time on a slow afternoon—that the woman named Mara, who had come from over the seas, and had once been acclaimed as the most beautiful woman in the nation, had died.

David had much to concern him and many worries on his mind, but he took a few minutes to mourn for the woman whom, he had recently learned, his beloved King Solomon, one of the greatest the world had ever known, had loved.

David watched the sun set through the tears in his eyes.

About the Author

Susannah Clements was born in Savannah, Georgia while her father was the pastor of a Presbyterian Church in America congregation. However, shortly after her first birthday, the family was off for ten years in the Navy, while dad served as a Chaplain in San Diego CA, Pensacola FL, Norfolk VA and Newport RI.

After her father returned to the pastorate, she completed high school at a small Christian school in Blacksburg, Virginia, where the influence of her headmaster and English teacher helped mold her love for literature and solidify her career decisions. After attending a summer workshop on creative writing at nearby Hollins College, she knew she not only wanted to teach literature; she wanted to write, as well.

She attended Belhaven College in Jackson MS, graduating with honors, with a B.A. in English. She enrolled in the Graduate School of the University of South Carolina, Columbia where she received an M.A. and Ph.D. in English, with a concentration in Victorian Literature. Her dissertation explored theological perspectives in three Victorian novelists.

Knowing that she preferred an emphasis on teaching rather research, after graduation, she pursued a teaching career at the University of Sioux Falls, a Christian liberal arts college in South Dakota.

Under the Sun was the first full novel Susannah completed. She is now working on a new novel exploring the incongruous lives of single, Christian women in contemporary culture. She lives in Sioux Falls with Leila, her chocolate-colored Cocker Spaniel.

www.ingramcontent.com/pod-product-compliance
Lightning Source LLC
Chambersburg PA
CBHW050512260626
47157CB00004B/1299